THE ENI(
13 SANDOWN ROAD

1st Edition

Published in 2012 by
Woodfield Publishing Ltd
Bognor Regis PO21 5EL England
www.woodfieldpublishing.co.uk

ISBN 1-84683-137-7

Printed and bound in England

Cover design by Christopher Turrall

The Enigma of 13 Sandown Road

A Botanical Mystery

JEFFREY PACK

Woodfield

Woodfield Publishing Ltd

Bognor Regis ~ West Sussex ~ England ~ PO21 5EL
tel 01243 821234 ~ e/m info@woodfieldpublishing.co.uk

Interesting and informative books on a variety of subjects

For full details of all our published titles, visit our website at
www.woodfieldpublishing.co.uk

This book is dedicated to my sister-in-law, Marilyn,
who will be remembered with love by all the family.

*"I knew them all by eyesight long before I knew their names
We were in love before we were introduced"*

From *On Reading A Book On Common Wild Flowers* by Patrick Kavanagh

~ CONTENTS ~

Disclaimer

None of the characters in this book is intentionally based on any real person, other than as explained in the postscript. Some are perhaps an amalgam of the many people I've met, known or read about over the years but they are otherwise purely imaginary. References to botany are as accurate as I, a non-botanist, could make them. The story is set against a background of Kew Gardens for dramatic reasons but is again purely imaginary; no aspersions against that fine organisation are intended.

The Author

My professional life was a tedious round of humdrum meetings, goals and objectives, reach-out targets and all the usual trappings of modern corporate life, which thankfully came to an end when I was in my 50s, which gave me the chance to write and do something creative.

I wrote two non-fiction books before this one.

Writing fiction, I have discovered, is considerably harder than non-fiction!

❖ ❖ ❖

Love Is In The Air: *The wartime letters & memories of Joe Pack and Margaret Dillon* edited by Jeff Pack | Woodfield 2008
ISBN 1-84683-046-X | 280 pages | softback | 140 x 205 mm | £9.95

This book is compiled from two main sources ~ the wartime memoir of Joe Pack, an RAF pilot and the many letters he exchanged with his wife-to-be whilst serving overseas during World War 2.

Joe saw plenty of action, both in the air and on the ground, firstly in Europe and later in Africa and the Indian Ocean. Born in 1918 and raised in the village of Egerton in rural Kent, Joe volunteered for the RAF in 1940 and was rapidly trained as a pilot. Just over a year later he was posted to an operational heavy bomber squadron (No.35) based at Linton-on-Ouse in Yorkshire. He flew a Halifax bomber on operations over enemy territory between January and June 1942 until the night of 7/8 June when, on his 18th 'Op', his aircraft was shot down over the Dutch/German border.

His evasion and return to the UK involved the famous Comète line ~ plus the efforts of a Dutch Inspector of ditches, a Basque smuggler and many other extraordinary people who put their own lives at risk to help stranded allied airmen evade capture.

On his return he was reassigned to flying boats ~ first Sunderlands and then Catalinas ~ and while undergoing the extra training this required, his eye was caught by a certain Margaret Dillon, a WAAF Officer serving at RAF Oban. His amorous advances were rejected, however, and she was subsequently posted to RAF Davidstow Moor in Cornwall, whilst he was destined to join 265 Squadron on patrol in the Indian Ocean.

Romance seemed well-and-truly off the menu, but at some point ~ and it is not clear exactly when or why ~ they began corresponding. The many airmail letters they subsequently exchanged, charmingly document their developing courtship and reveal many fascinating details about the wartime lives of two young people separated by extraordinary events.

A Cornucopia of Packs: An informal history of the Pack family by Jeffrey Pack (Woodfield, 2010)
ISBN 1-84683-104-0 | softback | 205 x 290 mm | 240 pages

In this enjoyable family history, Jeffrey Pack takes a look at the activities of the Pack family over several centuries and demonstrates how addictive genealogy can be.

The author succeeded in tracing his own forebears back about 250 years but, in the course of his research, he also discovered many additional bearers of the Pack surname who were quite possibly related to his own branch of the family but with whom he could not definitively establish a link.

This wider history of the Pack family name goes back 500 years and includes such luminaries as Sir Christopher Pack, Lord Mayor of London in 1654 and a close friend of Oliver Cromwell; Sir Denis Pack, second (after Wellington) most decorated hero of Waterloo; Thomas Pack, who ran the Whitechapel Bell Foundry, the most famous in the world; Packs who emigrated to the USA and elsewhere; Packs who ended up in the workhouse; a possible Mormon Pack; a Barnardo's Pack ... and much more besides. The author sets the stories of these colourful individuals in context within the wider history of the times in which they lived and, in some cases, played significant roles.

He also examines the history of Egerton – the village in Kent where the Pack surname proliferated and which has been home to many generations of Packs over the centuries.

The outcome is an entertaining and informative journey through several hundred years of English social history that will prove fascinating to present-day members of the Pack family in particular, but also makes for agreeable reading in its own right.

Prologue

It is a cold, rainy midwinter evening in a south London street. A figure is walking slowly along the road, head down and hunched against the rain, looking neither to the right nor to the left, appearing briefly in pools of streetlight, then disappearing into the darkness. The figure arrives at a terraced house, number 13 Sandown Road, finds a key and enters the house. He takes off his wet coat and hat and puts them, together with his gloves and scarf, near the front door. He also puts down a file he has been carrying under his coat to keep dry. He pauses for a moment and then goes up the staircase to the first floor of the house. At the top of the staircase, on the landing, he pauses again. To his left is his bedroom and it is late and he is tired; to his right is his study. After a moment's hesitation, he turns right into the study, carrying the file.

He sits down at his desk, sets his file in front of him, opens it, gets a pen from the drawer and starts to write. He writes for hour after hour, frequently pausing to think. Many hours later, he is still writing. He writes all through the night, breaking off only to make a hot drink and then resuming his work. As dawn breaks, with icy fingers of light entering the window opposite his desk, he finally completes his task and a small smile of satisfaction appears on his face. He puts down his pen, closes the file, eases back in his chair and falls asleep...

Chapter 1

It is Tuesday, just after 9.30am, and Kristina Kovalevsky lets herself into 13 Sandown Road. She is a cleaner and has worked at the house for about two years. She is paid to do two hours' work from 9am to 11am, once a week. She knows that her employer will not know what time she arrives and has been getting lazy. As she enters the house, she senses immediately that something is wrong. Normally the front door is double-locked but today it is not. And her employer has always left the house by the time she arrives but today his coat, hat, gloves and scarf are all in the hallway. It is cold and wet outside; surely he would have taken them with him when he left? And there is untouched post on the hall mat. She goes into the kitchen. Usually there are the remnants of his breakfast to be cleared up but today there is nothing. And her wages, customarily left on the kitchen table, are not there. She goes upstairs to his bedroom. In all the time she has worked here, he has never made his bed in his rush to leave for work. She always does this for him but today his bed has not been slept in.

She calls out, heavily accented, "Hallo, is there anyone there, this is Kristina the cleaner, Hallo..." There is no answer. Now she is getting worried. She has been all over the house except one room. Her employer told her that the only room that she was not to clean, or even go in, was his study. This was because "I have all my papers and books in there and I don't want things to get mixed up." He had told her this when he appointed her, which was, in fact, the only time the two had ever met. Should she look in the study? She is very worried now; the study is the only room she has not looked in and since she has never even been in it before, she doesn't know what she will find. She decides first to look again at all the other rooms in the house to see if there is anything she has missed, calling out all the time, "Hallo, it is Kristina, Hallo!" She finds nothing that could explain things to her, just an empty house where nothing has apparently happened for a while. She goes back to the closed study door and, heart pounding, stands in front of it, wondering if she is brave enough to enter. Eventually she opens the door...

The man is sitting in his study chair, leaning back with his eyes closed, a faint smile on his lips.

"Hallo, this is Kristina, your cleaner..." she shouts. There is no response. She shouts again, touching his hand this time to try to wake him. His hand is cold and she can see he is not breathing. She screams but cannot move: she is frozen to the spot, staring at the old man, seeing him for only the second time. Eventually she recovers and runs from the study, down to the hall and stands frozen, again, by the front door. What to do? She has recovered her senses now. He was an old man and old people die eventually; she had seen her grandmother die. These things happen. But she was a Ukrainian with no work permit, no national insurance and no tax records. If she called the police they would ask questions. She could just run away but she was a responsible person and that would be wrong. She decides to see if the neighbours will help her and rings the bell of Number 15 Sandown Road.

Number 15 is occupied by the Wellingtons, a West Indian family. The mother is Bertha Wellington (known to her friends, inevitably, as "Boeuf" Wellington) and she has two sons, Nelbert and Delbert, but no husband. Nelbert and Delbert are twins but totally unalike. Nelbert is 6 feet 7 inches tall, a beanpole described by his mother as "thick as two short planks" whereas Delbert is 5 feet 5 inches, tubby and "sharp as a tack". They all come to the door when the bell rings. They find a tearful and shocked blonde girl of about 23 years of age, who speaks in a very heavy accent.

Kristina explains in her broken English what has happened and asks them to help her.

"I cannot go to the police, I am frightened of them," she says.

Boeuf Wellington takes charge.

"Delbert, you come with me to take a look, Nelbert, you take this young lady into our house, sit her down and make her a cup of tea."

Ten minutes later, Boeuf and Delbert come back.

"Yup, he is definitely dead, but don't worry love, he was an old man and his time was up. We'll call the police and they'll want you to make a statement but I don't suppose they'll ask about work permits or anything like that," said Boeuf. "Oh, and Delbert and Nelbert, just in case the police want to come in here, there's one or two things that need tidying up beforehand, aren't there?" she winked.

Boeuf phoned the police, who arrived within an hour, an Inspector and a very junior PC. They inspected the body, looked carefully around the entire house and finally took statements from Kristina and the

Wellingtons. They did not ask about work permits, although they did want an address from Kristina, which troubled her a bit as she didn't have a fixed address, she was simply staying with alternating groups of Ukrainian friends. She just gave her current address, which seemed to satisfy them. What the Wellingtons forgot to tell the police, until later, was about a conversation over breakfast the previous day. Delbert had come home at about 3am from a party the previous night. He told the others that he had seen next-door's light on and he saw the old man working through the window. Then Nelbert said that when he had gone out at 6.30am to do his paper round the light was still on and he was still writing. Boeuf said that he often seemed to do this, every week or so he would stay up all night writing, she often saw him. "I wonder what on earth he could be writing?" They didn't tell the police then because they didn't think it important, although it could, of course, have helped to establish the time of death.

Then the police called their doctor to officially ascertain the cause of death. When all the formalities were complete, the Inspector addressed Kristina and the Wellingtons.

"We've had a good look round. There's no sign of a forced entry, no sign of violence or a struggle, nothing is apparently missing and the doctor has confirmed that the cause of death was natural causes. There is nothing at all suspicious; he just died of old age. Case closed. We'll deal with the rest; you can all go home now."

The Wellingtons returned to Number 15 and Kristina walked sadly down Sandown Road; she didn't have many jobs and now she had one less. Worse still, she had spent the last of her money on the bus fare to Sandown Road and had been relying on her wages for her dinner tonight.

The police had missed just one detail. When Kristina entered the study, the man's file was not on the table in front of him. Neither she nor the police had any reason to expect that there would be a file and therefore did not notice its absence.

Chapter 2

As the Wellingtons and Kristina went their separate ways, the police returned to the house to deal with the formalities. The main task now was to find a next of kin to take responsibility for the funeral, probate, the house and contents and to receive and register the death certificate, which the doctor had left with them. They split the task into two. The Inspector would search the house for details that might help and the junior PC would make enquiries up and down the road. Normally, the Inspector would have allocated these duties the other way around and he would have interviewed the neighbours, having found from experience that neighbours often know more than personal papers show, but his junior PC had only just qualified, did not like being in the house on his own with a dead body and seemed a bit queasy and worried.

In fact, it turned out the other way around. PC Dafydd Myrddin Rhodri, from the depths of West Wales, on his first assignment at his first posting after qualification, knocked at every door in the road, was lucky to find quite a lot of people in, but got almost no information. His "Good morning madam, I am making enquiries into..." was well practised but yielded almost nothing. Everyone in the road knew about and had seen the tall, elderly gentleman at Number 13 but almost no one had ever spoken to him or knew anything about him. The only exception was the Wellingtons at Number 15, who invited PC Rhodri in for a cup of tea. They remembered their conversation of the previous day and told him about the old man's occasional late-night writing sessions and that they had spoken to him once or twice when post was wrongly delivered but otherwise they knew nothing about him except his name, gleaned from the mis-delivered post, which was Havergal Wyllyams. As Boeuf had said; "You couldn't forget a name like that!" PC Rhodri thought nothing more of the late-night writing but was pleased to have at least confirmed the man's name, a name he recognised. He made his way back to Number 13 to report to his Inspector.

"Is that all you found out?" said the Inspector. "I found his name an hour ago from his gas bill!" The Inspector was rather brusque with his junior colleague, mainly because, other than the name, he hadn't found out much either. PC Rhodri was going to explain to the Inspector that he recognised the man's name but then decided not to.

"All the usual papers, gas bills, council tax and so on but no personal letters, no address book, no will, nothing to help at all. But loads and loads of what seem to be academic papers, some written in a foreign language and loads of books. I've never seen such a mass of books and papers, but I haven't found anything that could give a next of kin or even a friend. This looks like it's a job for social services, not us," said the Inspector.

The Inspector's exhaustive search had also failed to locate the file in which the man had been so busily writing on his last night; an item whose existence the police knew nothing about, but which might have helped them considerably had they done so.

Later an ambulance came to take away the deceased and peace then returned to Sandown Road ... for a while anyway.

Havergal's demise caused the authorities some consternation. With no will and no next of kin, there was nobody to take responsibility for the usual formalities. As far as the police were concerned, there was nothing suspicious and their job was done. In a case like this, the local authority will arrange a funeral. If no will or blood relatives can be found, the deceased's estate passes to the Crown, a process conducted by the Treasury, but only after all reasonable efforts have been made to find potential beneficiaries. The Treasury may agree to meet some of the local authority funeral costs from the estate they eventually realise. All of this can, of course, take a long time.

The woman at Social Services was called Leia Edeffu. She was from Nigeria and had started as a temp in this department but now, only 2 months later, such was the staff turnover, she found herself running it. She was a kindly woman and persuaded her superiors to fund Havergal's burial quickly and not to wait for agreement from the Treasury. Leia received only one call about Havergal, which was not either internal or from the Treasury. In fact, she had been occupied at the time and a colleague took the call and passed it over when Leia was free. It was a lady asking where Havergal's body was; she wanted to go and pay her last respects. Leia gave her the information and suggested that she should phone the hospital beforehand, so they were ready for her.

"Not many people go to see the body. Would you like details of the funeral when I have arranged it?" she asked.

"No thanks," said the caller. "I'll pay my respects personally."

They both rang off.

A little later Leia asked her colleague, "Did that caller leave a name or a number? She might be a friend or family and I'd hate to see everything this man owned go to the government. I should have asked her when I had her on the line."

"She gave me her name but not a number. Let me see... I wrote it down somewhere... Here it is... I wrote it on a Post-It note. She was a 'MISS MARY MIDLOTHIAN-SUTTON'. She insisted on the 'Miss' and sort of spoke in capital letters. She said she was calling from Wales and asked how long you would be because she was calling long distance."

Leia made a note of the name on the file but there was nothing more she could do with this information.

The funeral took place about 3 months after the death. Leia had left the social services by then. She hated working for the petty officialdom of political organisations, but she decided to attend the funeral because she had arranged it. Other than the officials, there was no one else there.

The man at the Treasury handling Havergal's case was one Roger Whalley. He had joined the Treasury's probate and recoveries department 32 years earlier as an assistant consultant and had risen to the position of consultant two years later. Now, 30 years later still, he held the same post. His job was to take all reasonable steps to find blood relations and then, if none were found, to realise the estate for the benefit of the Treasury. He made all the usual enquiries, which yielded nothing, and then he advertised in the usual channels for anyone related to or with knowledge of Mr Havergal Wyllyams. He received replies from all the usual chancers and conmen, whose style he recognised easily and discarded, but none from any genuine relations or friends. He had allowed a reasonable period for responses, so now set about realising the estate.

He had appointed a probate firm to investigate what financial assets the old man had had but they were very small and just covered a contribution to the council's funeral organised by Leia. He then engaged a house clearance firm to realise as much as possible from the contents of the house: the furniture, bed, desk, curtains and so on. This process took a considerable amount of time and many of the contents ended up at the dump. The only asset which had any value was an ancient Morris Minor car. Lovingly maintained, it had only 25,000 miles on the clock and was a collector's item. The house was also stacked with papers and books and several times a day Whalley received calls asking what to do about this and what to about that. In the end, the books were all sold or given as a job-lot to charity shops. Whalley instructed that the papers should be put into a pile and he would come and inspect them sometime. He had been through them once, looking for a next of kin, but found none, and now had to decide what to do with them. He forgot about this and never did visit 13 Sandown Road again, so eventually the house was completely cleared, except for a large pile of papers in the corner of the living room. Shortly after this, Whalley put the property on the market.

And so the case of Havergal Wyllyams was, apparently, closed.

Chapter 3

Meanwhile, thousands of miles away, Mrs Letitia Huntingdon-Brown was bored and, in case anyone in the vicinity was in any doubt, she shouted, "I am bored, bored, BORED!" She went over to her drawing room window and looked over her immaculate grounds, which stretched as far as the eye could see, but this did not lift her mood. She was just plain *bored*.

Her staff knew what to do when she had these outbursts, which were becoming more and more frequent, and that was to stay well out of the way, usually by hiding in the kitchen.

Letitia (Lettie to her friends; in fact, to almost everyone) had a wealthy and privileged English background. The Huntingdons could trace their ancestry back 1000 years. Lettie had been to Roedean, where she was head girl, of course. After that came a Swiss finishing school and then the plan was for a gap year before going up to Cambridge. Her gap year took her to New York, from where she never returned. She met Arvin Brown, a Greek oil trader with his own business, who had anglicised his name and was seeking a wife to further integrate himself into New York society. For some strange reason, despite, or perhaps because of being from such totally different backgrounds, they hit it off and married. Now they had to find somewhere to live and Lettie's approach to this had been somewhat unconventional.

Lettie had been born in Suffolk and her family still lived there in some style. Suffolk County, on the north shore of Long Island, was one of the most desirable and wealthiest areas just outside New York City and so this was a starting point. Of the many delightful townships in the county, Huntington was the nicest and the similarity of the names was the clincher. Lettie imagined herself as Lady Huntingdon (a title to which she would succeed in due course) of Huntington; of course it was a pity that the spellings were not quite the same; perhaps she would lobby the township to change their name to hers. So, having established the town to live in, it was just a case of finding the largest and most expensive property in it. Unfortunately, that property was not for sale but Arvin made the owners an offer they could not refuse and the Huntingdon-Browns moved in two weeks later. They hired seven staff to serve them and then Arvin got on with his business. That was 25 years ago and Lettie now was an American through and through.

But Arvin had died six months earlier. His working schedule had been punishing. He was up at 5am to be in the office before anyone else. It was his own business, after all, and he had to be there for the closing of European markets. He stayed until mid-evening, worked when he got home unless there was a dinner to attend with Lettie back in the City, and if there was then he would have to work again late in the evening. He just wore himself out and died of a heart attack.

Lettie's life then changed totally. Arvin had had three younger brothers who were also involved in his oil trading company. For Lettie, the six months after Arvin's death had been a nightmare, mostly spent with lawyers and in court, protecting her inheritance from Arvin's rapacious brothers, who had conspired to steal Arvin's share in the company from her. "We worked in the company, she didn't, why should she get the lot?" They thought she might be a soft touch. She was anything but and fought them all the way. That was now, finally, resolved and Lettie was a very wealthy woman living on her own in an enormous mansion with immaculate grounds extending to the far horizons with seven staff to serve her but with nothing to do. When Arvin had been alive she had often spent all day preparing for a dinner that evening, had enjoyed bridge sessions with the wives of Arvin's brothers or had planned vacations for the two of them that frequently did not get past the planning stage. Now all that was over and she was "bored, bored, *BORED!*"

Arvin and Lettie had had no children; Arvin had been much too busy for that. As she once told a friend, "We didn't just have separate bedrooms, we had separate wings in the house." Arvin's room and wing were geared up with screens and telephones for business action at any time of the night or day; Lettie's was as far away as possible from the telephones, fax machines and printers. After the business tussles, Lettie had lost her husband's family and a lot of friends as well, many of whom had sided with the brothers, and now she felt totally alone, rattling around in this enormous house with nothing to do.

One day, after another rant, Lettie decided things could not go on like this. She would have to do something. But what? Then she re-membered something someone had said at a dinner party when Arvin had been alive. She had been describing her family's 1,000-year history and someone had said, "Gee that's really interesting... why don't you do the complete research and write a book?"

Lettie had said, "Hey, that's an idea, maybe I will."

Arvin had then said, "Honey, just hire a geologist to do it for you." Arvin had a way with words.

Now she was excited. This was something *she* could do. As she thought further about it, an idea formed in her mind. She would go back to England for an extended stay, catch up with her history, look up friends from long ago, if they were still alive, take in the shows and maybe research her family history properly. In fact, the more she thought about it, the more she liked it. She would go for six months, perhaps a year, a complete break from here. And she would not stay in a hotel, she would be completely independent, no servants, no staff, on her own, doing as she pleased. Most of all, what she hated about her empty, lifeless house was the thought of all the staff watching her, arranging her clothes, tidying up after her and wondering what she would do next. She would get a break from that. "Wow, that's it!" she said to herself. "I know... I'll buy a house to live in for a year and just get away from here and think and be myself again."

Since her gap year she had only been back to England twice – for the funerals of her parents. On neither occasion had there been a chance to meet friends or relatives; Arvin had had business commitments that meant they both had to get back to New York immediately after the proceedings. She had never really taken much interest in her family and now her parents were gone, she had no siblings and knew nothing about aunts, uncles or cousins. This was the time for an extended trip back to the old country. She did not think further about the idea, she had *decided*.

She called her secretary and told him. She instructed him to lay off all the staff and close up the house; he would remain to look after things and await her return. He should arrange for her packing (she had no idea how to do this) but she would arrange her accommodation in London and her travel. She was loving the feeling of independence already.

The first thing Lettie did, striking while the iron was hot, was to book a flight to London. She booked an economy flight with an open return. Then she called Hiram Koenswater, the President of United Airlines. Hiram was an old friend of Arvin's. On Arvin's many business trips to London he would regularly book an economy ticket and then call Hiram to ask if he could be upgraded to first class. Hiram's *quid pro quo* was to be regularly invited to Arvin's dinners, ballet performances and the many social events sponsored by Arvin's company. Lettie saw no reason why she should not ask a favour too. The problem for Hiram was that since Arvin's death the invites had dried up and it had all been a bit one sided anyway when Arvin had been alive. He was reluctant "I'd better just check if there are any spare seats..." This was a red rag to Lettie. "Arvin always said what a great friend you were for him, that you'd do anything for him or his family... and then he invited you to that New York Yankees game that no one else could get tickets for.... and there was that trip to..." Hiram realised he was beaten and would get no work done that day unless he agreed, which he then did. "Gee, thanks Hiram. Oh, and by the way, I'll have 13 pieces of baggage and I'm sure I won't have to pay any excess."

"Yes, Ma'am, you bet," said the President of United Airlines.

Now Lettie needed somewhere to live. She hadn't really thought much about this. She did not want to stay in a hotel. She would just be surrounded by servants, which is exactly what she hated at home. She wanted to be independent.

"I know," she thought. "I'll buy a small house; it could be a good investment and I will be over there for at least six months, maybe more." Her flight was booked for four days hence, so she would have to move very quickly to buy a house and for it to be available by then. Normally she would have got her secretary to research all this but she thought, "I'm independent now, I'll do it myself, and besides it has to be done quickly." So she got onto the Internet and twenty minutes later she had bought a small house. It was Number 13 Sandown Road. She had bought it unseen and unsurveyed, cash down. As she told friends later, "I wanted a small house, convenient for Kew and the National Archives for my research but also for the West End and the shows, and it was cheap, so I bought it." The solicitors had taken a bit of persuading to get the paperwork done in time for her arrival but, somehow, the key for 13 Sandown Road arrived on the day of her departure.

Lettie was now packed, had a flight and somewhere to live in London; she was all set and very excited to go.

Chapter 4

Lettie's arrival at Heathrow four days later was almost as dramatic as her departure from New York. She had needed three porters at either end to deal with all her luggage and, even though they knew exactly what to do, this did not stop her from directing them. "This way..." "Mind that!" "Careful with my hat boxes!" and so on. Then, with so much luggage, she had needed three taxis at Heathrow, which rather upset the rest of the taxi line. She then instructed her convoy to "take me to 13 Sandown Road."

"Where's that then darling?" asked the lead cabbie."

"You should know, you're a cabbie," she replied.

"Listen sweetheart, there are at least three Sandown Roads in London," said the cabbie.

"Well here's the full address then," she said, pulling a piece of paper out of her purse, and they set off.

After Havergal's death, 13 Sandown Road had been empty for several months while things were sorted out by Social Services and the Treasury, so the arrival of three taxis and a rather domineering American lady caused quite a stir in the road and a small crowd gathered to watch.

On arrival, Lettie strode up to the front door with her key, telling the cabbies to start unpacking while she would just visit the washroom. Five minutes later she came storming out. "Hold it guys, I made a big mistake, this place is no good, there's no furniture, it's filthy, there are piles of papers and most of all... there's no shower! Take me to the Savoy," she shouted.

"What you gonna do then darling?" asked one of the cabbies as they started to reload the taxis.

"Sell it," she said. "I made a big, big mistake."

"Well, hold on..." said one of the cabbies, "perhaps my brother can help. He's a builder and decorator. He'll have it furnished, painted and a shower installed in next to no time." The cabbie sensed a highly lucrative business opportunity for his family with this clearly very wealthy American woman; he was already hoping for a large tip just for the taxi ride. Then a voice piped up from the watching crowd. It was Delbert.

"I could help as well Missus. I've got contacts and I live right next door. I can oversee things for you, be a good neighbour like..."

"When can your friends start, tomorrow?" Lettie asked "and how long will it take?"

"About a month darling," said Delbert.

"OK," said Lettie. "I want you and your guys here tomorrow morning at 8am, and now, cabbies, take me to the Savoy!"

When they were out of sight, Delbert turned to his mother.

"We'll do well out of her. What does *she* know about the cost of turnips?"

Meanwhile the cabbie who was driving Lettie was cursing under his breath that he had been beaten to such a potentially lucrative piece of business.

On arrival at the Savoy, Lettie once again instructed the cabbies to take her luggage in.

"Shouldn't we wait to see if they've got a room for you first?" said one of the cabbies.

"They will," she replied.

On his frequent trips to London on business, Arvin had always stayed at the Savoy and had got to know the General Manager, Francesco Molinari, very well. Lettie went straight to reception and, as the cabbie had expected, they were full up, no rooms at all.

"Would you ask Francesco Molinari to come here please? As soon as possible," Lettie more or less commanded. The General Manager of the Savoy arrived and received the same treatment as the President of United Airlines and somehow, magically, a room was found.

"It is not one of our best rooms but we will move you to a better one tomorrow when it becomes free, Madam."

Three months later, Lettie arrived for the second time at 13 Sandown Road with the same three cabbies and all her luggage. She had used the three months staying at the Savoy to see every show in London, visit every monument and museum and now she was bored with that and ready to start work. She had made the lives of Delbert and his builder friends a complete misery. They had thought she was a sucker but she had arrived every morning at 8am to inspect yesterday's work and agree what would be done today. Everything had to be done perfectly and if it wasn't it had to be done again. The one month for the work promised by Delbert had turned out to be considerably longer.

Lettie had learnt all about business from Arvin and she wanted it done just right. The builders had redecorated everything, carpeted everywhere, furnished the entire house, installed the latest kitchen and bathroom equipment, with a huge shower (which had to be imported from the USA) and Lettie now had exactly the house she wanted. Havergal would not have recognised his old house. But Delbert and his builder friends did not make a killing; Lettie had worn them down just as she had the President of United Airlines and the General Manager of the Savoy. She paid cost for the materials and a modest hourly rate for the time it took, which was paid only for hours worked and she was the judge of how long a job should take, not them. They had worked exceptionally hard for a modest return. Delbert was no longer flavour of the month with his builder friends. But for Lettie now the house was spick and span, except that in the corner of the immaculate lounge there was still the large pile of papers left by the house clearance firm. Lettie had told her builders to leave them and she would look at them when she moved in; they looked too important and intriguing to just throw away. Now she had moved in, she would have time examine them.

The builders said, "Is that all now Ma'am, can we go now?"

"Yes," she said, "I'll call you if I have any problems."

The builders gratefully slunk away and immediately changed their mobile telephone numbers! Delbert, unfortunately, had no way of hiding, unless he moved house or arranged to be out all the time.

Lettie looked about her new house and was very pleased. She had everything she needed and she had done it all herself – or at least arranged for it to be done. She was glad to be out of the Savoy, now she had no staff or servants, the builders and trades people had all now gone and finally she was on her own and independent in exactly the way she had dreamt of. Now she could start doing the work she had come to England to do. She would go immediately to the local super-market for some basic provisions, make a cup of tea and then begin looking through those papers that had been left behind. She would get down to her own 'geology', as Arvin had called it.

The supermarket was a bit of an adventure. She had never been to one before in her life and certainly not one in a foreign country. She also had no idea what she would need or how to stock up a house. She decided she would eat out for a bit but would still need the basics, so went next door to ask where the nearest supermarket was. Bertha was in. Sensing another business opportunity she said, "Why not make a list and I'll get Delbert to go for you?" But Lettie wanted to do it herself now that she was independent. Bertha said that there were three supermarkets nearby, one was the cheapest, another was good at vegetables and the third had a good delicatessen.

Lettie strode out but soon got lost. She asked a passer-by, "Can you tell me the way to Waitbury?"

"Never heard of it love," came the answer.

"You must have… It's a supermarket."

"Oh, you mean Waitrose… next left and you're there," he said.

Lettie entered the supermarket. She had no idea of what she wanted except tea and milk to make a drink. But there were 20 different choices of tea and a similar number for milk. Back home her staff knew exactly which tea she wanted at different times of the day but now she had to decide. Eventually she made her choice and, having fortunately remembered to bring some money, she paid and made her way home. This was the first of many supermarket visits to come, since she only realised what she needed when she found it was not in her house. She would return for toilet rolls, soap, tissues, bread and much else, but for now she could settle down with a cup of tea (the first she had ever made for herself) like a real Englishwoman, take a look at those papers and then prepare to get on with her own project.

The papers were in a complete mess. As the decorators had worked around them, they had been moved and thrown about and dropped and gathered up roughly. They had got dusty, had paint spilt on them and then, when everything was finally finished, they had been dumped unceremoniously in a corner of the lounge. Most people would long ago have scooped them up into a plastic bag and thrown them away. But Lettie was not "most people", she was incorrigibly nosy. Or, as she used to say to friends, "I'm just interested in people". She didn't really expect to find much in this messy pile but, after all, these had been someone's possessions and someone's life and to just chuck them out seemed wrong. And she had actually become rather interested in the previous owner of her property. How was it, she thought, he was writing one night and dead the next, as the Wellingtons had told her? And how come nobody seemed to know anything about him or that he apparently had no relations or friends? And why had the authorities been so stupid as to leave behind all sorts of personal paperwork that should have been taken away and destroyed and which now gave Lettie an opportunity to do what she most enjoyed – to pry into the lives of other people.

The final attraction was that name, Havergal Wyllyams.

Her cup of tea finished and her investigative juices flowing, Lettie set to work.

Chapter 5

As you may recall, the papers that had been left at 13 Sandown Road were only there due to the lethargy of Roger Whalley from the Treasury, who had been somewhat distracted by news from his boss that he was to be transferred to the Ministry of Agriculture in Newcastle as an Assistant Clerk Grade 3, and to the warm-heartedness of Leia in Social Services, who made sure that the house clearance firm engaged by Roger Whalley did not just dump the papers, even though she had no idea what was in them.

The papers may once been in some sort of order but were not now. The police had been through them several times looking for next of kin, as had social services, and for the builders and decorators they had been a complete nuisance, always getting in the way of whatever they were doing and they had not been careful with them, so now the pile was a complete mess.

The more Lettie sifted through the papers, the more she realised how disgracefully incompetent the authorities had been. They should never have been left in the house. There was the man's passport, his utility bills, his national insurance details and tax codings, bills and invoices, bank statements and much else besides; the opportunities for identity theft or for attacking the bank accounts were endless and there had been all sorts of workers in the house in recent months.

"These bureaucrats should be ashamed and I'll tell them if I get a chance," Lettie thought.

But such personal items were only a small part of the total. In addition there were what appeared to be academic papers that Lettie couldn't remotely understand, even though, apparently, they were written in English. Other papers were written in a foreign language that Lettie did not recognise at all. Lettie had thought that the papers might take her an hour or so to sort through but, many cups of tea later, she realised this would not be the case. She had also anticipated that most of the papers would be of no interest and therefore disposable but this proved not to be so; almost every document seemed to demand attention, if only because she couldn't understand most of them.

The best thing, she decided, in order to make a start, would be to sort the papers into three separate piles. There was a very large pile of what appeared to be academic papers. "These should surely go somewhere. Someone may be able to use them. This looks like a life's work on something, but Lord knows what it's about," she said to herself. Then there was a medium pile of all the foreign language writings, some of which appeared to be poems. "And what the hell is this all about?" she said to herself. "I'm guessing from his name that he was Welsh so perhaps these are written in Welsh. They have their own language there, I seem to remember. Perhaps I'll get them translated".

Finally, there was a small pile of all of Havergal's personal and official papers: gas bills, bank statements, council tax demands and so on. She decided to start with the small pile.

From these she discovered that Havergal had been 76 when he died.

"Gee," she thought, "these days that's not very old. I wonder what happened?"

He was 6 feet 3 inches tall and weighed 12 and half stones. His passport photo showed a serious looking man, only slightly grey with an aquiline nose and penetrating eyes. In none of the documents that required notification of a next of kin was one entered. His full name was Havergal Ulric Wyllyams and every time Lettie saw the name she could not stop herself saying, "Heck of a name that". He had been born in West Wales at Llandysul in Ceredigion and appeared to have been employed at one time by the Royal Botanic Gardens at Kew. There were no employment details but there were some modest expense claims. That was about all she could glean from the papers. She was puzzled to have found nothing very personal; no address book, no letters, no diary, in fact nothing very helpful at all. Getting this far had taken several hours and Lettie was tiring of going through dusty and stained paperwork and was not in the mood for more just now. She decided to ask about Havergal in the street, calling in on her neighbours, just as the police had done several months earlier. She had a bit more success than PC Rhodri had had, but not much more.

She started with the Wellingtons next door. They repeated what they had told the police; they had known his name from misdirected post, he was a quiet and gentle man and he sometimes stayed up very late to write and that was all they knew about him. They had lived in their house for 20 years and he had been there when they moved in. But they did have a little extra to add. Because there was no next of kin, Havergal's funeral had been arranged by "Someone called Leia" at

Social Services and the immediate neighbours had been invited to attend, although the Wellingtons didn't go (and neither did the other neighbours, for that matter). Leia had told them that because he had no next of kin the house and all his other assets would go to the State or the Treasury. "Someone called Roger Whalley. I remember because she made a joke about him being a complete wally and said it was a pity the old man's affairs were being handled by someone like that," said Boeuf.

The rest of the road yielded little. Most of the residents had seen the old man as he walked along the road, some had nodded in recognition but almost none had ever spoken to him. One family, at number 18, were Welsh, judging by their accents. Lettie asked if they spoke Welsh and mentioned Havergal's papers, which she thought were in Welsh. "No, sorry love, we are from Cardiff. Not much Welsh spoken there, I'm afraid," was the answer. "But I'll tell you who does, that police constable, PC Rhodri, I think it was, he interviewed everyone on the day the death was discovered. He noticed my Welsh accent and asked if I spoke it. He was sad when I said I didn't because he did. I remember him saying, 'you don't find many Welsh speakers in London'".

The very last call was at number 32. This resident had spoken to Havergal once in all the 20 years he'd lived there. They had both been waiting for trains at the local underground station; they were going in different directions but waiting on the same platform. Number 32 had addressed Havergal. "Where are you off to then?"

"Kew Gardens," came the answer.

"Lovely day for a walk in the gardens," the man had said.

"I'm going to work," had been Havergal's reply.

The arrival of the northbound District Line train had terminated the conversation. They'd bumped into each other occasionally at the station after this and nodded but never spoke again.

Lettie was a little deflated by her lack of success but there was one last possibility, the local pub on the corner of Sandown Road called 'The Crows Nest'. Lettie somehow doubted Havergal was a big drinker but it was worth a try.

She approached the barman and asked if he had known the tall, elderly gentleman who had lived at 13 Sandown Road and died recently.

"Oh yes," said the barman, "he used to come in quite often. I heard that he died. A pity. He used to eat in here quite a lot, lived on his own so it was easier, I guess. He'd just have a pint and a bar snack. Never really said very much. I asked him once what he did and he said he was a botanist, but he said it in a way that seemed to say, 'no more questions please'. Is there a problem? Why are you investigating?" he asked suspiciously, he had quite liked the taciturn old man.

"Oh no, there's no problem," Lettie replied. "I bought the house after he died and there were some of his papers left behind that I want the right person to have. Trouble is, I don't know who the right person is."

"Perhaps Ron can help," said the barman, "he was the only person I know that the old man used to chat to. They used to meet most Sunday nights, just for a pint or occasionally two."

"Which one is Ron?" said Lettie, turning to face the bar.

"He's not in tonight, I'm afraid. He doesn't come in every night and in fact we've been seeing less of him since the old man died," said the barman.

"If you see him, will you ask him to call me please?" said Lettie. She wrote a note with her mobile phone number and a brief written message saying that she had just moved into Number 13 and found some possessions of the previous owner and thought that Ron might be able to help her decide what to do with them. The barman agreed to pass on the note the next time he saw Ron and wondered if this American Lady was ever actually going to buy something.

She didn't. Lettie went home to think about all the things she had discovered during the day. As she thought through the day, she realised she now had a number of lines of enquiry. There was Kew, he was a botanist, and then Ron at the pub. She would try to contact Leia at Social Services and Roger at the Treasury, and then there was PC Rhodri who might translate the papers, if indeed they were written in Welsh. That seemed like quite a good start to her investigation and she was pleased with her day's work.

Lettie was now intent on finding out all she could about Havergal Wyllyams and his mysterious papers in order to 'do the right thing' with them. Her own geology (sic) could wait until she had sorted all this out.

Chapter 6

Lettie was up early the next morning. She had slept well and was now anxious to get on with her work. Breakfast was toast and coffee, during which she remembered that she still hadn't bought any marmalade, amongst many other things. She would start by making some telephone calls. The first would be to Roger Whalley; she would give him a piece of her mind about his carelessness. Then she would call Leia, then PC Rhodri and then Kew and she was still waiting to hear from Ron. Then she might start to look through the rest of the papers.

Her first call was to the Treasury to try to hunt down Mr Whalley. She had no idea which department he was in and was transferred all over the place until finally she arrived at the Probate and Recoveries department, who told her "he's not here any more, he was transferred to Ministry of Agriculture at Newcastle about two months ago". Lettie asked for his number but his replacement was reluctant to give it. "Why do you want to talk to him? If it is about an individual case then we are not allowed to discuss them with just anyone, unless you're family, of course."

"Oh no", said Lettie, "I just wanted to thank him for the fine job he did with Sandown Road," biting her lip. She got the number and called him. He was also reluctant to talk about an individual case but eventually Lettie opened him up, as she always did. He confirmed that he had visited 13 Sandown Road only once, at an early stage in the proceedings and mainly to see if anyone had missed next of kin information in all the paperwork. He was much too distracted by his imminent move to Newcastle to do much else with the papers but thought he had told someone else in his department to deal with the personal ones. "Didn't anyone deal with them?" he lied, trying to infer that it was not his fault. Otherwise, this was just a perfectly normal case. He'd advertised the probate process looking for next of kin, he'd received no useful replies so he'd appointed a house clearance firm, then advertised the property and then sold it, "apparently to you" and then, two days later, he moved to Newcastle. He knew nothing more about the papers; he'd dealt with this case the same as he had with hundreds of others. Somebody else must have saved the papers; it wasn't him. If asked, he'd have instructed for them to be disposed of. He remembered nothing about Havergal Wyllyams personally.

Lettie listened to all this politely and when it was clear that no useful information would come from him, she blasted him for his lethargy and incompetence to such an extent that Roger Whalley eventually had to put the phone down. But Lettie felt better that she had made her point.

The next call was to find Leia of Social Services. Finding the department where Leia had been was easy enough but Lettie was told that she had left the department two months earlier, just like Roger Whalley.

"Do you have a contact number?" asked Lettie. Once again, the authorities were reluctant to release any information, even just a contact number for an ex-employee, but once again Lettie eventually persuaded them to do just that.

Leia was more than happy to talk. She had hated her job and this case had really brought things to a head. Her bosses had been reluctant for the Council to bear the costs of the funeral, at least until the Treasury had indicated that they would recompense them later. They were quite happy to arrange funerals for penniless tramps that died but this man had a house and assets and they should not have to bear the cost. But to Leia it was undignified and inhuman to let all this drag on. Eventually she got her way and she arranged the funeral. Leia had been all through the papers looking, like others, for a next of kin but without success. It was her who instructed the house clearance people not to throw away the papers. She had assumed that Roger Whalley would deal with all the personal effects and she just couldn't bear to think of what was obviously a lifetime's work just being dumped. She had had no idea what would happen to the papers, perhaps a miracle would happen.

Lettie had never thought of herself as a miracle but thanked Leia profusely for saving them. "You did absolutely the right thing and I think they might reveal something quite interesting."

Leia confirmed that she had attended the funeral but that there had been no one else there.

"Did you get any calls about Havergal while you were working on the case?" asked Lettie.

"Just one," came the reply, and Leia recounted the call from Mary Midlothian-Sutton.

"Well, I wonder where she fits in?" mused Lettie.

Lettie's next call was to PC Rhodri to see if he could do any translation for her but once again, just like the others, she found that he had moved on. She was told that he had been posted to the Newcastle force and, once again, she was told that they would not be able to divulge any private information.

"Oh no, I don't want any private information, just some translation," she had said.

She eventually got through to PC Rhodri although she had had to wait until he was back from a patrol. Lettie then explained the situation and asked if he could take a look at the papers to confirm if they were in Welsh and, if so, what they said. PC Rhodri said he would be delighted to help. He loved the Welsh language, was proud to be a Welsh speaker and was pleased to help another, albeit deceased. He then revealed that, in fact, he sort of knew the deceased.

"What?" exclaimed Lettie. "Explain that to me."

"Yes," said PC Rhodri. "I didn't actually know him but we both come from the same village, Llandysul in West Wales. It's a small village where everyone knows everyone else's business and my father, and especially my grandfather, knew the Wyllyams family quite well. In fact, my grandfather went to the same school as Huw, although they were in different classes."

"Huw? Who's he?" said Lettie.

"Havergal was often known as Huw, in fact I don't think I ever heard him called Havergal," said Rhodri, "it comes from his initials HUW."

"Well that explains a lot," said Lettie, "I've been going through his papers and found lots that were signed "Huw" and assumed they were someone else's."

"When I found out who he was on the day of the death I was gobsmacked that it was him and I was going to tell the Inspector that I knew of him but I didn't. It didn't really add anything and the rest of the chaps in the force were always taking the mickey out of my Welsh accent," said Rhodri. "Besides, I didn't really know him at all, just the stories from my family about his family."

"Do you know where the Ulric comes from?" asked Lettie. "Surely that's not a Welsh name?"

"Huw's mother was unmarried," said Rhodri. "They were the only single-parent family in the village, so they stuck out a bit. The story my grandfather told was that Huw's father was a Swedish sailor on leave from Pembroke Dock, who was never seen again but whose name was Ulric. I don't know if that is true."

Lettie then delared, "We must have a long talk as well as going through these papers. When can I come up to see you?"

But PC Rhodri was going off on a short holiday the next day so it would be a while before he could help. He was also a bit concerned about having a mass of papers dumped on him.

"Don't worry," said Lettie. "I'll bring them up and be your shorthand typist and we can go through them together and decide which ones are important and which ones aren't. I'm sure we won't need to translate them all and that it won't take very long"

They arranged a date in a few days' time, after his holiday and when PC Rhodri wouldn't be working. Lettie was excited about the prospect of a trip to Newcastle, she had never been there before and it wasn't far.

"About the same as New York to Washington," she thought. It would be a good reason to buy a car.

She decided to buy a car immediately, to give herself a little time to practice before the trip to Newcastle. She thought of going next door for advice but realised that the advice would not necessarily be impartial. She had noticed a car dealership nearby and went along to see them. Just like the builders and decorators, the car salesman thought he knew a mug when he saw one, and, just like them, he was wrong. Lettie had cash and no car to sell and she knew how to bargain. She was a bit dismayed at how small the cars were and surprised, compared to the US, at how expensive they were, but she drove a very hard deal and emerged some hours later, at the wheel of a small convertible. She understood about insurance and was not fazed by car tax but could not get over the fact that she apparently lived in a controlled parking zone and would thus have to pay to park her car outside her own house. The car salesman did not normally deal with administration like this for his customers but for this one he found himself doing everything.

Mrs Letitia Huntingdon Brown was very satisfied with her day's work. She had told Roger Whalley exactly what she thought of him, had thanked Leia for saving the papers, had made an invaluable contact in PC Rhodri, which she would follow up, and had bought a car, another first for her. Now she deserved a shower, a bite to eat and a glass of something – but just as she was about to relax the phone went. Her day of discovery was not over yet.

The caller was Ron. He had been in the pub and the landlord had given him Lettie's message and number. Lettie explained that she had bought Havergal/Huw's house, found the papers and was trying to do the right thing with them. Ron was initially suspicious and asked, "Are you anything to do with Kew?"

"Kew what? Kew Gardens?" she answered,

"No, Kew research laboratories," he said.

"No, I've only lived here for a few months and all I'm trying to do is to find out about this guy and his papers."

Then Ron said, "Look, I haven't got much time, I've got to go out. I'll happily come round and go through the papers with you but for now I just have one important question, have you found Huw's red file?"

"No, I haven't found a red file, is it important?"

"Damn," came the reply. "If all the other papers are there, then it means someone must have taken it. I'll come round tomorrow morning and explain all. In the meantime, just go through everything again would you and make sure that a red file is not there."

"OK," said Lettie. "I'll see you in the morning but I am certain I haven't seen a red file." She put the receiver down and went through the papers again but there was no red file.

"Boy oh Boy, how am I going to sleep after all this?" she thought.

Chapter 7

Ron presented himself at 13 Sandown Road the next morning at 10am, as agreed. Opening the door, Lettie surveyed him. He was not a very imposing figure. He was about 5 feet 6 inches, about 12 stones, about in his early 50s; everything about him was *about* something. He was not very smartly dressed but was apparently clean and was sociable enough, although very shy. What Ron saw was a lady slightly taller than he was, plumpish, in her mid to late 50s, with greying hair, darting eyes and a forcefield of a personality that almost gave off electricity. She made Ron very nervous. He and Lettie exchanged formalities and she invited him in.

"Well, this has all changed a bit. Huw would never have recognised it," said Ron in a slightly south London drawl.

Lettie explained that she had redecorated the entire house. "Have you been here before?" she asked. "I was told Havergal never had any visitors."

"Only a couple of times." said Ron. "I was dropping off papers for him. He didn't always ask me in but he did once or twice. I think he may have stopped when I once told him that the house was getting a bit dusty and recommended a cleaner to him. He took on my cleaner but I think he was a bit put out by my suggestion about his hygiene. It was from the cleaner that I learnt of his death."

"Did you go to the funeral?" asked Lettie, knowing that he hadn't.

"No, I couldn't bear to." said Ron. "It was all so desperately undignified for such a dignified man, to be found by your cleaner, then have social services dealing with you. I wanted to remember him the way I knew him."

"Let's sit down," said Lettie. "I want to know how you remember him, but first, will you have a cup of tea?"

"Before we start," said Ron. "Have you found Huw's red file?"

"No," said Lettie. "After our conversation last night I looked again but there's no sign of a red book or file or anything like that. You can go all through the papers if you want, there they are," she gestured towards the pile.

"Damn," said Ron. "The red book is critical. It was his life, in effect. That's really the reason I responded to the message you left in the pub, I was hoping you might have it."

"You've got a lot to tell me," said Lettie.

"And I've got a lot of papers to sort through, by the look of it," said Ron, gazing thoughtfully at the pile in the corner.

Ron started his explanation. "Huw was a botanist, just like me, but a lot better. He worked at the Royal Botanical Society's research facility at Kew, just as I do now. He retired about 10 years ago but we kept in touch ever since. We'd have a pint or two at the local pub almost every week, just discussing botany and what was happening at Kew. He was almost a father figure to me. We worked in the same department and both loved our work but hated the environment we had to work in, especially recently. All the others in the department were super competitive, they all have PhDs from Cambridge or Harvard or the Sorbonne and they're always trying to score points off each other."

"Do I take it that you and Havergal do not have PhDs?" asked Lettie.

"Huw went to university but was mostly self-taught, one of the old school. But I do have a PhD, I'd never have got in otherwise," said Ron, "but unlike the others I didn't brag about it. My PhD is just as good as theirs but was from Durham and not Cambridge. In fact, I'd probably not have got in at all if Huw hadn't backed me. He was on the interview panel then, although they took him off later, probably because he appointed me. He was always looking for good scientists but not necessarily good PR people."

"What do you mean by that?" asked Lettie.

"The whole ethos of the department was, and is, to publish papers, make discoveries and get plants named after you – *Gladioli Wilsonii*, that sort of thing. The research didn't really matter as long as you were doing things that publicised yourself, the department and Kew. For Huw, the research was all that mattered and he couldn't care less about the rest. He made numerous discoveries for which he could have had a name attribution but he allowed others, especially the departmental head, to steal the glory."

"Who is this departmental head?" asked Lettie.

"Huw joined Kew more or less straight from university, I think, in the late 1950s and the head of botanical research then was Professor Sir Lancelot Swann, known as "Lance" to everyone. He was a delightful man, very old school, an old Etonian, I think, a real amateur enthusiast. He freely admitted he knew little about botany and had got his job via the old boy network; his passion was Lepidoptera, butterflies to you and me. He kept a butterfly net by his desk and would charge outside every time he saw a specimen fly past his window. He was as nutty as a fruitcake but everyone loved him and no one minded his lack of botanical knowledge. In fact, Huw helped him out whenever interpretation was needed. He and Huw got on very well; they were very similar characters, very enthusiastic about their passions."

"Lance retired in the mid-1990s, just after I joined, and it was generally assumed that Huw would take over; he was certainly the most experienced and knowledgeable botanist in the department and he'd been there for 30 years. But the trouble was that Huw was not in the slightest bit political and didn't bother sucking up to the powers that be or even telling the wider world about his theories and discoveries. I think I told you that he made numerous discoveries but never bothered getting his name attached to the new genus. And in fact the person who stole most, actually probably nearly all of Huw's discoveries and got his name attached was the person who got the department headship, a truly nasty man who is still there now, Doctor Carl Wiseman. Huw and I called him 'Carlos the Jackal'. He was a scavenger after everyone else's work. He's got an affected mid-Atlantic sort of accent, even though he is as English as I am. In fact, he's from Croydon. He was and is only interested in self-promotion and publicity and has no interest in the beauty of plants. I don't know what he's a doctor of but it's certainly not botany and not divinity either."

"Well how on earth did he get the top job?" asked Lettie.

"You need to know a bit about what's been happening at Kew to understand that," started Ron. "Originally, and I'm going back to the war, Kew was a classic Victorian public good. The entry price was one old penny until 1951 and it only went up to three old pennies then. Even with decimalisation in 1971, entry was still only one new penny. But gradually in recent decades public funding was reduced and is now totally withdrawn, so Kew had to become commercial. Both Lance and Huw hated this trend. When a new botanist was needed, about four years before Lance retired, they appointed Wiseman because of his commercial credentials and the deals and sponsorships he claimed he could get. And then, when Lance retired, they chose Wiseman for departmental head, even though he'd only been in the department a few years. Huw didn't mind that much; he told me that he'd have hated all the meetings and personnel issues and reports. All he ever wanted to do was to get on with his work. But when Wiseman became head, the atmosphere changed totally, as I've said. But the biggest shock was when Huw got to 65 and expected to be asked to stay on, which was what he wanted, Wiseman insisted he retire, although he did agree to allow Huw continued access to the departmental records and facilities."

"He must have been crazy," said Lettie. "Why insist that such an experienced man retire when he wants to stay on?"

"Easy," said Ron. "Huw regularly embarrassed Wiseman at departmental meetings, not intentionally but because he just knew so much more. Wiseman couldn't allow that to continue happening; it could damage his ambitions if it got around. But he allowed Huw access to the department so he could keep an eye on what he was doing and steal it if possible, and that's exactly what he regularly did."

"Huw knew what was going on and that is why he kept all his papers at home and left nothing in the department," said Ron. "And that, I expect, is what that pile of papers is."

"But what's the story about the Red Book and what exactly are all those papers?" asked Lettie.

"Well," said Ron, "Huw was very old school in his ways of working. He never used a computer or had things typed, everything was handwritten. He would make copious notes and lists but when he finally reached a conclusion he would write it up and it would go into his Red Book. In fact, it wasn't really a book, it was a sort of file that zipped up, a freebie from a supplier, everyone in the department got one with their initials on them. I lost mine years ago, his just happened to be red. He kept all his findings and conclusions in there, as well as his personal things. I know that because a couple of times I asked for a telephone number or a date and he would go to this folder; he kept everything in there. It was pretty much his life, and that's why it is such a pity it has disappeared."

"What do you think has happened to it? "said Lettie. "I've no idea but I can think of several people who would like to have it, especially the scientific papers he kept in there," replied Ron.

"Did Havergal have a speciality?" asked Lettie. She couldn't bring herself to call him Huw, just as Ron didn't think of his friend as Havergal.

"Huw was a very knowledgeable all round botanist but his passions were palms, orchids and cacti – and especially Madagascar," said Ron.

"Palms, orchids and cacti I can understand," said Lettie, "but what's with Madagascar?"

"Well," said Ron, "it all began with Lance. He had made a field trip there in the late 1980s, just a few years before he retired. Madagascar had been very difficult to get into for many years but was then just starting to open up. Lance was there for about two months and came back with loads of specimens but, to the consternation of Kew's senior management, most of his specimens were butterflies. In fact, he confided to Huw later that that was really all he had done until the last few days, when he realised he had better bring back some plants to satisfy the botanists back home and so scurried around grabbing armfuls of whatever he could find. But even such an unscientific survey was enough to enthuse Huw. He'd never seen anything like these randomly collected species and quickly persuaded the finance department to support another trip but with him going with Lance this time. He made many later trips on his own. He was gobsmacked by what he found. Madagascar was becoming the world hotspot for botanists and they were flocking there from all over the world. Ninety per cent of the plant species there grow nowhere else in the world. The palms were of particular interest, including climbing palms, bush palms, alpine palms and especially the self-destructive palm. There are 180 known palm species in Madagascar and 100 of them were discovered by Kew; 70 of them have been discovered in the last 20 years. There is *Tahina spectabilis,* the self-destructive palm, which has leaves up to five metres across; when it flowers it produces a mass of shoots and then dies. Then there is *Ravenea delicatula,* a climbing palm, and *Beccariophoenix madagascariensis,* the window pane palm and Madagascar's most iconic plant. Huw was fascinated by what he found there and until the day he died he was working through his notes, trying to link up the botany of the various species."

"Do you know what Havergal died of?" asked Lettie, "and when was the last time you saw him?"

"I saw him just a couple of weeks before he died. We'd meet in the pub just to chat about botany. Huw wasn't really interested in departmental politics," replied Ron, "he was well and quite excited, or as excited as he ever got. He said he was "onto something". I didn't think too much of it, Huw was always "onto something" and I knew that he wouldn't tell me until he had got to the bottom of it."

"Is it possible that Kew or Wiseman knew that he was on to something and could it have been something to do with the Madagascan palms?" asked Lettie. "Perhaps they found out when he was in the department?"

"I don't know," replied Ron, "but I do know that they were always trying to steal his file or look in it; every time he left the room someone would sidle over and look in the file while he was away. I warned Huw about this and from then on he never let the file out of his sight."

"Is it possible that someone at Kew perhaps stole the file from the pile over there when the workers were here? asked Lettie.

"It's possible," said Ron, "there's plenty of Kew staff living around here and in fact Wiseman himself only lives just round the corner."

"WHAT?" exclaimed Lettie. "Wiseman lives around the corner?"

"He lives two houses from me, about 600 yards away in the next road. Of course, it's only his weekday home, he has a big place in the country for weekends. Lots of Kew staff live around here, it's handy for getting to work."

Lettie's mind was racing.

"I'd better be going soon," said Ron. "I told them at Kew I would be an hour or two late because of a dental appointment and if I don't show up soon the Jackal will have some snide comment or another to make. I haven't gone through the papers yet and I can't now, and there are an awful lot of them, the best thing would be if I take them to my house to go through tonight, if you are happy with that. In fact, it might take me a few trips to get them all to my place."

Lettie said she was happy with this and it did indeed take Ron three trips to take all the papers to his house. On his final trip he and Lettie agreed to meet again at the weekend, which would give Ron more time to go through the papers and more time to talk.

When Ron had gone, Lettie sat down to review what she had learnt. Her head was spinning with so much new information and so many possibilities. But one thought troubled her greatly, something she had not mentioned to Ron. Was it possible that someone had come round to the house on the night Havergal died and taken the book or file or whatever it was, perhaps Wiseman himself? The police had found nothing suspicious and no evidence of forced entry so if this was true Havergal must have let someone in so it must have been someone known to him.

"Surely even such a nasty man as Wiseman obviously is would not have committed murder?" she thought. "Did Wiseman come round on the pretext of asking for some paper or another, they had an argument, Havergal perhaps had a heart attack, sat down in the chair and Wiseman took the book and ran off?" How could she pursue this? Then she realised that the front door was the key. She'd lived long enough now in London to realise that people locked their front doors when they were home for the evening. If the front door had been locked when the cleaner arrived, it would mean that no one had been admitted to the house that evening. But what if it had been unlocked? Only the cleaner would know. So how to find the cleaner? And, what's more, had anyone come to the house while her workmen were there and taken away anything? Lettie was beginning to feel she knew Havergal and was beginning to like him and nothing was going to stop her getting to the bottom of this.

Chapter 8

Lettie decided the first thing she must do is to try and get to the bottom of whether the front door had been locked or not when the cleaner arrived; if there was any suspicion of foul play she must tell the police and she hated the thought that perhaps Havergal had experienced violence. But how to find the cleaner? Then she remembered that she had been Ron's cleaner as well and she called him.

"She gave me her resignation about two weeks after Huw died," said Ron. "She said she couldn't earn enough money here and was going back to the Ukraine. Why do you want to find her?" he asked. Lettie explained. "Wow," said Ron, "then you had better contact the police. I know she had to make a statement for them, she told me about it. Maybe she said something there?"

"Yes," said Lettie, "and I know just the man to call to find out..."

It took a while to get hold of PC Rhodri in Newcastle. He had holiday and work commitments but eventually she did.

"Well," he said, "to be honest I don't remember all that much about the case. I've dealt with hundreds of cases since then. All I remember is that it seemed a pretty open and shut case but whether we asked the cleaner if the front door had been locked, I can't remember. The only way to find out is to call the local station and ask to see the case notes and the actual statement itself. They won't give that to you so I'll call them and call you back."

"Thanks," said Lettie, "but if the notes say nothing about that, what then?"

"Let's wait and see what they do say first," said PC Rhodri. "It might take me a bit of time to persuade them to give me what they have; it messes up the performance targets if old cases get reopened, I'll have to be very careful. I'll call you when I have some information and anyway we are meeting soon aren't we?" They rang off.

While she was waiting for PC Rhodri, who was now Dafydd Myrddin Rhodri, Lettie decided to go next door and ask about visitors while the work had been going on. As usual she found them all there. "Don't they ever do any work?" she thought.

"Oh yes," said Delbert, "loads of people came to the house while we were working, one or two a day, almost every day. Most of the neighbours up and down the street came round to ask about the old man, what had happened and who was moving in, they were all nosey and wanted to see what was going on. Then there were painters and trades people asking if there was any work, and then there were one or two people I didn't recognise, and one in particular, who just asked if he could look around. He said he wanted to see our work and I was hoping there might be a job in it for me but he didn't seem to take much interest in the paintwork, he was more interested in that pile of papers. He asked who the new owner was and did I have a contact number he could call so he could ask if they were satisfied with our work. I gave him your number. He was dressed in a suit and seemed respectable. I hope you didn't mind. Did he call you?"

"No," said Lettie, "no one called me. Did this man leave a name and did he take anything?"

"No to both," said Delbert. "Why, is there something missing?"

"There could be," said Lettie. "Oh, and by the way, do you know what happened to the cleaner's keys, she must have had some keys to let herself in, what happened to them?"

"They were just left in the house," said Delbert, we were using them to let the painters and plumbers in and out. Do you want them back?"

"No, that's OK," said Lettie. "I was just wondering. I've changed the locks anyway, thanks for your help." After Lettie had gone, the Wellington family looked at each other, wondering what that was all about.

A little later Dafydd Rhodri called. He'd had no luck. The local station had been very suspicious at first. "Why do you want to know? You're not going to reopen the case are you?" he was asked. It didn't help that he was only a young PC and he was asking his old station sergeant who had never thought very much of him when he was there and had been fairly instrumental in getting him posted as far away as possible to Newcastle. PC Rhodri had had to tell some white lies to persuade his old station sergeant. "I took the notes and statements that day and recently I found a page from my notebook and I'm not sure if I put it in the filed papers. It was nothing startling but just for completeness I wanted to be sure if it was in there or not." The station sergeant eventually relented. "I always knew he was useless," he thought, went to fetch the papers and read them to PC Rhodri.

"Ah, yes, it's in there so no problem," Rhodri had said, and then rang off.

Rhodri reported to Lettie that there had been no question to the cleaner about whether the front door was locked or not and that the conclusion had been that nothing suspicious had occurred and it had been a natural death that needed no post mortem or further investigation and therefore the case was closed.

"You'll have a heck of a job getting them to reopen it," added PC Rhodri. "And what's more," he continued, "you'll have a job finding the cleaner. In my experience they all use false names to avoid tax and she was apparently living with friends and moving around." "It's worse than that," said Lettie, "she's gone back to the Ukraine. She used to clean for someone else I know and he told me."

"Then you won't find her; she'll be back to her real name by now," said Rhodri. "I'll see you in a week or so when we meet up here to look at those Welsh papers." They rang off.

"So," thought Lettie, "someone, quite possibly from Kew, possibly Wiseman, came round to look at the house and took an interest in the papers but we don't know whether the front door was locked or not and probably never will. Where does this leave us?"

Her thoughts were interrupted by her telephone. It was Ron. He had finished sorting the papers and was ready to bring them round.

Chapter 9

Being a good botanist, Ron arrived at 13 Sandown Road, somewhat theatrically, with the papers stacked in his wheelbarrow. Because they were now sorted into individual related stacks there appeared to be even more of them than before.

"If I'd carried these round it would have taken 5 or 6 trips," he explained. "I thought about driving round but the controlled parking zone gets complicated, so this seemed the easiest way, and I can park the wheelie in your front garden."

"Havergal's botanical papers delivered in a wheelbarrow. It couldn't be more appropriate, could it?" said Lettie, smiling. "I'll bet he would have enjoyed it!"

Lettie made some tea and they sat down to start.

"I'm sorry it's taken so long," said Ron, "but the papers were in a complete mess. It's such a pity because Huw was so well organised and tidy and they would have been neatly filed and classified but when I picked them up they were in a complete jumble, some of them covered in tea stains and others with footprints on them. Huw would have been horrified."

"Well, at least I saved them," said Lettie. "If I'd known about them while the work was going on, I'd have done something sooner."

They sat facing nine piles of papers of varying sizes.

"I think I told you that Huw was very old school in his ways of working," said Ron. "He never threw anything away, he hand wrote everything, he would draft things until he was happy and only then produce a final copy. And for his botanical work he would make prodigious lists and notes before finalising a last conclusion that would go into the red book. The first two piles are easy and quite small. When you divided the papers up into three groups; the academic papers, the administrative papers and the foreign language papers, you missed some. This first small pile is some utility bills and council tax demands that you missed and the second small pile are some presumably Welsh letters that you missed."

"Thanks," said Lettie. "I'll destroy the first pile, as I did the others, and add the second pile to the Welsh papers over there that I am going to have translated by PC Rhodri."

"Now as to the next seven piles," Ron continued, "we'll be getting down, eventually, to some serious botany, but first this pile..." Ron gestured to a neatly stacked pile about 6 inches high. "These are all of Huw's school notes and exercises from his school botany lessons. I think I said he never threw anything out, well he doesn't seem to have kept his History or French notes, or any other subjects, but does seem to have kept all his botany ones. Reading these and some of the later ones will give you a good grasp of basic botany..."

"Why don't you just give me a quick overview of what botany is all about before we go any further," said Lettie. "I always thought a daffodil was just a daffodil!"

"Well OK," said Ron, "if you're sure that's what you want. Just stop me if it gets boring. You see, I do a lot of lecturing about botany, we all do at Kew, we're encouraged to do it and I enjoy it. I do a 40-minute introduction to botany class for the lower schools. You have to finish dead on 40 minutes otherwise you're crushed mid-sentence by the stampede when the bell goes. I do a practical class for sixth formers who are studying botany. I do an introductory lecture for volunteers at Kew and I do evening classes wherever there is a demand. Which one do you think you would like to hear?"

"Give me a mixture, you know how little I know, just a taster."

"OK," continued Ron. "I'll try and make it brief and as understandable as possible for a layperson. Botany is a branch of biology and biology is the study of life itself, so what could be more interesting than that?"

"Nothing, I guess," said Lettie, not yet convinced.

"Well, if you need convincing, consider this," said Ron. "Plants do something magical called photosynthesis, they take carbon dioxide from the atmosphere through their stemata, on the underside of their leaves, add some water and some light that has travelled 150 million kilometres from the sun and from this they produce sugars for their growth and then expel the oxygen into the atmosphere as a waste product; without plants there would be no oxygen and therefore no animal life on earth. We need plants to survive. Photosynthesis is the most important natural process on earth. By photosynthesis plants produce 100 trillion watts of energy each year and they produce nectar with three times the sugar concentration of Coca-Cola and this led to the evolution of insects – bees, butterflies and moths and this led to birds either for the pollen or eating the pollinators and all this led eventually to us."

"OK, I think I sort of knew that," replied Lettie, and then asked, "Who discovered photosynthesis?" although not quite sure why she wanted to know.

"It's an interesting story, full of personalities," said Ron. "It's very rare in science for there to be a 'Eureka' moment where one person suddenly finds the complete solution to a problem, usually it's lots of people adding little bits over a long time that eventually fall into place and photosynthesis was typical of this, in fact it's only finally been properly understood in quite recent times. Originally it was thought that plants grew by consuming the soil they grow in but that was disproved in the 17th century by Jan Baptista van Helmont. You can probably imagine how he did it. He just measured an amount of soil, stuck a plant in it, watched it grow for three years and then measured the soil again and found that it was exactly the same. Simple. So if it wasn't the soil, how was the plant growing?

About a hundred years later Jan Ingenhousz proved that plants give off oxygen when they have sunlight and water, and this was the first real breakthrough. Then, about a hundred years later again, Julius von Sachs showed that plants produce sugars, which are stored as starch, because of the light and then it was proved that they take in carbon dioxide through their stemata but it was not known what they did with the carbon until the 20th century when, using particle accelerators, two scientists at the University of California, Andrew Benson and Melvin Calvin, made the final breakthrough and identified the microbiology and showed how it all worked. So you see it evolved over 300 years or more. But there's an interesting story there. Benson and Calvin were pursuing quite different theories and were working completely independently. Benson was the one who got it right but Calvin was nominally the departmental boss. Guess who got the Nobel Prize and all the fame and is credited with being the discoverer of photosynthesis? Calvin. Does that sound familiar at all?"

"It's a pretty lethal world, botany, huh?"

"Probably the same in all walks of life. There are plenty of decent people but there are also some scoundrels," replied Ron.

"But if plants are so good at processing carbon dioxide, why is there all this fuss about greenhouses gasses?" asked Lettie.

"That's a bit of a big subject," said Ron, "but in a nutshell carbon dioxide is not the only greenhouse gas, there are others, but the main thing is that with the burning of fossil fuels for energy, there is now much more carbon dioxide in the atmosphere, much more than occurs naturally from volcanoes and geysers and so on and more than the plant world can process, especially as rain forests around the world are being cut down. But I think we should we get back to some of the basic botany, just to give you the framework?" Lettie nodded. "I hope I'm not boring you already?" said Ron.

"On you go," said Lettie, impressed by this new Ron, full of confidence and enthusiasm, his shyness abandoned. "To tell you about botany I need to tell you a bit about the history of the earth," Ron continued, "and all about Darwinian evolution, something some of your creationist fellow countrymen don't believe in. I hope you are comfortable with that?" Lettie nodded. "I'll give you a quick summary first. The world began, as we all know, with the Big Bang. Then, for millions of years there was no life on earth, just swirling toxic gasses, no atmosphere and no protection against the sun's rays. The first life forms were microorganisms, bacteria really, that survived in the sea and produced oxygen from the sun's rays. Gradually these life forms crept out of the sea to the water's edge and became plants, but they were rootless and leafless. Over many millions of years they developed roots and leaves and the roots started to break up the rocks to produce soil and the leaves produced more and more oxygen and so created the ozone layer, which protects the earth. Gradually, some of the bacteria evolved into animals. Primitive crabs were the first, and as the plant world made the earth habitable so the animals came ashore and developed too, and then, of course, over millions of years life evolved into us, as Charles Darwin has shown, so you see, there would be no life on earth if it weren't for plants. Plants drove the evolution of all animals.

"Originally there were no separate continents, there was just one land mass, called Pangaea, and by now plant life had evolved into just two plants, conifers and ferns. Conifers reproduce by windblown spores, the pollen has to find female cones, 10 billion grains are released by a single tree; ferns have to live by water and release their seeds into the water. There were only these two plants, about 1% of today's range and the animal kingdom was just dinosaurs, although there were 700 species of them. There was no colour, only green; rain forests covered most of the earth.

"Then, about 65 million years ago, a 10-kilometre wide asteroid hit the earth with a force of a billion Hiroshima bombs, this killed all the dinosaurs and the acid rain killed all the plants, but the seeds of some plants survived and gradually plant life recolonized the earth. At about this time the supercontinent was breaking up into the continents we know today.

"The next big development was between 30 and 50 million years ago, as the continents developed huge mountain ranges formed made of limestone and this sucked the carbon dioxide out of the atmosphere and CO_2 levels fell to one sixth of where they had been. This killed off many of the forests but grasses processed CO_2 more efficiently and prospered and gradually they would become the dominant force on the planet, with very important consequences. The earth at this time was also very dry and fires were a constant hazard. Trees could not survive fire but the grasses developed an ability to exploit fire, they are the most fire resistant plants on earth and could recolonize very quickly after fire, to this day the savannahs are regularly burnt to control the trees but in the knowledge that the grassland will regrow. By then there were 8,000 different species of grasses covering a quarter of the land.

"Grasses also transformed the animal kingdom. 6-7 million years ago herbivores diets changed to grasses and the animals that adapted to grasses survived, and this was all down to their teeth and their ability to adapt to the plants.

"And then, about 5 million years ago, one group of primates left the forest to go to the savannah/grasslands, they started to use tools, and they started to stand up, to see over the grasses and look for predators or for prey. Over the next 5 million years, these apemen turned into *Homo Sapiens* and 100,000 years ago they migrated from Africa over the rest of the world. They were hunter/gatherers then but became farmers, starting with wild wheat, giving them bread and they evolved into societies.

"Along the way a lot of other things happened too. Colour came into the world as flowers developed. Flowers reproduce much more quickly than conifers and ferns, so mutations can occur more quickly. They have very rapid lifecycles. Plants evolved colour to get noticed by insects, specific colours for specific insects, plants also developed seeds, seeds are almost indestructible, surviving droughts and fire they can lie dormant for years but then regenerate and, of course, the primates ate the fruit and thereby spread the seeds.

"So, let's just summarise… plants give us oxygen, they formed the soil so life could colonise the land, they gave us colour and food, they shaped the animal world, they drove our ape ancestors and created us and our world. They have been the central driving force of life on earth. Of course I'm biased but I believe botany, the study of the plant kingdom, is the senior of all sciences because nothing else would exist without it, and yet most people are entirely uninterested."

"That's probably because most people haven't heard you talk about it," replied Lettie. "You have a gift, you're a real teacher, you transmit your enthusiasm. I really enjoyed that. Now what's next? That can't be all?"

"No, there's quite a lot more," said Ron. "Let me tell you about the Tree of Life, you must have heard of it?" he continued.

"I'm afraid I may have missed that, is it some kind of vitamin supplement?" replied Lettie sheepishly.

"Let me give you a simple non-botanical example," said Ron, walking over to the window. "You see that lady walking her pet, what kind of dog is that?"

"It's a King Charles spaniel," replied Lettie, pleased to have got something right.

"Well let's see if we can define a King Charles spaniel through the Tree of Life. This is a method of defining every living thing in 10 easy steps. The first step is simple, is the dog animate or inanimate?" asked Ron.

"Animate," was the reply.

"Correct, it is not a rock, we'll leave those to the geologists. Now animate things are divided into three *domains*. Put very simply, these are; number one, bacteria with genes, number two bacteria without genes and number three, *Eukarya*, which are organisms whose cells contain complex structures within membranes; which does our spaniel sound like?"

"The last one, I guess," came the answer.

"Correct," said Ron. "Next, *Eukarya* are divided into four *kingdoms;* simplifying heroically these are; firstly *Protista*, which are microorganisms that are usually single celled, secondly, *plants*, thirdly *fungi* and fourthly *animals*. It's pretty obvious which kingdom our dog is part of isn't it? It's called the *Kingdom Animalia*. The next stage is that this Kingdom has about 40 different *Phyla*. What that means is different body constructions. I won't go through them all but one is called *Chordata* and that, in simple terms, means animals with backbones.

The next stage is called *class,* and I won't go all through it except to say that one of the classes is *mammalia,* which includes our dog. The next stage is to determine the *order,* and one of these is *carnivoro,* which is self-explanatory, then the *family,* and one of these is *canines,* then the *genus,* which is spaniels, and then the *species,* which is King Charles."

"Now let's try the same with your daffodils. There are about 50 different species of daffodil and the most common is called *narcissus pseudonarcissus* and they are all part of the genus *narcissi,* which itself is part of the *amaryllis* family and so on. Obviously the botanical definitions are different to the animal ones. The basic divisions of the *Kingdom Plantae* are microbes and bacteria, algae, fungi, liverworts and mosses, ferns, club mosses and horsetails, conifers and angiosperms. Each of these groups has a different method of reproduction. For *angiosperms,* which are all flowering plants, it is by seeds, for ferns it is by spores and so on. There are 300 families and 250,000 species of flowering plants. When we think about botany we tend to think just about the *angiosperms* but the others are just as important, and in some cases more so.

"Gee, you know so much," said Lettie, in admiration.

"Well, it's 30 years of work and I still don't know half what Huw did, and anyway this is all basic stuff, you'll find it all in Huw's school and university notes."

"But there's one thing I've never understood," said Lettie. "Why are some of the names so complicated. What's wrong with just daffodil rather than *narcissus pseudonarcissus?*"

"Well," said Ron, "as I said earlier, there are about 50 different species of daffodil, including my favourites, *narcissus jonquilla* and *narcissus odorus plenus,* and if they were all just called daffodil then no one would know which one you were talking about."

"OK," said Lettie, "I can see that, but why are the names so complicated?"

"Good question," said Ron. "The history of the naming and classification of plants is fascinating. Sit back and I'll tell you..." Ron was warming to his subject and growing in confidence. "It's called Taxonomy and the name everyone has heard of is Carl Linnaeus, who was an eighteenth century Swedish botanist, have you heard of him?"

Lettie indicated that she had not.

"There are some interesting stories here too, so I'll start at the beginning," said Ron.

"Three hundred and more years ago, there were no supermarkets or chemists, foods and medicines were not packaged and labelled and you had to know what you were eating or what might help you to get better. Everybody had to be a sort of botanist. A simple example is given in school botany lessons today where you are shown three apparently identical small black berries. One is St John's Wort, which is good for treating depression, the next is deadly nightshade, which is fatal and the third is a blackcurrant. Knowing which is which was fairly important.

"Attempts to explain how plants work and therefore categorise them go back thousands of years to the Greeks and the Romans and Theophrastus and his *Historia Plantarum*, Pliny and *Historia Naturalis*, Plato and many others. In the early days, the study of plants was intimately connected with the study of medicine and magic. In England the Society of Apothecaries started in the 16th century to try and standardise definitions.

"Classification is the basis of botany. From the start botanists were trying to classify plants into related families and groups. If one plant in a family was poisonous, the chances are that they all are so you need to try and find the relatives. The first botanist to try to identify families was John Ray at Cambridge in the 17th century. He was looking for patterns of similarity and focussed particularly on similarities between different seeds – were they *dicots* and split into two or *monocots* and so on. He published *Historia Plantarum* and this was the start of the attempt to classify plants.

"About 50 years after Ray came Carl Linnaeus, who I mentioned. He made two contributions to botany, one useful, the other not. The first, which was the useless one, was that he said botany was all about sex. The schoolchildren all sit up when I say that. He classified plant families by their reproductive arrangements, in other words all plants with the same structure of sexual parts, the same number of male genitalia (stamen) and female genitalia (pistils) must be related. He published *Systema Naturae* in 1735 and made himself very rich from it. But the Royal Society rejected him and society was shocked to hear such ripe language in a scientific book. A famous newspaper quote at the time said, "Who would have thought that bluebells, lilies and onions could be up to such immorality?" In fact, he was wrong. Since then it has been shown that there are plenty of species with identical reproductive systems that are not related and the reverse.

"But his valuable and enduring contribution was to define a *binomial* naming system for plants and this what he is known for to this day. The binomial system is like a surname and a Christian name.... I hope I'm not boring you," Ron broke off.

"Not at all, I always like listening to enthusiasts," purred Lettie, "even if I don't understand everything."

"Well, the naming of plants was becoming a real problem. The same plant might have different names in different countries or even in the same country and even in the same county and the names were often 5 or 6 words long. A simple example, the humble tomato was called, in Latin, *Solanum caule inermi herbaceo, foliis pinnatis incises,* which means "the smooth stemmed herbaceous solanum with incised pinnate leaves", which is a bit of a mouthful and something simpler had to be found, also herbal medicine was becoming more popular and you needed to know what you were getting. Linnaeus introduced a standard binomial naming system for plants which survives to this day and which he published in *Genera Plantarum* in 1753.

"With just two words, the genus and the species, he classified about 9,000 plants. Today it is estimated that there are 370,000 plant species with 1.6 million names of which about a third are still unresolved and, what's more, there are 2,000 new species being discovered and named every year, so goodness knows where the total will end up. Linnaeus' methodology was largely by physical examination; if things looked similar they must be related. Since then there have been numerous reclassifications and changes but the basic system hasn't changed. What he didn't really take into account was that plants adapt to their environments. If it is a hot and dry environment then all plants will develop defensive mechanisms and may come to look similar even if they are not. *Cacti* (in the Americas) and *Euphorbs* (in Africa) are both succulents that deal with hot and dry conditions and look very similar but are unrelated. Huw did his University thesis on Taxonomy so you can read all about it there, it's in that pile," and he gestured to the second pile.

"It is only by classifying plants that you can understand them. And with that understanding comes an ability to propagate them, to control disease, to exploit them, to avoid poisonous plants and to use good ones for medicine and food and much else. The *Kingdom Plantae* gives us the oxygen we breathe, the food we eat, the clothes we wear and often the medicines we need, it is crucial to all human life, in fact plants really are the origin of life on earth, we simply wouldn't be here if there were no plants, that's why botany is so fascinating."

"But, you know what?" continued Ron, "even though I like all the scientific stuff, I like the simple beauty of plants so much more. Huw was the same. Despite all the dreadful office politics, I'm so happy to work at Kew, each day something new is budding, snowdrops in January, daffodils in February, I never tire of it. But I think you must be tiring of me, I've lectured you long enough, let's get back to the papers."

"Thank you Ron," murmured Lettie in admiration. "I hope I remember some of that."

The second pile was about twice the size of the first. "These," said Ron, "are his university notes. As I told you, I didn't realise he'd been to University, he never mentioned it, I always thought he was self-taught. These are all the lecture notes, the essays, the field trips; he even kept the exam papers. His final dissertation on Taxonomy is actually rather good, considering he was only in his early twenties; of course it's a bit out of date now."

"Let me just butt in for a moment," said Lettie. "I'm interested in his handwriting; it seems to have hardly changed from his school and university days to his more recent writings."

Ron agreed. "That is exactly as I remember his writing at Kew, it hadn't changed one jot. He was left handed, so writing was always a bit more laborious for him, especially in the old fountain pen days. Although his writing was always very clear, it had a very distinctive style."

"Left-handed, huh?" thought Lettie, she didn't know why she found that interesting but tucked it away in her mind.

"Well that's the first two piles," said Ron. "The next two piles are all of Huw's working papers, developed while he was working at Kew over all those years. I have tried to arrange them chronologically and in subjects. The early ones record some simple projects he was given in his early days and they then get progressively more challenging. In all cases the papers are missing the final synopsis or conclusion, which he kept separately .There is nothing earth shattering in them and any botanist will be able to see what the conclusion was because things quickly enter the public domain. But what these papers are is a record of one man's working life and it would be nice if something appropriate could be done with them."

"But the last three smaller piles are very interesting," said Ron, "these are what Huw had been working on since retiring from Kew, and one certainly and possibly two could be *very* interesting. I think I told you that Huw's interests were orchids, palms and cacti. Well, he was working on a project on each of these. I'm pretty sure that I recognise enough of the orchid project to know what it's about and that it is almost certainly concluded and in the public domain. I'm also pretty sure that the palm project is definitely completely new and could be very significant. The cactus project is somewhere in the middle. He was definitely onto something but it's not clear exactly what."

"And Wiseman could well have known about these?" asked Lettie. Ron did not answer.

"You know Ron," said Lettie, "I am going to get to the bottom of what happened to Havergal and I am going to try my best to find out what his discoveries were and make sure that he gets the credit if credit is due. Will you help me? I am not a botanist and I'll need all the help I can get."

"Of course," said Ron. "Huw was my mentor and my friend. I will help all I can but I will have to be careful at Kew. And remember I am a working man and don't have total free time."

"We can work around that, you're just round the corner anyway," said Lettie. "You know what I'm going to do? I am going to read all of those papers, or as many as I can, I'm going to copy the three project piles, then I am going to call Wiseman at Kew and offer him all the papers, I'll suggest he sets up a Havergal Wyllyams library and it will give me a chance to have a good look at him. I am going to become a botanist! With you helping me Ron, we will get to the bottom of all this!"

"Oh, and thanks Ron for sorting through all these papers. I can see you've got to go soon, but since we are going to be allies in this, first, tell me a bit about yourself."

She could tell immediately that Ron did not much like talking about himself.

"Nothing much to say really," he said. "I'm 53, I never married, live on my own, I love my work but not the people. Huw was a great friend and I don't have many, so his death was a big loss. I'm a bit solitary but I will help you all I can. And yes, I should be going. Thanks for the tea, you know where I am."

Lettie now knew exactly what she was going to do. The first step was to become a botanist and this she would achieve by reading Havergal's papers, so she sat down and made a start.

Chapter 10

A few days later, Lettie was sitting in the kitchen, enjoying her morning cup of tea but she was not happy. In fact, she felt like a complete fool. After Ron's lecture on botany she had felt inspired and energised and for several days she had been reading enthusiastically through the papers, trying to become a botanist. As well as going through the papers, she had even bought herself some books. "Botany made easy" and "An Idiot's Guide to Botany". But she was getting nowhere. With much help from Ron, she had understood most of the school notes and some of the University papers but nothing else. It was like a foreign language. She now realized that to think she could absorb Havergal's 40 years of work and research experience in a few days was madness and she felt depressed by her stupidity. She decided she would make copies for herself of the small number of pages she had understood and the three research files that she certainly hadn't, and then let Kew have the lot. She was not going to become a botanist but she would still get to the bottom of what happened to Havergal and, somehow, perhaps with Ron's help, his three discoveries.

She phoned Kew and asked for the Head of Research (she deliberately did not ask for Carl Wiseman; it might have seemed strange that she knew his name and she must protect Ron). She got his secretary and was told, "I'm sorry, Mr Wiseman is on a trip and will not be back for a few weeks. Can I help?"

Lettie explained about Sandown Road and the papers, whereupon the secretary jumped in. "Ooh, did you find the red book?"

"I don't know, it's just a pile of papers," Lettie lied, registering the fact that after all this time even the secretary knew about the red book. "Would you ask Mr. Wiseman to call me when he is back? When do you expect him to return?"

"You can never tell with these field trips," said the secretary. "If they make a discovery they will stay as long as it takes to pin it down. It could be several weeks."

Two hours later, Lettie's phone rang. It was Wiseman.

"My secretary passed on your message. I'm in Argentina. Did you find a red book among Huw's papers?" he came straight to the point.

"I don't know," Lettie lied again. "There's just a large pile of papers. What is this about a red book? Your secretary asked the same question. Oh, and by the way, did you visit my house while it was being renovated? The builders told me that someone called by and seemed interested in the papers."

"I can't hear you," said Wiseman, "the line is terrible. I will be back early next week and will make contact with you then, but in the meantime please keep all those papers safe and do not let anyone else near them. I'll explain why when I'm back."

Even after such a short conversation, Lettie knew she was not going to like Carl Wiseman and would never trust him.

Lettie now had the best part of a week to wait before Wiseman was back, so she decided to go and visit PC Rhodri in Newcastle with the Welsh letters. She had confirmed they were in Welsh by picking a few at random and consulting the internet. She called Dafydd Myrddin Rhodri and they agreed to meet in Newcastle in two days' time.

Chapter 11

Lettie was excited; this would be her first big trip since coming back to her home country. She had really hardly used her car: a trip to see Windsor castle, a trip to Oxford and another into the Surrey country-side was about all that she had managed. It was useless in London and she'd been tempted to sell it but now it would prove it's worth. She couldn't take the train because of the mass of papers, so she would have to drive to Newcastle.

The first minor problem was Newcastle itself. She had assumed you just put the name into the satnav and off you go. But there appeared to be two Newcastles – Newcastle-under-Lyme and Newcastle-upon-Tyne. Which was it? Then she remembered that P.C. Rhodri had mentioned having to fish someone out of the Tyne, so that must be it. Putting the postcode of the hotel into the satnav clinched it.

She set off early, to miss the rush hour, successfully navigated through London and was on the M1 heading north with no trouble. She drove for about three hours and then, just as she had entered Yorkshire, she decided it was time for a break and pulled off the motorway into a small village called Hampton Magna. She would spend a few hours here before resuming her journey, she thought, after all, she had plenty of time. It was a lovely little village with a green in the middle where several marquees had been erected. A large crowd was gathered around them and there seemed to be a bit of an argument going on. Ever nosey, Lettie strolled over to see what was happening.

It turned out to be the annual Hampton Magna village fête. There was a bouncy castle, a beer tent, a coconut shy, marmalade and chutney for sale and much else besides. There was also a flower and vegetable competition and this was where the crowd was gathered, surrounding two men outside the entrance to the flower and vegetable marquee.

It took Lettie several minutes to tune in to the broad Yorkshire ac-cents all around her but as she listened to the exchanges she gathered that the problem was that one of the judging committee had suffered a last-minute illness and they had to have three judges but only had two and did not know what to do.

"Just carry on with two," someone said.

"You can't. The rulebook says three, the results won't stand if you don't follow the rules," said another.

"Cancel it till next weekend, when Bill will be fit again," said a third.

"Not likely, my brassicas are ready now!" said a fourth.

"Well then," said one of the judges, "we will just have to co-opt someone to join the judging committee for today only, but who knows enough about it to be able to judge?"

"Tell you what, we'll have a competition," said his fellow judge. "Whoever wins it joins the judging committee for today only. That's fair isn't it?"

No one in the crowd dissented. After all, they now had a judge's competition as well as a flower and vegetable competition and this could be interesting. So the two judges withdrew briefly into the marquee to decide on the questions they would pose to the crowd.

A few minutes later they came back.

"We need to keep this fairly simple otherwise we'll be here all day and we're late already. We've got three questions and whoever answers first and gets most right will join us as the third judge. Right, we'll start off with an easy one... how many different species of daffodil are there?"

Lettie could not contain herself.

"50!" she shouted, before anyone else could speak. The crowd, all of whom were Yorkshire locals, turned as one to see who this stranger with an even stranger accent was.

"That is correct madam, and who, may I ask, are you?" said one of the judges.

"I am just passing through. I'm a botanist and I studied under Havergal Wyllyams at Kew," she lied.

"Well that's very interesting I'm sure, but I don't know if non-members of the society can be judges."

"Nothing in the rules that says they can't," said someone.

"And a non-member would be more impartial than a member," said another.

"OK," said the judge, "is everyone happy if this Lady should happen to win?"

Nobody dissented.

"Well I happen to be a bit of a botanist myself, so I'll make the questions a bit harder, and the next one is this; brassicas developed from a single species of wild cabbage, does anyone know its proper botanical name?"

Everyone turned to Lettie.

"*Brassica oleracea,*" she said before anyone else.

"Correct madam."

"OK, we'd better move on to the last question," said the judge, thinking to himself that now he would really test her. "Do you know the botanical name for the Madagascan self-destructive palm?" smirked the judge, confident that she would not.

"Well of course," said Lettie, "*Tahina spectabilis.*"

The judge was considerably taken aback. "Well, it looks like you know your botany, so I guess you'll do. Does everyone agree?" he asked.

"But what have all these botanical names got to do with judging my courgettes?" someone asked.

"Absolutely nothing," said the judge, "but it shows she is a botanist and she is neutral. She won't be voting for her next-door neighbour like some do and there is no one else so I propose this lady joins the committee for today only, does everyone agree?" Everyone did. "Well, I suppose we'd better know your name Madam," said the judge.

"Mrs Letitia Huntingdon-Brown from New York City at your service, but you can all call me Lettie," she replied.

Lettie felt very excited as well as a little bit of a fraud. She'd been very lucky with the questions but was also very surprised at how much she remembered from Havergal's papers and Ron's coaching.

"Right then, we'd better get on with things, there's a lot to do and we are running late, let's start the judging..." And with that, the three judges, now including Lettie, went into the marquee.

The show had been supposed to open at 11.30, fully judged, with the winning rosettes in place. It was now 11.15 and there were 12 vegetable categories to be judged and then three others before the public could be admitted, so the judging would have to be brisk. They had to judge the largest, this would be easy, and the best quality, not so easy, for potatoes, carrots, courgettes, leeks, cabbages and onions and then the best summer floral display, best dried flower display and finally a best in show category for either a vegetable or floral display.

From the start it was clear that Lettie was going to disagree with almost everything except the size categories. Lettie called things the way she saw them. The other two seemed to judge things according to favours they owed or neighbours they knew or local issues. It took twice as long as usual to finalise the awards and Lettie's two fellow judges were exhausted and rather angry when they had finished.

"Why on earth did you agree with her about Arnold Sidebottom's carrots when Arthur Youngman, my neighbour, has won the carrots category for years?" asked one.

"Because I hoped she would agree with me about Percy Entwhistle's leeks, but she didn't. But why did you agree with her about Billy Wainwright's cabbages? They were nowhere near the best, mine were better!"

The two judges were a bit shell-shocked from the whole experience.

"We're going to have to open the marquee to the public in a moment and there'll be all hell to pay. Billy Bolton will probably never let us into the Dog and Duck again; he's always won the courgettes prize."

Just then Lettie was walking to the entrance to leave. "And may we ask, Madam, how you made your choices? They were quite different to ours but you seem to have persuaded us and we will have to explain all this to the members."

"Well..." said Lettie. "I thought all the exhibits were good, so I allowed a few extraneous factors to influence me."

"What does *that* mean when it's at home?" said one of the judges.

"Well," said Lettie, "in the Leeks I chose the Musselburgh leeks because Arvin and I had a holiday in Scotland many years ago and went to Musselburgh, which was lovely; for the carrots I chose the variety called Trevor because it's just a ridiculous name for a carrot; for the onions I chose the variety called Golden Bear because that's what I used to call Arvin; for the potatoes I chose Charlotte because I have a goddaughter with that name, for the courgettes I loved the name Costata Romanesco and for the cabbages the variety Victoria Pigeon just sounded hilarious. I had no interest in the dried flowers, so I just picked the first display I saw. For the best floral display anything that has Alium Schubertii in it gets my vote and anything with chrysanthemums doesn't and for the best in show I just could not get those carrots called Trevor out of my mind, so that was my vote."

The other two judges looked at each other. "How on earth do we explain this?" they both said simultaneously. They were speechless. Then one of them said, "and, what's more, how are we going to explain this to Ben Hatcher the Mayor, he's won the potatoes category for years and Bettie Hatcher has won the dried flower prize for years. They'll be livid. They'll drum us out of the village!"

"I'll tell you what," said the other. "SHE can explain it. Let her do it, where is she?"

But Lettie had gone. She was back in her car, heading for Newcastle, a smile playing on her lips. She had enjoyed herself mightily. She felt like a real botanist now. Havergal would have been proud of her. Hampton Magna, however, would never be the same again.

Lettie had called Francesco Molinari at the Savoy to recommend the best hotel in Newcastle for her and he had suggested the Hilton and she had said, "that sounds just fine, please will you be good enough to call them and book me a suite for a couple of days. I'll have work to do." Francesco Molinari had been unaware that the General Manager of the Savoy was also responsible for the travel arrangements of Mrs Letitia Huntingdon-Brown but nonetheless did as he was asked. The General Manager at the Newcastle Hilton was a friend of his and he would warn him of the force of nature that was coming his way.

Chapter 12

Lettie arrived at the Newcastle Hilton in the same way that she arrived everywhere. noticeably. The General Manager of the hotel, Eduardo Cinqueterra, had made a point of being around for her arrival, after his forewarning by his friend at the Savoy. He heard the hullabaloo outside as she arrived and immediately mobilised three porters to carry all her luggage to her suite. She clearly did not believe in travelling light. When everything had been removed from the car, Lettie turned to the General Manager and asked where the valet was who would park her car for her. Cinqueterra thought quickly. "I guess he is busy. Give me the keys and I will park the car for you."

Lettie was pleased with her suite – a large bedroom, a large bathroom and a very large sitting room, with all the seating and office facilities she could want. One small thing troubled her. The luggage and all the papers sat neatly in the middle of the sitting room.

"Not quite the Savoy," she thought, "they unpacked for me there."

Lettie had never been to Newcastle before, neither in her youth, when living in England, nor since. She had always imagined that it was all shipbuilding and coalmining and grimily industrial, but the city centre was magnificent. From her suite she overlooked the Tyne and could see the impressive Baltic Centre and the redeveloped area all around it. She was looking forward to exploring but another thing worried her; she had discovered from talking to the porters that the Newcastle accent was even more impenetrable than the Yorkshire one.

She had arranged with PC Dafydd Myrddin Rhodri to come to her suite the next morning at 9.30 am to go through the papers and he duly presented himself at that time the next morning, escorted by Eduardo Cinqueterra, who wanted to make sure nothing went wrong for his distinguished guest. PC Rhodri was in uniform, he had just come off an unexpected night duty, and this was an added reason for the general manager to escort him, just to make sure none of the guests panicked at the sight of a policeman.

Lettie greeted the PC warmly, he was 'Dafydd' to her now.

PC Dafydd Myrddin Rhodri was enormous. Six feet plus and an ex rugby player, dark complexioned with curly hair and bulging with muscles everywhere, he seemed to bang into everything clumsily. For safety, Lettie sat him down and asked Cinqueterra, just as he was leaving, if he could "possibly rustle up some coffee?"

Dafydd looked at the papers and letters Lettie had brought. They were contained in four large box files, each full to the brim.

"I'm not going to be able to do much today with all those," he said. "I've been working all night and need to get to bed soon. And anyway, that lot will take me days to go through when I get some spare time."

"I didn't expect you to be able to do much here and now," replied Lettie. "All I hoped is that you would take them away and go through them when you do have time. There's no need to translate everything, there'll probably be a lot of routine stuff that we won't need to keep, it's really just to know what is there and what might be worth translating, and whether there is anything that could explain what happened to Havergal. Are you ready for some coffee?"

"Yes please," said Dafydd, rather crestfallen at the quantity of paperwork and what he had let himself in for.

"Now," said Lettie, "tell me about yourself and your background in Llandysul and what you knew of Havergal's family, you mentioned some of it on the phone."

"Well," said Dafydd, "I probably told you most of it when we spoke on the phone. Llandysul is a small village in West Wales where everyone knows everyone else's business and when I was growing up it was largely Welsh speaking. It's the only thing I regret about coming to England, that I don't get to speak Welsh, because I love the language. I left Llandysul when I was 18 and joined the police force and have never regretted it. I never knew Havergal Wyllyams, of course, he had left for Kew long before I was born, although I sort of knew of him because my father and especially my grandfather, knew the Wyllyams family quite well. In fact my grandfather went to the same school as Havergal, although they were in different classes, so everything I know is what they've told me. When I found out who he was on the day of the death I was gobsmacked that it was him and I was going to tell the Inspector that I knew of him but I didn't. Havergal's full name, as you know, was Havergal Ulric Wyllyams and his mother was unmarried. They were the only single parent family in the village, so they stuck out a bit, apparently. The story is that Havergal's father was a Swedish sailor on leave from Pembroke Dock who was never seen again but whose name was Ulric, which is how Havergal got the name but I don't know if that is true or not."

"Do you think anyone in the village would remember the Wyllyams family now?" asked Lettie.

"I very much doubt it," said Dafydd. "His mother, of course, is long gone, he had no brothers or sisters and I don't know if he ever visited the village after he left, and anyway Llandysul these days is overrun by English second homers, the Welsh have all gone."

"That's a pity," said Lettie, "but maybe sometime I'll pay a visit to Llandysul, just to look around. "Now," she continued, "I think it's probably about time you were going, you'll be needing a sleep after your night duty."

"I do feel a bit tired," said Dafydd, "and I'm not sure how I am going to get all those boxes back to my flat or how long it's going to take me to go through all that lot."

"Don't worry," said Lettie, "just take one box to get started and I will get that nice Mr Cinqueterra to deliver the rest to your flat if you give me your address. And as to how long it will take, again, don't worry, I'm up here for a few days, just call my mobile when you're ready."

Dafydd bit his tongue. He was thinking in terms of a few weeks or months to go through such a large pile, not just a few days. "Are you sure they actually are all in Welsh?" he asked.

"Take a quick look at some of them," said Lettie, opening one of the boxes.

"They are in Welsh all right," said Dafydd, his fate sealed.

Chapter 13

For the next several days Lettie had a wonderful time and completely forgot about her main purpose for being in Newcastle. She toured a vibrant city with art galleries and concerts and then toured more widely to Edinburgh and Musselburgh. There was just so much to do and see. And then, quite suddenly, and for the first time in ages, her mobile phone rang. She'd almost forgotten she had it. It was a secretary at Kew. "Mr Wiseman is now back from his trip and would like to see you at the earliest opportunity, when can you come in to see him?"

Lettie replied that she was in Newcastle at the moment and it would be a couple of days.

"Mr Wiseman asked me to make the appointment for as soon as possible," said a rather pushy secretary.

"Well, the day after tomorrow then, at 9.30am, how would that be?" replied Lettie.

"Thank you and we will see you then," came a rather abrupt reply.

"Wow," thought Lettie, "things are beginning to move. I'd better get hold of Dafydd and see where he's got to with the letters and papers and then get ready to head back down south." She called Dafydd and they agreed to meet the next day at the Hilton to review his progress.

The general manager of the Hilton escorted Dafydd, as before, to Lettie's suite and this time took it upon himself to arrange coffee before being asked. Lettie greeted Dafydd like a long lost friend, which rather embarrassed him as he stood there in his rather ill-fitting police uniform. "Well? How's it going, how much have you done?" Lettie got quickly to the point.

"I really haven't got very far at all," came the reply. "Let me explain. I've been on nights ever since we met the first time and I've had overtime as well. I tried to explain to my sergeant that I needed some time off. He asked why and I explained but he was not too impressed. And there was just so much paper and so many letters I was never going to be able to do it all in a couple of days. So really all I've been able to do is to sort all the papers into several related piles and I've done a little bit of translation but I've probably picked the least interesting stuff. Let me just say a few things before I tell you what I have done, Lettie," and this was the first time he had dared use her first name. "I am not going to be able to translate all of those papers and letters, there are just too many, it would take years. I will read them all and if you tell me what you are looking for I will translate or summarise those parts. So, what is it you are hoping to find?"

Lettie thought about this for a few moments and then said, "Well I guess it's three things; first, is there anything to indicate how and why he died so abruptly? Second, is there anything about the botanical breakthroughs he is believed to have made? And third, what sort of a man was he? I find him intriguing."

"OK," said Dafydd, "you will have to trust me. I will read all the papers and extract just the things which help with those three questions and I will email them to you as I find them."

"Thank you Dafydd and I trust you implicitly," said Lettie.

"But before I show you the piles I've arranged I'll tell you a bit about Havergal's writing style," Dafyyd continued. "Havergal had a very individual working style, he drafted everything and kept everything so sometimes there are several drafts of the same letter or paper. But there is a strange thing – there are no reply letters in the papers you gave me, only the drafts of sent letters. There definitely were replies because he refers to them in his letters, but there are none here. Did he keep the replies in a separate file which perhaps is lost?"

"That's all there was in the house when I bought it," replied Lettie, "so, yes, I guess they are lost," she said, wondering whether they were, in fact, taken by someone. Or perhaps they were in the little red book, wherever or whatever that was.

Dafydd continued. "OK, let's start going through the piles I have sorted into. This first small pile is a Welsh pile. Havergal was a member of the Welsh language society in London and various other Welsh groups and this lot is all to do with meetings and committees and agendas and so on. I don't believe they'll help with any of the questions you've asked. One thing that interested me was that Havergal attended a poetry reading by Dylan Thomas in London in 1952, lucky man, but I'll now give all of these back to you, untranslated."

"Could they be of interest to anyone?" asked Lettie, "or should I just junk them?"

"Junk them," said Dafydd. "Right then, let's move on to the next pile... I have only read some of these but they appear to be all draft letters to people in Llandysul, where he was born. There seem to be quite a lot of "congratulations on the birth of your child" and "well done in your rugby match" and quite a lot as well to his mother saying how he is getting on at Kew and "hope all is well at home" but all of these types of letter dried up about 20 years ago when presumably his mother died and he lost contact with the village. There seems to be just one stream of correspondence which continues after that, and I haven't read much of it yet, and it is with someone called Mary Midlothian-Sutton, and at first it is sympathetic because her husband has died, but then it carries on right up to when Havergal died. There is an address here, you might like to write to her."

"I surely will," said Lettie, "and I look forward to what you can find in that correspondence, it sounds promising."

"So I'll hang on to this pile," said Dafydd, "but, as we've agreed, I'll just email you the gist of the useful letters and the uninteresting ones I will junk on your behalf, OK?"

"As I said, Dafydd, I trust you."

"Thank you again. Right... that brings us to the two largest piles, the poems and the botany."

"Wow!" exclaimed Lettie. "The poems and the botany might explain everything. I can't wait!"

"Well you might have to, I'm afraid," said Dafydd. "I haven't got very far with either of them except just sorting them into related piles."

"Let's start with the poems," he continued. "As you can see there are literally hundreds. Look at that pile there, I will not be able to translate all of them, there are just too many. And anyway, I'm not a poet, so they won't sound like poems when they are in English, they will just be a collection of clumsy words that don't rhyme."

"What are they about?" asked Lettie. "Are they just about day to day things, the weather, Trafalgar Square and so on, in other words poems for himself or were they written for somebody and if so in what sort of terms?"

"I've only looked at a few but they do seem to be written for somebody and I only really say that because they're all drafts, in some cases rewritten several times with crossings out and changes and so presumably the final version went to someone."

"Are they any good?" asked Lettie.

"Well, I've only read a couple but, yes, they do seem to be quite good, or at least, the ones I read were."

Dafydd was deliberately not saying much and Lettie sensed it. Poems are a very personal art form and these could very well reach right into Havergal's soul, so there must be no rush into conclusions. She instinctively felt they would tell her much about Havergal but now was not the time to press Dafydd.

Lettie asked a question she knew the answer to. "Should we consider publishing them?"

"No, not yet," replied Dafydd, "better wait until I've been through them all. These are all drafts, the originals have been sent to someone and they will be their property. Let's wait until I see what's there. I won't try to translate them all but, as I said, I will read them all and give you an overview of what they're about."

"OK," said Lettie, "shall we move on to the botanical papers?"

"Well, I've made even less progress here," said Dafydd. "The papers are stacked with scientific and botanical words that mean nothing to me. I can translate the "ands" and "buts" and the words in between but what it all means I have no idea. But there are some interesting things. These papers are all recent. The paper is still crisp and the writing hasn't faded and some are even dated; they all appear to have been written in the past 10 years or so."

"Dafydd, that is very interesting. The key to Havergal may well lie in those papers, if we can only find it. If the papers were all written in the past 10 years, then they were written *since* Havergal left Kew and I wonder if they were written in Welsh to protect them from prying eyes. If these ones are dated then they are final versions so they weren't being sent to someone, they were his final versions. Do you have any vacation coming up?" asked Lettie.

"If you mean holiday then yes I do," replied Dafydd. "I have a week off next week, in fact. I am going to go walking in the Trossachs with some friends."

"How about you come down to London?" suggested Lettie. ""you and Ron between you can get to the bottom of these botany papers." Lettie explained who Ron was.

Dafydd took a bit of convincing, he had been looking forward to his mountaineering holiday but he also realised quickly that he was not going to win and so eventually and reluctantly agreed.

"You can stay with me," said Lettie. "I have a spare room. So, see you at 13 Sandown Road next Monday."

Lettie now had just two pieces of administration to do before packing for her return to London. She dashed off a letter to Mary Midlothian-Sutton, although with no great expectations. 'Probably just a local friend,' she thought, 'certainly not a botanist.' Then she called Ron to tell him about the meeting at Kew and about Dafydd and the botanical papers. To her surprise Ron knew about the meeting because he had been told to attend. "I don't think that it's because they suspect I am talking to you, I think it's only because they know I knew Huw well. And yes, I'd be delighted to help Dafydd. By chance I've got next week off as well."

"That's great," said Lettie. "Now, don't tell me anything about the guys at Kew or what will happen, it's better if it's a complete surprise. I'll see you at Kew the day after tomorrow and we will have to act like strangers."

The next day Lettie was up bright and early for her trip back to London and the Kew meeting on the following day. Just as she had on the way up to Newcastle, she stopped about half way back to London for a break. She pulled into a lovely village in Derbyshire called Tissington and, once again, found crowds of people and lots of activity.

"What's going on?" she asked someone.

"It's our annual well-dressing festival," came the reply.

"And what's that when it's at home?" Lettie asked.

She was lucky. She had picked the local historian to ask.

"It's a tradition that goes back almost 1000 years and is unique, as far as we know, to this part of the country. The wells around here have given pure water for all that time despite droughts and the Black Death in 1348 and so the custom started on the eve of Ascension Day to have a thanksgiving service and create these dressings to celebrate our good fortune and it has continued to this day."

Lettie wandered round the village. There were about a dozen wells that had been 'dressed' – adorned with pictures on boards using natural materials such as petals and cones and coffee beans and each with a message. She came to one that had been made by the local school, its message was "Flowers make the world" and a little further on was a board made by the local Women's Institute "Eat vegetables, Dig for Victory."

"Well," thought Lettie, "if I needed inspiration for Kew tomorrow, this is it. I am gonna dig for victory!"

Chapter 14

Lettie was up even earlier than usual the next day. She had hardly slept for tossing and turning the whole night, wondering what might happen at Kew. She had given a lot of thought as to how to present herself and decided to be an innocent and sweet American Lady who didn't really understand what this was all about. Above all, she must protect Ron and not allow any suspicion that they knew each other.

She arrived at Kew much too early for the meeting and spent some time wandering around the beautiful grounds. When the time came, she presented herself at the offices and asked for Dr Carl Wiseman. The receptionist asked her to take a seat and phoned someone. Lettie did as she was told. After nearly half an hour, Lettie asked the receptionist if she had informed Dr Wiseman that she was waiting for him.

"Yes I have, but they're always very busy, they'll be along soon." Eventually a secretary entered reception and asked Lettie to follow her. On the way the secretary asked, "Have you found Mr Wyllyams' red book?"

"I don't know, what is that?" replied Lettie innocently.

"Oh, it's all they talk about. They think some answers lie in it and will do anything to find it," she replied.

"Interesting," thought Lettie, "even the secretaries know about it."

They entered a meeting room and someone stood up and introduced himself.

"Good morning, I am Dr Carl Wiseman and you, I take it, are Mrs Letitia Huntingdon- Brown?"

"That's correct," Lettie replied.

"Please sit down," said Wiseman, "no, not there, that seat there if you wouldn't mind." He gestured towards a chair that faced Wiseman and the other four people in the room, who were seated in a semicircle; the seat placements felt like an Inquisition.

"Now, let's make a start," said Wiseman. "I understand you have some of Mr Wyllyams' papers, is that so?"

"Well, before we start would you introduce me to your four colleagues please, just so I know who I am talking to?"

"Yes, of course, how remiss of me," replied Wiseman. "To my right here is Roger Griffiths, our Legal Director, and to his right is Sharon, who will take the minutes of this meeting. And to my left is Eileen Tinker, our HR Director and to her left is Ron Carter, one of my botanists, who knew Huw quite well."

'Wow,' thought Lettie, 'they've really rolled out the big guns for little old me, but if they think they can bully me they've got another think coming. The sweet little innocent American Lady persona might not last long.' Already Lettie felt uncomfortable. Wiseman was a short, thin, middle-aged man with a weedy, sneering transatlantic sort of accent and he spoke in jarring commercial clichés, not at all like a botanist. And the others in the meeting were clearly his acolytes, there to do his bidding, except, of course, Ron. There was a jug of coffee and also some water in the corner and all the others had coffee cups or water glasses in front of them; no effort was made to offer anything to Lettie as she sat in her inquisitional chair, and that seemed to sum things up.

"Well, shall we get down to things now then?" said Wiseman "I've got lots of things to do today and can't spend all day in this meeting. I'll get straight to the point. When Huw Wyllyams died he left lots of papers and research and I believe that when you bought his house you acquired those papers and, since the papers are the property of this department, I would like you to give them back. In particular there is a red book in which Huw kept all his research and that is important to us. Will you please arrange to return all the papers, files and books which are in your possession at the earliest opportunity?"

"In a word, no," said Lettie, and sat back to watch their reactions of incredulity. No one had ever spoken to Wiseman like that before. But two expressions turned from incredulity to smiles. Ron allowed himself a hidden half smile and the secretary, who clearly did not like Wiseman either, allowed herself a full smile.

"I beg your pardon?" said Wiseman. "Those papers are the property of Kew. If you do not return them then I will have to call the police."

"I'll explain, if you give me a chance," said Lettie. "I've taken the trouble to sort all through the papers and there are lots of different things there. There is correspondence with his mother, there are poems that he wrote and much else besides that is none of your business. As to botany, there are two groups of papers. The first group is written in English and contains all his notes from school onwards, including notes while he was working here right up to about 10 years ago, which is when, I believe, he retired. You can have all of those right now. They are in my car outside and I would like to think you will set up some sort of Havergal Wyllyams library to make them available to all. Then there is a second group of papers, all written in the past 10 years during his retirement and all written in Welsh and they, I suspect, are the ones you are interested in, but they are not your property because you did not employ him when they were written. They are Havergal's property and since he is no longer with us and since they were in the house when I bought it, they are now my property. Go ahead and call the police if you wish, or consult your lawyers. I think that you'll find that I am right." Lettie's sweet little American Lady was now a thing of the past. "Oh, and by the way, I wondered why Havergal wrote those papers in Welsh and I can only assume it was to keep his work private and to keep it from you!"

Wiseman's face screwed into a snarl. "I accept that Huw was not employed here when he wrote those papers but we did allow him access to our facilities and the work he was doing was a continuation of work done here when he was employed here so I think," said Wiseman, smiling now at his Legal Director, "that you will find that Kew owns the intellectual property rights to what is contained in the papers and thus in that way you should return them immediately, otherwise you may find yourself in serious trouble."

"Intellectual property rights?" Lettie sneered. "Well, I have some experience of that. When my husband Arvin died, his brothers and nephews all tried to use that argument to overturn Arvin's will, which was in my favour. I used some top New York City lawyers to refute it and I will call on them again if you make that necessary. The papers are at the moment in Newcastle, being translated into English. I will give you copies when the translation is finished. I would have told you that much sooner if you hadn't started so aggressively"

"How long will that take?" asked Wiseman. "We will pay to have them translated."

"I don't know, it could be months," said Lettie. "You will have them when I am good and ready."

"But those papers could be of international botanical importance!" exploded Wiseman.

Lettie came back equally strongly. "Then why did you retire Havergal against his wishes? Why didn't you keep him on the staff and continue to pay him? If you had acted properly, the papers would be yours now."

Eileen Tinker, the HR Director, looked up and took an interest for the first time, but said nothing. Lettie realised she might have gone too far. How could she know so much about this? She was risking revealing her connection with Ron, who was looking a little glum, but no one seemed to notice this. Instead Wiseman replied, "Mr Wyllyams' employment status is none of your business, I insist that you return the papers or I will instruct my lawyers," he said, turning to Roger Griffiths, the Legal Director.

"Well, I'll see you in court then," said Lettie, "but I have already told you that I'll give you translated copies in due course and by the time you've briefed a lawyer and started an action, which you will almost certainly lose, you'll have them anyway, and what's more, if you do try that I will not hesitate to go to the press with stories of Kew harassing an old lady and mistreating a past employee. It will all come out."

Ron's previously glum face turned into another private smile.

"Why are you so interested in all this?" asked Wiseman. "And what do you think you can do with the papers?"

"It's pretty clear to me, from things he wrote, that Havergal did not have a very high opinion of you, Mr Wiseman, and I want to make sure that whatever discoveries there are in those papers are properly attributed to Havergal. Why do you suppose he wrote the papers in Welsh? It was so you couldn't steal them! And while I'm on that subject, did you come round to my house while it was being redecorated to try to get the papers?"

"Yes I did," replied Wiseman. "I came round, not to *your* house but to Huw's old house, to see if there was any of Kew's property still there, which was a responsible thing to do. I was dealt with rather abusively by your agent, called Delbert something."

"Serves you right," Lettie smirked, "you can't go barging into someone else's property. You should have asked me."

Wiseman immediately came back. "But you are not a botanist. What on earth can you do with scientific papers?"

"I don't know yet, but I guarantee Havergal will get the credit for whatever he found," she said.

Wiseman felt more comfortable now. She would not be able to do anything with the papers; only a skilled botanist would be able to understand them.

"OK," he said, "you let me have the papers as soon as they are translated and then let the race begin."

"I will let you have copies of the papers when they are all translated and when I have read them all," said Lettie. "And now, since you are not going to offer me any coffee, I will take my leave."

The occupants of the room were speechless but then the secretary rose and said she would show Lettie out.

"Hold on," said Wiseman. "If you will wait in reception I will get someone to come to your car to collect the English papers."

"I will wait in reception for 5 minutes only," said Lettie. "I will not be kept waiting half an hour as you did at the start of this meeting." She left a silent room.

The secretary escorted Lettie back to reception. When safely out of earshot, she said, "Well done! No one has ever spoken to Wiseman the way you did. He is a horrible man. Everyone hates him. I wish you good luck. If I can help at all, I will. I liked Huw, everyone did – and Wiseman was beastly to him."

"Thanks," said Lettie. "I am going to do what I said and make sure Havergal gets his credit. Tell me, this might sound crazy but do you think Wiseman could have murdered Havergal in trying to get the red book?"

"I don't think he is a murderer but I would put nothing past him," came the reply. "Huw had been here on the day he died and he had his red book with him then, so something must have happened."

They had reached reception so the conversation ceased and Lettie sat down to wait. She only had to wait four minutes before Ron appeared. "Dr Wiseman sent me to collect the English papers. Shall we go to your car?" he said, in an official manner, in case overheard.

When out of the office, Ron told her, "Wiseman went absolutely ballistic after you left. I won't tell you the names he called you. He told Roger Griffiths to immediately check the legal situation and instructed Eileen Tinker to find out who decided Huw should be an unpaid consultant without a contract. He is already looking for a scapegoat because it was him who decided that. He also tried to get me to give up my holiday to prepare a paper on what is known about what Huw was doing. I told him I couldn't give up my holiday because my mother is ill. It was the first thing I could think of. In fact, my mother died four months ago and I had compassionate leave then. Eileen Tinker knows that but she said nothing; so she is probably an ally. Then Wiseman said I had better go to collect the English papers and told me to try and find out from you who has the Welsh papers."

"Well, I guess the race is on now," said Lettie, "and we have a start of a month or two. I told Wiseman he would have a copy of the papers when they are all translated and when I have read them all. If the very last page is so complicated it takes weeks to translate that will be his bad luck and if it takes me weeks to read everything because I'm so busy with shopping at Harrods and watching tennis at Wimbledon, that's bad luck too. I can string it out if we need to. Dafydd arrives tomorrow and your holiday starts then too, so you guys will have to get down to some serious work. And I will have to tell Dafydd to forget about the poems. You don't know about those yet. I'll explain later. You'll just be concentrating on the botany."

"Can't wait to get started," said Ron, "but I will have to be very careful about my movements. Remember I live almost next door to Wiseman and he mustn't see me going to your house every day, but I can handle that."

They reached Lettie's car and, not for the first time, but this time without a wheelbarrow, Ron was responsible for moving large piles of paper.

Chapter 15

The next day Lettie was again up early. There was much to be done. Dafydd would arrive late morning, having caught the early train from Newcastle, and she had asked Ron to come around at about the same time. She was fully prepared for their arrival. She had stocked up with tea and coffee and food, had installed a computer and had arranged with Delbert, next door, for the services of a shorthand typist to be available when and if the men needed it ('Is there anything the Wellingtons can't find or arrange?' she thought). Dafyyd's bedroom was ready, with towels and soap. After years of having servants, she was pleasantly surprised at how domesticated she was becoming.

Dafydd and Ron arrived at almost the same time and she introduced them to each other, although they both knew about each other already. "Before you start I just want to say how grateful I am to both of you for giving up your holidays to help me with this. You've both helped so much already. And now, perhaps we can get to the bottom of things." The two men mumbled something in return. Neither was quite sure how they had got into this and both felt they had somehow temporarily lost control of their lives. Then Dafydd said, in his lilting Welsh accent, "Can I just ask something. Why are you doing this? We have a reason to be interested in Havergal; Ron was a colleague and a friend of his and as for me, I would always help a Welshman from my village who knew my family, but what is your connection, other than the fact that you bought his house?"

Lettie thought about this for a few moments and then said, "Well, at its simplest I am, I suppose, a retired, middle-aged widow with not much else to do, and having a project is kinda fun. But of course it's more than that. I never knew him but I feel that I have come to know him, mainly through you two and the things you've both told me and the writings he left. I picture a quiet, decent, academic man who wouldn't harm a fly, who just wanted to get on with his work, to which he was devoted, slightly unworldly, not able to deal with people like Wiseman, and not really caring much about that anyway and I just thought 'I will try and get to the bottom of this if I can'. I have known tons of nasty people in my life, some of them even in my late husband's family, and wherever I can, I stand up to them. Meeting Wiseman yesterday just made me all the more determined in this and especially to make sure that Havergal gets the credit for anything that is important in those papers, because it's pretty clear to me that Wiseman thinks there is something important there and has already made one attempt, while the house was being refurbished, to steal them, so it will be my pleasure to stop the guy. So, that I guess, is my motivation, boys."

The two men looked at each other and silently echoed her words.

"I've laid everything on for you," continued Lettie, pointing out the facilities, "and I think the best thing I can do now is to leave you alone to get on with it. I'm going to go to Kew to see the gardens. You have my mobile and I can be back very quickly. If I don't hear from you I'll be back around 6pm to cook you both dinner. You've both got a weeks' vacation and none of us know if that will be enough to get through all those papers." They all glanced nervously at the huge pile. "As you know, I've told Wiseman he can have copies of the papers when they are translated and when I have read them all. If we're lucky then there may be several different subjects in there and it may be easy to translate one complete subject before moving on to the next. There could also be a lot of extraneous stuff that doesn't add much but does delay handing anything over. One way and another, I think we can keep Wiseman at bay for a couple of months and, hopefully, that will give us enough of a start to find out whatever it is that is in there. Now, if you guys have got everything you need I'll tootle off to Kew and see you this evening, if I don't hear from you before." And with that Lettie went out to her car and off to Kew.

Ron and Dafydd looked at each other and then at the pile.

"I guess we'd better get cracking then," they said simultaneously.

As Lettie drew away in her car, she could not help thinking what an odd couple she had left behind in the house. Ron, small, softly-spoken, academic and slightly weedy and Dafydd, a generation younger, enormous, clumsy and outgoing.

"Will they get on?" she wondered, "and will they succeed?"

Chapter 16

Arriving at Kew, Lettie decided to join a guided tour. The tour leader was Isobel Gardiner. "Yes, I do get my leg pulled about my name," she had begun. She was a very good guide but Lettie was not concentrating, her mind kept wondering what the boys were up to and she kept checking her mobile to see if she had had a call. But little bits of Isobel's talk stuck in her mind. "Kew was started in 1759 when Princess Augusta opened a nine acre botanical garden, so it is now 250 years old and has been progressively expanded to its present size of 300 acres over that time."

"Gee," thought Lettie, "its even older than the good old US of A"

"... our mission is to inspire and deliver science based plant conservation worldwide, enhancing the quality of life. Kew is a UNESCO world heritage site and there are 450 volunteers working here, including me."

This woke Lettie up. "You mean you do this for nothing?" she asked.

"Just for the love of the place," came the reply.

"Wow," thought Lettie, "such a beautiful place and such lovely people. How does a nasty creature like Wiseman end up in the middle of it?"

When the guided tour was over, Lettie had heard almost none of it, her mind was elsewhere. She would come back and do it again. It was still too early to go home; she didn't want to disturb her boys, so for the next hour or two she wandered around the gardens on her own until she could contain herself no longer and practically ran to the car park to drive back to 13 Sandown Road.

She burst through the front door and dispensed with any formalities.

"Hi guys, how's it going?" she blurted.

Ron answered, "Lettie, I suggest you sit down, we've got a lot to tell you and it's almost all good news. The first thing to tell you is that although there is a mass of paper it's not nearly as bad as it looks and we will easily be finished this week. The papers are all dated and numbered and, miraculously, they seem to all be in order. And there is lots of repetition. Sometimes there are five or six drafts of the same paper, it's the way Havergal worked as we know. But they're all drafts, there are no final papers here, those must all be in the red book, wherever that is. I'll give you an example. The Madagascan self-destructive palm, *Tahina spectabilis*; there are six drafts of this paper. There is no final version, as we know, but the last draft is clearly virtually final, but, and this is important, this species is all now in the public domain, so that is 60 pages we do not need to translate and this is repeated over and again. 'How come is it in the public domain?' you may ask. And the answer is because Wiseman clearly stole the finding. This species was announced to the botanical world by Kew, and specifically Wiseman, about ten years ago, yet here are all the field notes and the analysis. And this happens time and again. There are lots of Havergal's old discoveries, some made while he was still at Kew and some since. So you'll have to be careful about the legal situation, some of these papers actually are the property of Kew and I'm sure Wiseman could say that he needs them all to be able to decide which are which."

"To do that," said Lettie "Wiseman would have to admit that he had seen some of the papers, which would lead to questioning about how he came to do that when they were in someone's private property."

"I'm sure you're right," said Ron. "I'm not a lawyer, I just felt I should point out that Wiseman definitely knows about the papers and what is more it seems pretty clear to me that Havergal was rather integral to Wiseman's career. He has never been popular at Kew but he has kept making discoveries and announcements and the senior management liked that. And now it is clear that all or most of those discoveries were stolen from Havergal."

"Which means," said Lettie, "that he will go to any lengths to get these papers. But there is one question. How did he get the papers translated? Is there another Welsh speaker in the department?"

"Well yes, there probably is. There is Ifor Rodrigues, another nasty little character and a big friend of Wiseman's. He sat at the next desk to Havergal and was always skulking around. I never heard him speak Welsh but he is from Swansea, where there is a lot of Welsh spoken, so he probably knows it. I don't know if Havergal knew he was a Welsh speaker and it never occurred to me until now that he and Wiseman might be in league together but it does all begin to make sense now. Havergal only started writing in Welsh shortly after Wiseman joined which, I guess, says it all. He must have thought this would protect his papers from Wiseman but may not have known what Ifor Rodrigues was up to."

"Another question," said Lettie. "Why didn't Havergal do something when he discovered that his work was being stolen? I can understand that while he was at Kew it would be difficult to stop the departmental head making the announcements and it's tough but not unusual for the person who really did the work not to get a mention, but why didn't he make more of a fuss when his post Kew work was stolen, that is pure theft?"

"I am afraid that was Havergal all over," said Ron. "His only passion was in the science and the discovery, he had no interest in the fame or the kudos. So, in summary," continued Ron, "there is an awful lot of this that we don't need to translate. Once you take out the old stuff that is now public and the repetitions and the general stuff he copied out just have it handy, there is probably only about 10 pages or so of new material in each of Havergal's specialist areas; orchids, palms and cacti, 30 pages in total and we've made a start with that and done the first 3 pages of his notes on cacti. We'll have the whole lot done in a few days."

"Wow," said Lettie, "you guys are stars. It's good that it can be so quick because I just have a feeling that Wiseman might try and pull some kind of stunt. As you've said, this could be fairly serious for him. Have you enjoyed the work?"

"Well," said Ron, "I find I am beginning to learn Welsh...

"And I," said Dafydd, "am beginning to learn botany...

"And I," said Ottoline, the shorthand typist arranged by the Wellingtons, "am learning botany *and* Welsh!"

"You guys deserve a drink and something to eat; you have done very, very well. And, you know what? When you have finished the cacti paper, I'll give Wiseman a copy one week later, that's all we need, one week's start, and we'll find whatever it is." Lettie was excited at the prospect of the race, even though she knew nothing whatsoever about the subject matter. "And then later we'll do the same with the orchids and the palms when they are done. I can't really justify sitting on what might be new discoveries and even if we don't find them it will be enough that we have the proof that Havergal discovered them and not Wiseman, but we will find them, won't we, guys?"

"Yes Ma'am!" chorused the three of them.

❖ ❖ ❖

Chapter 17

It was blindingly, searingly hot. There was no wind but the boiling air currents moved like sea tides and the sand crept continuously. There could surely be no more hostile place on earth. And there could surely be no life forms. How could anything survive in this cauldron? Yet there were two life forms. Near a large rock there was a small depression and in it a small cactus huddled for protection from the heat. But there was also another life form. From under the rock, every 20 minutes or so, a small beetle scuttled from the shade over to the cactus for a few moments and then returned quickly to the protective shade of the rock. Somehow the beetle provided sustenance to the cactus and the cactus provided sustenance to the beetle. As well as sustenance, the beetle cleared away any sand accumulating around the cactus to maintain its life support system. It was almost as regular as clockwork, every 20 minutes, scuttle over, clear sand, feed, scuttle back. How this symbiotic system worked would need a botanist to find out.

Ron, Dafydd and Ottoline had finished the cactus papers by the end of the next day and proudly presented the translation to Lettie that evening.

"OK," said Lettie, turning to Ron, "what does it all mean?"

"Well..." began Ron. "As I have told you, Havergal had three special interests; orchids, palms and cacti. Of these, cacti were his least interest and we translated these first only because it was the smallest pile. Most of what is in there is not earth shattering. He made several trips to Morocco, especially to study cacti and there are a lot of field notes and observations that will be of interest to botanists but are really just detail. But there is one possibly very interesting subject. He found a cactus in the middle of the desert that he had never seen before but could not work out how it survived in those conditions, there was absolutely no water. There were very few specimens and he only brought back one but it did not survive. These days we routinely DNA test even dead plants and learn from them but there is nothing in his notes to indicate he did this. He did note that he would go back sometime and try again and he gave very precise coordinates for where he had found his specimen. It does appear, from what he has written, to be potentially a brand new species."

"Then we will go there right now and find another!" said Lettie.

The beetle scuttled from the rock over to the cactus and then soon returned.

Just then, the phone rang. It was Wiseman. "I want those papers and I am preparing legal proceedings to retrieve Kew's property. Will you see sense and hand them over now and save yourself a lot of trouble?" he asked.

"Mr Wiseman," Lettie replied. "I have already told you that I will let you have copies of the translations when they are all done and when I have read them. I have told you before I want to make sure Havergal gets full credit for what he has discovered. In fact, my translator has nearly finished translating one subject area and I will send you a copy of this when it is finished in a week or so. It is about cacti. I will then send you the other subject areas as they are done."

Wiseman muttered that he wanted them now and would continue with his lawyers and what was she doing messing about with things she did not understand and then he eventually rang off.

The beetle scuttled again.

"Well, he is piling on the pressure, isn't he?" said Lettie "The race really is now on. I guess we had better push on as quickly as possible."

"Is there enough detail in the notes for me to go to Morocco and find a specimen and could you show me how to do it?" asked Lettie. "Ideally, you'd come with me but I don't think there will be time if you two are to get the rest of the papers translated before your holidays run out."

"The coordinates are very precise," said Ron, "and specimen collecting is quite straightforward, provided you follow a few basic rules that I can show you."

"I guess I'd better find out where Morocco is then," replied Lettie.

Now Lettie was manically busy. She was determined to travel to Morocco as quickly as possible. She had to make flight and hotel bookings, get the special desert clothing that Ron had recommended, get some jabs and some currency, find out where the coordinates were and how to get to them, learn how to take specimens. Were there any visa requirements, she wondered, amongst much else. She must also fulfil her promise to Wiseman to let him have his copy of the translated papers. This she did immediately so as not to forget it. She copied the cactus papers and wrote a covering letter to Wiseman, telling him exactly what she was going to do. Then she sealed and stamped the envelope and gave Ron strict instructions to post the package exactly one week after her departure, which she hoped would be the next day, but no sooner than this. She expected to be back before then, so this was just in case of delay.

Ron said nothing but was secretly very pleased by this. Although he was totally loyal to Lettie, the botanist in him was thinking that, in truth, there really is nothing worse than an amateur messing around with science. This might, after all, be very important and a real botanist should be dealing with it, even if it was the hateful Wiseman.

The beetle scuttled again between its two life supports.

Somehow Lettie managed to make all the arrangements, which Ron, who was used to these things, had planned for her and the next day she was on a Royal Air Maroc flight to Casablanca and very, very excited. Ron's itinerary had her connecting in Casablanca with an internal flight to Ouarzazate, spending the night there and then, the next day, a driver would take her to Zagora, an oasis town about 100 miles away and then 34 miles south to the village of Oulad Driss, where she would find another driver with an all-terrain vehicle who would take her about five miles further into the desert to the coordinates given by Ron from Havergal's notes. This all sounded simple enough to Lettie.

The beetle made its regular scuttle.

Ron and Dafydd, despite their age and considerable size and personality differences, were getting on well and becoming good friends. They were a bit of an odd couple, a bit like Delbert and Nelbert, the twins next door. They both liked football; Ron supported Fulham and Dafydd Heart of Midlothian.

"What's a Welshman doing supporting a Scottish team?" asked Ron.

"I've always loved Edinburgh," replied Dafydd. "That's part of the reason I was happy to be transferred to Newcastle, which is close by – and I just liked the name Heart of Midlothian."

Lettie had now gone and the work was progressing well, so they decided to go to the local pub for lunch, the Crow's Nest, where Ron and Havergal used to meet, where they could discuss non-botanical matters. Ottoline did not like pubs and ate her sandwich at the house. Afterwards she decided to go for a short walk. As she left the house, she noticed a letter ready for posting and thought she would help the boys by posting it for them. She did not realise it was to be kept back and had not heard Lettie's instructions to Ron and she didn't even look to see who it was addressed to. When the boys got back, slightly late and slightly tipsy, Ron immediately noticed that the letter was gone. Ottoline told him what she had done. Ron immediately phoned Lettie, who was in Casablanca airport waiting for her connection, she wasn't unduly worried, she had a two day lead at least. "Well, I guess I'd better get on with things then," she had replied.

Lettie's journey was more or less straightforward. Mohammed V International airport at Casablanca was a heaving mass of people, mainly holidaymakers, but she managed to make her connection, just after having received Ron's call. Ouarzazate airport was similarly busy but this time with film crews, this being, she discovered, the centre of the Moroccan film industry. Ron had known nothing about hotels.

"Normally I just arrive and then look around for the cheapest, it's all Kew will pay for" he had said.

"My husband never came to Morocco so I don't have any contacts. Just book me into the most expensive, it should be alright," she replied.

She was booked, for three nights, into the Berbere Palace, the only 5 star hotel in the town, one that was favoured as well by the film industry. It was very comfortable. The next morning she met her driver, Abdul, for the next stage of her safari, again very excited. Abdul chatted merrily the whole way. He was used to Westerners, especially film crews, and hoped for a good tip. He was scheduled to bring Lettie back to the hotel later. They got to Zagora relatively easily, the road had started out as a highway and then gradually, as they neared Zagora, got dustier and smaller. Luckily, Abdul had air conditioning. Then after a brief stop at Zagora they continued on to Oulad Driss, the road getting ever smaller and sand covered.

At Oulad Driss they found Mohommed and his all-terrain vehicle for the next stage of the journey to the site itself, about five miles away. Mohommed spoke not a word of English and did not want to speak anyway, even if he could, so those five miles, which took nearly an hour, were bumpy, silent and felt dangerous as the road continually disappeared in the swirling sand. Then Mohommed suddenly stopped, right in the middle of the desert.

"I go no further" he said "sand is too heavy for my vehicle, now you go on foot, I wait here." So he did speak English.

They were still about a mile from where the rock was. Argument proved futile, he wasn't budging. She set out with her desert clothes, compass, map, notes, water and everything she needed. "You be here when I get back, no matter how long I take, OK?"

He nodded.

It was midday and as hot as it could be. The beetle made its regular perambulation. There were still only two life forms in that sand-blasted forever-moving landscape. Then suddenly there were three, as a figure appeared to the east, sheathed in white robes, head bent downwards against the glare of the sun and the sandy air, walking slowly and heavily in sand that was knee high. The figure neared the rock but was still 20 minutes away. The figure was now very near to the rock. It was time for another scuttle. The figure had arrived at the rock; the beetle did not complete its scuttle. Now there were two life forms again but this time it was the cactus and the figure, the beetle was crushed.

The figure circled the rock several times, as if looking for something, then gradually walked further and further from the rock, peering all the time at the sand. Eventually the figure walked out of sight but later returned to the rock and walked around it again. The figure then stopped and bent down and picked something up. It was the crushed beetle. Somehow, magically, the sands which had buried the beetle had then brought its body back to the surface and the figure saw it and put it in a specimen box that had been intended for the cactus.

The figure then returned in the direction in which it had come. There were now no life forms in that hostile hothouse.

Mohommed was waiting for Lettie as she struggled her way back to the vehicle. She was very disappointed and now, on the way back to Zagora, it was she who did not want to talk. She was as near as she ever would be to tears. She had failed. She was not a botanist.

That evening she phoned Ron from the hotel to tell him what had happened. She was very unhappy but Ron had some news that cheered her up immediately.

"You know it was such a rush to translate the papers and then the rush to get you ready to go that I didn't really read the papers properly. All we did was translate them and not study them or think about them. Cacti are not my speciality but since then I have read the papers more thoroughly and consulted some text books and from Havergal's description I am certain I know what the specimen was and, what's more, I don't think he was actually interested in that cactus in itself at all. I am virtually certain that the cactus was *Ariocarpus fissuratus*, the living rock cactus; it lives in the hottest deserts by keeping as much as possible of itself underground, by root contraction. It was actually discovered and analysed about five years ago and is not new. Wiseman will be furious he's gone all that way looking for something that is in the public domain, assuming he finds it. The interesting thing though, and what Havergal writes about in his notes, is how such a specimen could survive *there*, and he actually speculates about insects or beetles being important to the plant. He wasn't interested in the cactus but only how it survived. So the beetle you found could be the real discovery and, even if it is crushed, we can DNA it and find out how all this worked. So you don't need to feel badly about it, you may have made the real find. We are going to need an entomologist to figure this out and I think I know one."

"Wow," said Lettie, "but I still can't get over the fact that I probably crushed it, there was no one else there to do that so it must have been me."

"That's probably true," said Ron, "but that often happens when we take specimens, and anyway if it was living on the cactus you would never have been able to bring it back alive. At least we can DNA test it and hopefully learn something new."

Lettie felt much happier now. She had booked into her hotel for three nights, not knowing how long her work might take. Now she had a free day before her flights home. She decided that the next day she would investigate the town.

She had a fascinating day in Zagora. Not for nothing is the town called, "The Gateway to the Desert". To the west are the towering Atlas mountains, to the east the Sahara where she had been the previous day. Of course she had to try a camel ride but immediately afterwards said 'never again'. The Berber people of the town were gentle and hospitable although it felt strange that she was probably the only person in the town not dressed in a skirt. In the late afternoon she decided to go back to the hotel to prepare for her return the next day.

As she went to reception to collect her room key Lettie noticed someone she knew in the queue to check in. "Well, Dr Wiseman I presume? Fancy meeting you here."

"Ah, Mrs. Brown, thank you for the cactus papers, have you found anything?"

"No, Mr Wiseman. I went to the exact coordinates and all I found was a dead beetle."

"A dead beetle? Oh dear. Well, that's the trouble with amateurs messing around with things they don't understand. You should have left it to a professional scientist like me," he said sharply.

"Good luck then," said Lettie. "I'm off home tomorrow. I'll let you have the other papers as they are completed."

The next day it is just as hot and another shrouded figure appeared in the now lifeless desert following the same route as the first figure two days before. The figure went straight to the rock using a handheld instrument, walked around a few times and then started digging at a precise spot and found the dead cactus, now buried several inches in the sand. It was then transferred to a specimen box for DNA testing, whereupon the figure tramped back the way it had come.

The very next day Abdul and his cousin Mohommed both came to the same spot with spades. Twice in three days wealthy Westerners staying at the best hotel in town had come to this spot looking for something. This was a big coincidence; in 15 years as drivers they had never been asked to come here. Was there gold there or diamonds? But they found nothing except sand.

Lettie arrived home tired after a long day's travelling but elated with Ron's news. Both Ron and Dafydd were there to greet her but she was briskly down to business.

"Now we are going to need an entomologist you said, Ron?"

"Yes, and I have one, he is sitting in the front room right now, let me introduce you," said Ron. "This is Dr Geoffrey Livingstone of University College, London, Geoff is an old friend and lives just three doors from me. We often have a drink at the Crow's Nest and he even met Havergal a couple of times. I've given him copies of the notes and a full briefing, all he needs now is the specimen." Geoff and Lettie shook hands.

"I really am most grateful for your help," said Lettie.

"Well... let's see first if I *can* help," he replied cautiously.

Just then the phone went.

"Excuse me a moment," said Lettie. It was Wiseman phoning from Casablanca airport. "That cactus you were looking for was just an *ariocarpus fissuratus*. It was buried in the sand, dead, but there are thousands of them all over North Africa, you wasted my time."

"I didn't tell you to go," said Lettie. "I just told you I was going. You made your own decision, and if you aren't impressed with the specimen you found, can I have it?"

Lettie was thinking that an entomologist might find that the cactus had adapted in some way to the circumstances in the same way as perhaps the beetle had.

"I threw it away," growled Wiseman. "Now I really do strongly urge you to give me the rest of the papers. I have started legal proceedings but it seems stupid to waste time like this."

"All in good time," said Lettie. "I've told you that you will have copies of the other papers when they are translated and when I have read them."

"I'm stuck here in Casablanca for a few days because of a sand storm, there are no flights, but I want the papers by the time I get back," threatened Wiseman.

"If the cactus papers were a waste of time, why do you want the others? They may be the same," asked Lettie, but Wiseman had exhausted his threats and rung off. It was pretty clear he hadn't read the cactus papers and wasn't really scientifically interested in any of the papers; he just regarded Lettie as a threat that must be dealt with.

"It was Wiseman, issuing threats again. He's just a bully, all hot air, I'm not worried about him. He's stuck in Casablanca due to a sand storm. Ha Ha! And he's confirmed that the specimen was *ariocarpus fissuratus*, just as you thought Ron. But he threw the dead plant away, which is a pity."

"It certainly is a pity," said Geoffrey Livingstone. "As well as being rather unscientific. But I can get other specimens of *ariocarpus fissuratus*. They won't be the same as the actual specimen, which may well have adapted in some way, but there could still be things to learn. I had better be going now. I will let you know as soon as I have anything on this beetle."

After he had gone, Lettie turned to Ron and Dafydd.

"OK guys, how are the other papers going?"

Six weeks later an article appeared in learned scientific journals in the USA and Britain, which set alight the small and cloistered worlds of botany, biology and entomology. It was written under what was presumably a pseudonym, Stanley Livingstone. The article was to do with the interactions of plants and insects. In itself this, of course, was not new. Some plants eat insects, insects eat pollen and spread seeds but for two single specimen species to live symbiotically off each other was unique. The article paid fulsome tribute to Mr Havergal Wyllyams, who first observed the phenomenon without being able to explain it. And also Mrs Huntingdon Braun (the only alias Lettie could think of) for finding the insect which had mutated considerably to adapt to the circumstances. It also said what a pity it was that the cactus specimen had been lost, without going into how, and opined that this will have shown mutation as well. The article did not pretend to be the final answer on this matter, it left many unanswered questions, in particular how exactly did the two single specimens nourish each other and how did two individuals reproduce, the article just took Havergal's observations further and posed these challenges to the botanical world. There was no mention of Kew in it.

It was the monthly executive meeting at Kew and it was the usual rather tedious agenda. During a break for coffee someone asked Wiseman about the article, which had just been published, and then they all chimed in.

"Who is this person, Livingstone?"

"You've just been to Morocco, is someone beating us to the botany, are you losing your touch?"

"Maybe this Mrs Braun should join us here at Kew?"

"Is she the woman who came here with Wyllyams' papers?"

"I don't know who they are," replied Wiseman, untruthfully, "probably just a couple of amateur botanists on their summer holidays who got lucky, but I will find out."

Wiseman now felt well and truly threatened. Round one to Lettie.

Chapter 18

The next morning Lettie, unusually, was up late. The boys were already up and busy. It was the last day of their holidays and they were just finishing up; everything was translated, there was just stapling, copying and some remaining typing for Ottoline; just an hour or two's work.

The work done, Lettie announced, "OK guys, we're going to the pub, I'm going to buy you all a slap-up lunch to celebrate a good week's work." At the pub they all ordered the landlord's best fish and chips. They were a noisy group, Ottoline, after a glass or two of wine, turned out to have a racy, not to say a risqué, sense of humour and an infectious laugh and kept them all in stitches. After coffee and brandy it was time to start saying goodbyes and to go their separate ways. Dafydd was heading for the station to catch the train back to Newcastle; he was back at work the next day, he had loved working in Welsh for a week and especially working with Ron. He would start again translating Havergal's poems and email them to Lettie as they were done. "Take your time, Dafydd" said Lettie, "I can't see that they will contribute much to the botanical work here but they will certainly be of interest in knowing more about Havergal."

Then Ron said, "I'd better be going too. I'll need a couple of days now before you see me again, I've got some work to do with Geoff Livingstone on the cactus article and I need to reread the new papers properly and do some research on them this time before I tell you what they are about. Don't worry, I won't take any longer than I need, I know about the urgency and I'm just round the corner anyway."

Ron and Dafydd left the pub. They had been preparing to shake hands with Lettie but she insisted on a hug of appreciation, which embarrassed them no end. Only Ottoline remained, finishing her brandy. Then, suddenly, Ottoline remembered that the postman had brought a letter for Lettie just as they had been leaving and she retrieved it from her handbag and passed it over. It was from a Mary Midlothian-Sutton. Lettie had completely forgotten that she had written to her when she had been in Newcastle with Dafydd. The letter was short and read as follows:

Dear Mrs Huntingdon Brown,

Thank you for your letter. I knew Havergal Wyllyams well and would be happy to meet you to talk anytime you are in Llandysul in West Wales.

Please contact me at the above address.

Yours sincerely,

"It's great I've got you here, Ottoline, can I just dictate one last letter in reply to this Lady?" Ottoline got out her notebook and hoped she would be able to read her writing after such a convivial lunch.

This letter was somewhat longer than the first. Lettie explained that she had bought Havergal's house after his death and that lots of papers had been left behind and that it had become clear that Havergal's botanical work had been underappreciated and that she, with help from some friends, intended to put this right. She explained she was very busy with this just now but would come down to Llandysul at the earliest opportunity but she didn't yet know when that would be.

"I'll type it up and put it through your letter box," said Ottoline. "If you want any changes you know where I am." And with that, and another hug, the two parted.

When Lettie got home she was tired. With nothing much to do now she switched the television on for almost the first time since she had bought it. It was football. She sat down on the sofa and within seconds was fast asleep. She woke up at 3am, stiff as an ironing board and then went properly to bed. The next day, having had a really good rest, and with nothing happening now for a while, she decided that she would go to Kew Gardens and visit them properly.

Chapter 19

Lettie arrived at Kew, pleased not to be in a rush and with the whole day to wander round and enjoy the gardens, and it was a lovely day. First off, to get her going, would be a coffee in the beautiful Orangery cafeteria, sitting on the terrace watching children scamper on the lawn. But then she saw someone she recognised, it was Isobel Gardiner, the tour leader on Lettie's last visit. They recognised each and Isobel came over to sit down. "I'm at a loose end," she said. "I was booked to do a guided tour at 10 this morning but there's no-one there waiting for the tour, it's most unusual, they're usually very popular."

"Well, in that case," replied Lettie, seizing her chance, "would you mind doing a tour for just little old me?"

"Of course not," replied Isobel. "I don't mind if the tour is for one or a hundred, the reason I do it is because I just love being here at Kew. If you have finished your coffee, shall we make a start?"

As they set off, Lettie asked Isobel how long she had been working as a volunteer at Kew.

"About 15 years. I wanted something to occupy me when I retired from full-time work and I've always loved Kew."

"Then did you know someone called Havergal Wyllyams?" asked Lettie cautiously.

"I knew someone called Huw Williams," she replied, "but he died a couple of months ago."

"That's him!" exclaimed Lettie and proceeded to explain that Havergal was also Huw.

"Why are you so interested in him?" asked Isobel.

Lettie launched into a long explanation about buying the house, the papers, the botany, Morocco and everything that had happened; she instinctively trusted Isobel but thought it best not to tell her about Wiseman. They had already passed several of Isobel's normal explanatory stops; they were both more interested in this.

"So tell me how you knew Havergal," asked Lettie.

"I'll have to get used to the name Havergal, he was always Huw to me. It started out many years ago," continued Isobel, "with us just choosing the same bench and the same time to eat our lunchtime sandwiches. We didn't meet every day, I only worked here three days a week and only two now, and he would often be in meetings that overran when he was working full time, so I suppose we met about once a week, sometimes twice, and just really for half an hour or so. But then he retired and we met more often. He still came to Kew almost every day after he retired and we probably met for lunch two or three times a week. Sometimes he would be asked to do a guided tour and sometimes I was asked to help with the annual orchid festival, which he was very involved with despite having retired; not in a botanical sense you understand, just fetching things and carrying messages and so on. So we met quite often and became friends."

"Would you describe him physically for me please?" asked Lettie.

"Hugh, sorry, Havergal, was tall, about 6 feet 2 inches, slightly stooped, from peering through microscopes for hours I suppose, he had a dark complexion but grey hair, always cut short, he was slim and had piercing blue eyes. He always dressed smartly but in a sort of scruffy country sort of way, not a City slicker way. And he also had a lovely melodious lilting Welsh accent."

"And what sort of person was he?" asked Lettie.

"He was as charming and gentle a man as you could imagine. He was very old fashioned. When we met for lunch he was often there first and when I arrived he would immediately stand up and he would remove his glasses as we shook hands, almost as if he missed having a hat to doff. He was also the only man I have seen for years that wore a cravat. He was very generous and thoughtful. Once, when he had some plums with his lunch, I said that they looked nice and he immediately offered me one. I couldn't take it, of course, but the next day he brought extra plums just for me. It was a great pleasure to be friends with him and I miss him terribly."

Isobel was slightly emotional and so Lettie waited a few moments before quietly asking, "Were you in love with him?"

"Oh no," came the immediate answer. "I'm married. It was just a lovely friendship with a lovely man, purely platonic, that's all. It's a shame that just that such a gentle and distinguished man was so solitary and was treated so badly here, yet he never complained and I tried to just add a small friendship to his life, hopefully to brighten it. I think he liked talking to me. I don't think he talked much to anyone else. And then suddenly he was gone." Now Isobel did shed a tear so Lettie waited again.

"Do you know what he died of?" asked Lettie eventually.

"No," Isobel replied, "I have no idea. All I do know is that he and I had our usual lunch about a week before he died and he seemed just fine, just as normal. I don't understand it."

"Why do you suppose Havergal never married?" asked Lettie.

"That's easy," said Isobel. "He was married to his work; that was all that mattered to him. Even after they retired him about ten years ago, he still kept on working. He lost none of his enthusiasm."

"But why did they force him to retire when all he wanted was to keep on working and even kept coming here every day?" asked Lettie.

"I'm just a volunteer guide," replied Isobel. "I don't know for certain about all the internal office politics but what people say is that the new Director, new 10 years ago that is, regarded Havergal as a threat. He was too clever and he was scared of being shown up by him. I don't know that for certain but that is what I have heard. Havergal himself never said anything about this and never complained; in fact he never said a bad word about anybody."

"Did he have any friends other than you?" asked Lettie.

"Well, as I've said, almost everyone liked him, but as to close friends... he often mentioned Ron. I don't know his surname. He worked in Havergal's group and seems to have been a friend. He also had a friend in Wales, in the village he came from, they used to correspond, Mary something. Havergal used to tell me her news. That she'd had another grandchild, that sort of thing, but I think it was just a sort of pen pal friendship. I don't think they ever saw each other."

Isobel's guided tour was coming to an end, although they had seen nothing and talked only about Havergal. She would soon have to collect her next group. They exchanged telephone numbers and agreed to keep in touch.

"Just before you go," said Lettie, "have you got time to show me the bench where you used to have lunch?"

"Of course," said Isobel, "it's just over here, overlooking the lake, near the Sackler bridge, it's a beautiful place."

"Do you think there should be some sort of plaque put on the bench, perhaps just Havergal's name and his dates, we couldn't really have your name on there as well, it might be misunderstood."

"I think that's a lovely idea but you would have to get Kew's permission to do it and I doubt they will allow it," answered Isobel.

"You know, why don't we just do it anyway?" said Lettie. "I know just the man to run up a nice plaque and he will just come here quietly and screw it on. I'll tell him to rub it a bit so it looks as though it's been there for years, then every time you come here for lunch you'll have a reminder, how would that be?"

Isobel approved greatly of the idea and so it was that a few days later Delbert appeared with a screwdriver and a rectangular object in his pocket and instructions on where to go and left, finally, a public recognition of Havergal Wyllyams at Kew.

Now it was time for lunch and afterwards Lettie wandered around Kew rather aimlessly, her mind consumed by what Isobel had told her. Once again she had missed the tour but would come back tomorrow and try again. She knew Isobel was not working the next day and it would be best to give her a rest. Ron was unlikely yet to have finished all that he had to do and so it would be another free day. Time now then to head off back to 13 Sandown Road.

As she was leaving Kew, heading for her car, who should she pass but Carl Wiseman coming in.

"Well, howdy Mr Wiseman, just back from Casablanca are you? Have a good trip?" she said, rather sarcastically.

"I have said all I have to say to you, Madam," Wiseman bustled past.

"Well I don't think I have much to say to you either," called Lettie over her shoulder.

Chapter 20

It was another gloriously sunny day. Lettie had phoned Ron but it would be another day or so before he was ready with the next set of papers so now, for the third time, she would go to the Royal Botanic gardens at Kew and try to see them properly.

To get her bearings for the 300 acres of Kew, Lettie decided to start by taking the Kew explorer train which covered the gardens in 40 minutes and had an interesting running commentary and showed all the iconic sights such as the world famous Palm House ("designed by Decimus Burton, it was completed in 1848 to accommodate the exotic palms being discovered and collected in early Victorian times from all over the world"), the Temperate house ("also designed by Decimus Burton it was opened in 1863 to house semi hardy and temperate plants, it is now in need of a major restoration"), the Japanese gateway ("a replica of the Karaman of Nishi Hongan-ji in Kyoto"), the Pagoda ("completed in 1762 it is 163 feet high and has 253 steps but it is closed for the time being I am afraid"), the Princess of Wales conservatory ("Named in honour of Augusta, Princess of Wales, who founded the gardens. It was opened by Diana, Princess of Wales in 1987"), Kew Palace ("built in 1631 and bought by George 3rd in 1781, Queen Charlotte died there in 1818"), the Orangery ("designed by Sir William Chambers in 1761 as a hothouse, it is now a delightful restaurant and a good place for me to end our tour so you can now seek some refreshment"). It was almost a lesson in English history as well as a botany lesson and all a bit too much to take in so Lettie took the advice and went into the Orangery for a coffee.

She needed something a bit more personal than a rush around the entire gardens in less than an hour so she decided to take another guided tour on foot. The guide this time was Clemacy Hill-Hughes and there were about a dozen others on this tour, which was a botanical and scientific tour. They started at the Order beds, where the system of plant classification, which Lettie had already heard about from Ron, was explained, but this was a practical demonstration with related plants side by side in families. Clemacy explained that they were forever having to change the beds as new classifications and interpretations evolved, especially with the advent of DNA. She then went on to talk about Kew's Millennium Seed Bank. This was a hugely ambitious project to collect seeds for the entire flora of the world.

"Several plants become extinct every day, especially because of intensive farming and deforestation and if we have the seeds we can reintroduce the species elsewhere but it is a race against time, we are rapidly losing plant diversity," she said forlornly. "Currently 10% of the world's plant seeds have been banked and the target is to reach 25% by 2020.

"When do you reach 100%?" someone asked.

"The trouble is that just as we lose species we also keep discovering new ones, so it's a bit of a moving target and we'll never be sure it is 100% but it will be a long, long time," said Clemacy. "It's a huge task."

She then went on to talk about climate change, which Kew is heavily involved in, and the many other smaller research projects undertaken including one into the anatomy of the *Dicotyledons*. Since everyone else on the tour seemed to know what this was, Lettie realised she had joined a tour of science students and, though she stayed with it to the end, just to hear the words, she understood little of what was said and just smiled a lot. When the tour was over Lettie waited until the others had left and then asked Clemacy if she had known Huw Williams.

"Oh Yes, he was a lovely man," she replied. "How did you know him?"

"I bought his house."

"Oh," said Clemacy, surprised. Lettie decided to leave it at that.

There were two places she wanted to go back to now to spend some time in; the Princess of Wales conservatory and the Marianne North gallery. At the conservatory she wanted to see the orchids, which she knew were a speciality of Havergal's. She was lucky because it was the annual orchid festival, with a stunning display of orchids from all over the world. She wandered round several times, hoping she would learn something, but at least drinking in the beauty of the displays. There was an orchid specialist on hand to answer questions. Lettie collared her.

"What a beautiful display," said Lettie. "Thank you," said Candida Moore-Templeton. Lettie could not restrain herself. "Did you know Huw Williams?"

"Oh yes," said Candida, "I knew him well. He was very involved in setting up the orchid festival every year, even after he had retired, and he was working on this year's festival right up until he passed away. In fact, this year we only just got the show ready in time for the opening, it was touch and go until the final day."

"Why was that?" asked Lettie.

"The content of the display kept changing," explained Candida. "First we were going to have Patagonian orchids, then we weren't, backwards and forwards, these things take months of planning and sourcing and it gets difficult if the script keeps changing. There was some sort of disagreement in the office that held things back, and then, of course, Hugh's death robbed us of the most experienced orchid specialist we've got," said Candida sadly.

"What was the disagreement about?" asked Lettie, innocently.

"I'm just a trainee botanist," replied Candida. "I don't know what happens in the office, we just hear stories second hand, but it seems that Hugh and the Director disagreed over which orchids we would have this year and this held things back quite a lot, but we got there in the end," she said cheerfully.

Then someone else approached Candida and Lettie decided that she had asked enough questions for now.

Her head still spinning with what she had been told about the orchid festival, Lettie made her way to the Marianne North gallery, which she found utterly inspiring, temporarily driving thoughts of dark orchid deeds from her mind. The paintings were glorious and, having inspected them all, Lettie bought a book about the painter and retired to the Orangery for a coffee and to find out more.

Marianne North (1831-1890) was the eldest daughter of a wealthy and well-connected family. Her father, Frederick, was returned seven times as Member of Parliament for Hastings and was a Deputy Lieutenant for Norfolk and Justice of the Peace. Her mother, Janet, was the daughter of Sir John Marjoribanks MP and 1st Baronet of Lees. When her mother died in 1855 she had promised her that she would not leave her father and they undertook many foreign travels and visits to Kew gardens together and shared a love of botany. When her father died in 1869 Marianne, inspired by her father's passion for exotic plants, determined to continue with his interests and travel the world, painting plant specimens. She was a 40-year-old spinster who would never marry now and although she could have afforded companions she travelled almost entirely unaccompanied, occasionally hiring just porters. There were cliffs to be scaled, swamps to be crossed and deserts to be navigated, often in dangerous and uncharted places to reach the specimens she wanted to portray. She completed 832 paintings in 14 years during visits to Sri Lanka, India, Australia, New Zealand, South Africa, the Seychelles, Egypt, Chile, America, Canada, Brazil, Tenerife, Japan, Singapore, Sumatra and Java. She was travelling most of her life, rarely staying at home in England for more than a month or two between trips. All her trips were long ones; she spent a year in Brazil and 18 months in India.

Marianne paid for the building of the gallery at Kew and donated all her paintings to it. She designed almost everything in it; the displays, the carvings and the building itself. She had wanted tea and coffee to be available in the gallery but Kew would not allow this so she carved tea and coffee plants above the two entrances. She was a highly accomplished artist as well as a true botanist and she had several species named after her, such as *nepenthes northiana*. Just as she had thought she had finished her life's work Charles Darwin, one of a group of friends that included Edward Lear and Sir Joseph Hooker, the Director of Kew at the time, told her she must go again to Australia to see some plants she had missed; this was her final trip. Her gallery opened in 1883 and is still there to this day. Under Marianne's bequest, nothing can be changed, even if the paintings are displayed by continent rather than by plant families.

Somehow Lettie felt a strong and inspirational affinity for this remarkably intrepid and philanthropic Victorian Lady; they were both middle-aged, single and determined women chasing specimens. Both came from distinguished families and both were dedicated to continuing the work of a distinguished forbear. Marianne made Lettie feel all the more determined to get to the bottom of whatever had happened to Havergal.

"And to think I used to spend $500 a week on flowers for the house back in New York and I didn't even look at them or know the names of any of them," thought Lettie.

As she was leaving Kew Ron phoned her mobile.

"I'm ready to go through the next lot of papers."

"Oh good, I've got lots to tell you too, come round tonight and I'll cook you dinner."

Chapter 21

Ron came round to 13 Sandown Road at about 7pm that evening. He accepted the offer of a glass of wine and then said, "Lettie, I've got a lot to tell you but it's not going to be straightforward."

"So you think Morocco was straightforward?" retorted Lettie.

"Compared to this, Morocco was a walk in the park!" came the reply.

"Well, sit down and eat your dinner first and go we'll through things afterwards."

Ron had finished his dinner when Lettie was barely a third of the way through hers, so he started. It was obvious he couldn't wait to unload.

"As well as reading through the papers properly, I've also made some discreet enquiries and checked out some of the standard texts," he started. "I think you know that even after he retired Havergal continued to be heavily involved in the annual orchid festival at Kew, which is on now. He planned it and was involved in installing it, he was the project manager in all but name. This was to be his last orchid festival, and presumably the end of his contact with Kew. I don't know that for certain, or what he was going to do next, but he had let Personnel know that he would not be doing the orchids any more. He had wanted this final festival to be devoted to Patagonian orchids, which were a passion of his, and the centrepiece was to have been a brand new orchid discovery, and I'll come back to that in a minute." Ron paused for breath and a sip of wine. "But you may want to know a bit about Patagonia before I go any further?"

"Yes please," his host replied.

"Patagonia is an area at the southernmost tip of Latin America, it's mostly in Argentina but some of it is in Chile. It's a geographical term rather than a political one. Now there are lots of interesting flora in Patagonia, including orchids, but there is another interesting thing... There is also a sizeable Welsh-speaking community."

"What?" exclaimed Lettie. "How did that come about?"

"There is a community of about 50,000 Argentineans of Welsh descent, of whom about three or four thousand still speak Welsh as a first language. It came about in the late 19th century when Argentina was encouraging immigration to some of the lesser developed parts of the country and at the same time there were Welshmen worried about the Anglicization of their country. They set off to Patagonia to establish a new Wales. To this day, lots of the towns and street names are in Welsh, even if not that many speak it now. The area concerned is the Chubat province and the towns of Gaiman, Trelew and Trevelin. It would appear that Havergal made contact with one of the Welsh speakers, a gentleman called Xavier Morgan. I suspect the contact was initially because of Havergal's interest in the Welsh language but it developed into a mutual interest in botany and orchids in particular. So that's Patagonia and I've introduced you to Xavier Morgan. I'll have another sip before I go on," Ron had two large sips and took a deep breath.

"Xavier," continued Ron, "was an active field worker, by the sound of it, always writing to Havergal about things he had seen, not all of them of great interest. But he did find something, probably accidentally, which was of great interest and does appear to be a brand new discovery. He wrote to Havergal about it and sent him a photograph of it; I don't have his letter or the photograph but I do have a draft of Havergal's reply, in which he says that he believes this to be a hitherto undiscovered orchid, and Havergal would not have said that if he didn't mean it. In the papers there's a written description of the specimen but a photograph would really have helped."

"It's probably in the red book, wherever that is," said Lettie.

"Unfortunately," Ron continued, "Xavier died a couple of months before Havergal. And it would appear that Havergal had wanted to travel to Patagonia to try to find the specimen, which would have been the centrepiece of this year's orchid display at Kew. But it would also seem that Wiseman stopped him. Whether he needed funding to make the trip, I don't know – Havergal wasn't rich – or whether it was because Wiseman wouldn't let him have the equipment he would need to borrow or perhaps Wiseman simply didn't want Havergal to have any limelight, I simply don't know, but I do know that he stopped him stone dead. Such a pity." It was time for another swig of wine.

"Well, boy oh boy, you've found out a lot. You've done well!" exclaimed Lettie.

"Perhaps," said Ron, unconvinced, "but it leaves us looking for an orchid known only to two men, both of whom are dead, in a region of about 50 square miles in a country 8,000 miles away. Oh, and by the way, I think Wiseman suspects someone is helping you. He is watching everyone like a hawk. I'm sure he won't allow me any time off, so you are almost certainly on your own. And he's bound to know a certain amount about this if Havergal was discussing it with him to try and get funding or whatever."

"Yes, Morocco was a walk in the park compared to this," said Lettie mournfully. "So how do we go about it?"

"I just don't know. I can probably do a drawing of it from the description but we have no idea of where you will have to look for it. Perhaps something will turn up. I'm going home now, thanks for dinner, let's sleep on it." And Ron slouched off into the night.

Chapter 22

The only thing Lettie could think of was to write to Mary MidLothian-Sutton in Llandysul, who seemed to have been a friend of Havergal's. Just maybe he had mentioned something in a letter to her. It seemed pretty unlikely but she could think of nothing else. For the next few days she spent hours pacing around the house and the garden, pouring over maps of Argentina, pestering Ron about the drawing he was trying to do, visiting Kew again and thinking all the time about how to find this orchid in such a vast area; what had they missed? Then, the postman called with a letter.

It was a reply from Mary MidLothian-Sutton and the envelope contained a photograph of an orchid. The letter read:

> *Dear Mrs Brown,*
> *Thank you for your letter. Havergal sent me the enclosed photograph of an orchid; in his letter he was very excited about it and believed it was a new discovery and he wanted me to see it and to keep the photograph. He must have sent the letter and the photograph shortly before he died. He had never sent me anything to do with his work before and it was so uncharacteristic. I tried to phone him in case something was wrong but I couldn't get an answer. I will be happy to meet you and talk about this if you can visit me in Llandysul. I don't have a telephone (I tried to phone Havergal from a public phone) and I don't have internet so you will have to write to me when you are coming.*
> *Yours sincerely,*
> *Mary MidLothian-Sutton*

"Wow!" exclaimed Lettie. "A breakthrough!" She immediately called Ron to come round as quickly as possible. Ron appeared almost immediately, which was strange because he was supposed to be at work at Kew. He was very excited. "I'll take the photo to Kew and check it against the books to make certain it's not already known," he said, and dashed out, returning a few hours later to say, "Yes, that orchid is completely unknown to the botanical world. It is a first, a genuine discovery!" Lettie and Ron almost embraced with excitement but at the last minute Ron thought better of it. "But that is only half of the puzzle," he said. "We now know exactly what we are looking for but we still don't know where it is any more precisely than a 50 square mile area, it is still a problem."

Lettie was thinking. "Why do you suppose Havergal sent the photo to Mary MidLothian-Sutton? It can only be because he wanted to protect it and there is only one person he would have wanted to protect it from, Wiseman."

"I think that must be right," said Ron. " I wonder if this Mary Mid-Lothian-Sutton knows more than she has said in the letter? Perhaps I had better visit her as quickly as possible. Oh, and by the way, how come you were able to come around so quickly, aren't you supposed to be working?" asked Lettie.

"Oh my goodness, in all this excitement I forgot to tell you. Wiseman isn't in the office today, he's gone to get some jabs, he is setting off for Argentina the day after tomorrow. I heard his secretary making all the arrangements this morning."

"What!" Lettie exploded. "But how does he know what he's looking for? Is he looking for Havergal's orchid or is he going for some other reason?"

"I think it's pretty clear from what I heard him saying in the office that he is looking for orchids in Patagonia and that must mean Havergal's orchid."

Lettie was flabbergasted. She didn't know what to think. One minute they had just made an enormous breakthrough with the photograph and then the very next Wiseman seemed to be somehow ahead of them.

"But what will Wiseman know that we don't? How will he know what he is looking for and where to go?"

Ron was feeling rather shell-shocked too. "I don't think Wiseman really knows very much," he said. "He will only know what Havergal has told him, and Havergal will have known he had to be careful not to say too much, for obvious reasons. He will have had to show him the photograph and perhaps tell him roughly where the specimen is to found, Wiseman would never have approved the funds for a trip without a certain amount of detail. But Havergal will have probably only shown him the photo together with the source books proving it to be unique and will not have let him copy it or let it out of his possession. Wiseman knows nothing about orchids, he must have just assumed that he could find the specimen on his own, that he would get lucky, and he may also think that you know more than you do and that he therefore had better get out there fast and be there before you."

"Is he taking anyone with him?" asked Lettie.

"I don't think so. The only other specialist is Cressida Dixon, we call her 'Watercress' because her specialities are orchids and water lilies. She was a good friend of Havergal, hates Wiseman, very old school, Roedean and the Sorbonne. Havergal may well have suggested to her that she go with him. I'll ask her, but Wiseman would never have asked her to go with him, he would know the answer he would get."

"So Wiseman is about to go haring off in search of an orchid he has probably only seen a brief picture of which is located in an area of 50 square miles or so just so that someone else will not get the credit for it. That is incredible behaviour," opined Lettie.

"That's the man," said Ron "but he may also be scared that all his previous "discoveries" will be revealed as thefts as a result of this and so he had better get on and make a discovery of his own, who knows."

"Is there any chance of you coming with me to Patagonia?" asked Lettie, knowing the answer.

"No, I don't think so," replied Ron. "I think I told you the department is like an armed camp now with Wiseman's cronies spying on the rest of us and even though he won't be there for the next few weeks, one of his acolytes would report me as absent and he would sack me. And although I hate Wiseman, I do love my job at Kew and would not want to lose it."

"I understand," said Lettie. She thought back to Marianne North and her gallery at Kew. 'If she could go specimen hunting all on her own more than 100 years ago, then, goddamit, so can I now,' she thought. Then Lettie remembered Mary MidLothian-Sutton. She would not be able to go down to Llandysul until after going to Patagonia and she dashed off another letter explaining what she was doing and that she would be back in touch as soon as possible. Ron then left to return to work.

An hour or so later, Ron phoned. He had spoken to Cressida Dixon. Havergal had discussed a possible Patagonian orchid trip with her but Wiseman had not been prepared to fund it, so it came to nothing. She had briefed Ron a bit, since he knew little about orchids, and Ron passed this on.

"Orchids, or Orchidaceae, are very exotic but generally not very rare. There are 25,000 species, that is twice the number of bird species and four times the number of mammal species, and there are now about

100,000 hybrids and cultivars, so they are very common and occur in almost every habitat except glaciers. Despite being so numerous, 'Watercress' told me that they're still discovering new angles. For instance, the first known night-flowering orchid, *Bulbophyllum nocturnum,* was recently found on New Britain, near Papua New Guinea, and, astonishingly, the flowers only last one night. Havergal did not share all his details with Watercress but she got the impression that there was something unusual about this one too; Havergal would not normally get excited about yet another orchid discovery, they happen almost every week. She thought it was possible that this one might be closer to a glacier than ever known before but she wasn't sure, the whole idea was stopped before it got very far."

"Thanks, Ron, that's very interesting." No sooner had she replaced the receiver than it rang again, this time it was Dafydd.

"Afternoon Missus," he greeted her, still not quite comfortable calling her Lettie and unsure what else to call her. "I just thought you might be interested in where I have got with Havergal's poems. I've not forgotten them."

"I'd love to hear where you have got to Dafydd," replied Lettie.

"Well, the first thing I did was to put them all into an order as best I could. Some are dated, others you could tell by how fresh the ink is and how crinkly the paper is and I got them into some sort of sequence. I started with some of the early ones. Many of the poems are written in what the Welsh call *cynghanedd*, which is a difficult verse metre using stress and alliteration as well as rhyme. Lots of the early poems are ones about natural history. There is a delicious one about Lancelot, the department head before Wiseman, chasing a butterfly (*Pili Plal*) that was fluttering by, in Welsh it is beautiful and it even translates quite well into English. I've had great fun translating them, it's been a real privilege. But I know this is not quite what you were hoping for from the poems so I switched to the more recent ones, and I found something that I think may mean something to you. This one is written in a different handwriting and it is signed by someone called Xavier Morgan. It's in Welsh, of course, and it is sort of a poem, but rather clumsily done, and it seems to be a set of directions. I haven't tried to make it rhyme in English, shall I just read it to you as it is?"

"Yes!" Lettie practically shrieked, "this may well be the missing link."

"OK, here goes...

In the land of loneliness and wind,
no shelter to be had
Near a Welsh mill town called Trevelin,
is a most unexpected friend
Head for Chile, Los Cipresses and then the mountain road,
to Lake Baggilt at the foot of Conico hill where a canyon
leads to the glacier and there, my friend, you will see
a beautiful new friend, which I would like to think
when I am gone, you may name after me.

"Compared to some of Havergal's poems it's absolute rubbish, even in Welsh," opined Dafyyd, "but I thought the instructions might be important."

"I think they might just be very important. I'll call you back later to explain why but for now I need to get hold of Ron quickly, we have some work to do, but keep working on those poems, the most recent first, you never know what else is there, oh, and email me those words would you, I haven't written them down and they could be crucial." And she rang off.

Lettie and Ron spent several hours poring over maps and looking at source books and it became increasingly clear that this was almost certainly the missing link. Trevelin turned out to be a small town in Chubut province in the lower Andes, about 20 miles from the Chilean border. The town had been founded by Welsh immigrants in about 1860 and Trevelin means 'mill town' in Welsh. Los Cipresses is a small place almost on the border and then a 12-mile mountain road leads to Lake Baggilt and the glacier. Lettie found an interesting historical twist in this; in the nineteenth century, Chubut province had been disputed between the Chileans and the Argentinians, one claiming the border should run along the mountain tops, the other that it should run along the water courses, and the issue was referred to the British Crown for resolution. The British decided to ask the inhabitants what they wanted. Apart from llamas, who didn't really care either way, the only other inhabitants were the Welsh immigrants and they voted for Argentina because of the other Welsh towns of Gaiman and Trelew, which were 250 miles to the east and firmly in Argentina and so it was resolved.

""A beautiful new friend, which you will name after me" can surely only mean the orchid that Xavier found?" said Lettie.

"Yes, that must be so," said Ron, "and I assume that when he wrote that he must have been ill and must have known that he would not be able to go back for a specimen and that is why he wrote, "when I am gone, you may name after me?" That is why he sent the instructions to Havergal. And what's more," continued Ron, "I bet that what's special about the orchid is that it grows in a glacial area, because that has never been known before. Orchids can grow in almost any conditions except those and if this is one that can survive there then it is truly unusual."

"Well, we've got a picture of it and we have instructions on how to find it, so I guess it's time to start packing again!" said Lettie.

"I wish I was coming with you," said Ron, "but I've been thinking, why did Wiseman go dashing off quite so quickly? He won't have these instructions, Havergal would never have given them to him. All he has is probably a glimpse of the photo and he will know the general area but nothing else. I think his strategy is to get there as soon as possible before you and then wait for you to arrive and then follow you. I can't think of any other explanation."

"Well, there is something that's been troubling me too," said Lettie. "Why did Havergal send the photo to Llandysul? Was he expecting someone to try and steal it? And why were the instructions in amongst the poems and not the botanical papers? Again, was he protecting them?"

"Add to that," replied Ron, "that Xavier died just before all this and then Havergal died as well."

"Do you think I should speak to the police?" asked Lettie.

"I don't know about that, you'd better ask Dafydd," said Ron, "but I do think you had better be mighty careful when you go to Patagonia."

Lettie called Dafydd and asked him if she should speak to the police. "When you put it all like that, it does sound a bit fishy," said Dafydd, "but I don't think you should call them yet. They won't do anything. Everything you've said is circumstantial. Don't forget there was no sign of forced entry when Havergal died, the doctor said it was natural causes and you would be casting aspersions against a director of Kew Gardens. I am sure they wouldn't do anything. But Ron is right, you will have to be careful from now on."

"Well, I guess I had better figure out how to get to Patagonia then," said Lettie to herself.

❖ ❖ ❖

Chapter 23

Three days later Lettie was at Heathrow airport, preparing to board a plane for Buenos Aires. The past few days had been a maelstrom of preparations; tickets to be booked, Ron's specimen equipment to be checked and fully understood, maps to be studied, clothes to be packed ("be prepared for all kinds of weather" had been Ron's advice) visas to be arranged, a hotel in Buenos Aires to be booked, jabs to be checked (fortunately none were necessary after her trip to Morocco), and now finally everything was done and she was ready for her next expedition. This time she had better instructions on where to go but she would be a long way from home if she needed help. But she was still very excited, she was on the next stage of her Marianne North recreation as well as the next stage of uncovering Havergal's story.

The airport was hot and airless as she waited in the economy line for check in. She had tried her usual trick, the one Arvin had taught her, of booking economy and then calling well-placed friends to get an upgrade but it hadn't worked this time. She hadn't managed to get through to anyone senior, only secretaries, and she'd been told that the plane was completely full and so there was no possibility, but she wasn't bothered much by this. Then, on the other side of the departures hall, she noticed a familiar face; it was Wiseman waiting in the first class check-in line. Lettie turned away. She did not want to talk to him and was now pleased that she hadn't been given an upgrade; she would have been in the same cabin as Wiseman. "That was a close thing," she thought. "I'll have to make sure I avoid him when we get there. But what is he doing travelling today? Ron told me he was going two days ago. Did he find out I was on this flight and change his plans?" But, just then, passengers were invited to board and they were soon on their way and for the next 11 hours Lettie hardly thought of Wiseman, in fact she slept for most of the journey, so busy had she been preparing for it.

On arrival at Buenos Aires, Lettie again managed to avoid Wiseman. First class were the first off the plane and when she finally got out she saw him at the front of a long line waiting for taxis and then soon he was gone. Although she had failed to get an upgrade on the plane, she had been successful in pulling strings with her hotel booking. Arvin had been a regular visitor to Buenos Aries and had always booked a suite at the Alvear Palace hotel and, as luck would have it, his old friend, Silvio della Santa Cruz was still the General Manager and only too happy to accommodate his old friend's widow in his finest suite. As Lettie stood chatting to the General Manager, while her cases were being taken upstairs, she noticed Wiseman, sitting in one of the reception chairs, watching her. This time there seemed to be no avoiding him. What was he doing in the same hotel as her? He must be following her. Silvio then announced that all her luggage had been delivered to her room and then left, and that was Wiseman's cue to come over.

"Well, we meet again," he said, in his usual sneering way.

"Why yes, we do," trilled Lettie. "If I didn't know better, I might almost think you are following me. We were on the same plane but you didn't seem to notice me..."

"Oh yes I did," interrupted Wiseman.

"And now we're in the same hotel," she continued. "What are the odds of that happening? I guess we'd better have a chat and, rather than standing here in the middle of reception, perhaps we should find a table and have a cup of tea?"

"OK," said Wiseman.

Lettie had no desire for a cup of tea with this man but there seemed no avoiding it. Wiseman started the conversation.

"So you're on the trail of Huw's orchid are you? Why are you taking such an interest in all this? You're not a botanist, or if you are you're just an amateur. You could mess everything up. Do you know where you are looking? Where are you going next? You won't find the orchid here in Buenos Aries, you know. And you must know that all of Huw's papers and findings are the property of Kew and that is why I am here. It's my duty to protect Kew's work. You must surely know how stupidly you are acting. My lawyers are still working on a case against you but if you're going to go charging off like this, it's my duty to keep an eye on what you are doing. Why don't you let me help you find the orchid, if you know where it is?" Wiseman even made this last sentence, intended to sound like a friendly offer, sound menacing instead.

"Yes, I think I do know where the orchid is to be found," replied Lettie, "but I'm not going to tell you and I don't need any help, thank you very much. This is nothing to do with Kew or any of the papers you claim belong to you; the discovery is a result of a private correspondence and a personal friendship which Havergal had. I have sent you already Havergal's translated orchid papers but you will have left before they arrived at Kew, and there is nothing in them about this. This was a private piece of research and so none of your business."

"Why should I believe you?" countered Wiseman. "You will have to show me whatever letters or photographs you have to prove that. You may or may not know that some months ago Huw asked me for funding to make a trip here to look for the orchid, that proves that this is Kew's matter, not yours."

"So why did you refuse the funding? Since I presume that is what you did." Lettie tried not to appear to know what had actually happened.

"Because I didn't trust Huw. He was always a one-man-band and not a team player. He would have gone charging off in all directions, looking for anything and everything and probably ended up attributing the specimen to some local botanist rather than Kew. Don't get me wrong, he was a very good botanist and from what he told me, which I trusted, this could be a very important discovery, but I couldn't risk him confusing the situation, so I refused the funding and decided that at some stage I would do it myself. I know all about the orchid from what Huw told me."

"Then you don't need to keep pestering me," countered Lettie.

"I know all about it, except where it is," replied Wiseman.

Then Lettie remembered a long distance conversation with Wiseman when he had said he was in Argentina on a field trip. "He's been here before," she thought. "Was he looking for this or something else? If he was looking for the orchid, then he obviously didn't find it and perhaps I am now his only hope. In fact, he is planning to steal from me just as he stole from Havergal. I had better be very careful."

"Well Mr Wiseman, it's been a long day and I have an early flight at 8.30 tomorrow morning and I think we've gone as far as we can. We're just going to have to agree to disagree. But I will promise you this; when I have found and named the orchid and given it its proper attribution, I will donate the specimen to Kew so that you can propagate it to your heart's content, how's that?"

"I'm sorry but that's not good enough. As I have already explained," he said. "That finding is the property of Kew and it is my botanical duty to pursue this. If you have an 8.30 flight tomorrow morning then that will be to Esquel, presumably en route to Trevelin? Thank you for that information. Oh, and by the way, may I ask you to refer to me as *Doctor* Wiseman, as everyone else does, just out of respect, please."

"Oh yeah?" now Lettie sneered, "and what are you a doctor of exactly?"

"My doctorate was in applied scientific marketing from the University of Buckingham," he replied.

"So you're not a botanist either!" Lettie exploded. "And you accused *me* of being an amateur! How are you going to find this orchid if you're not trained?"

"I have worked in the field now for a number of years and I've had a full briefing from my staff before I came," said Wiseman pompously.

'Yeah, I'll bet Watercress gave you a full briefing,' she thought. 'You really are just trying to steal from me now the same as you did from Havergal.'

"And by the way," and Lettie looked straight at Wiseman. "I'm also interested in what happened to Havergal. Several people have told me they saw him just weeks, days even, before he died and he was just fine, so what happened?"

Wiseman shifted uncomfortably in his chair. "I know nothing about that. It was a surprise to me too," he mumbled.

"Well, I'm going to bed," Lettie closed the conversation. "Please don't follow me, I don't want to see you again."

"I have to do my duty," Wiseman said, for about the third time. He was becoming very repetitious.

Lettie double locked her door that night and pushed a chair against it. She was going to have to be careful.

Chapter 24

Lettie left early for the airport the next morning. There was no sign of Wiseman. Arriving at the airport she realised why, he was already there. With time to kill she wandered round and so did Wiseman, never letting her out of his sight but making no attempt to talk; he was obviously waiting to see which flight she was catching so he could make sure he was on the same one. "This is going to be a real damn nuisance," Lettie thought. "How do I get rid of him? Should I speak to the police? I'd struggle to explain it all in English, let alone in Spanish. What do I do?"

No answer revealed itself. An hour or more later of aimlessly wandering round and her flight was called. As she made her way to the departure gate, she sensed Wiseman following. "This is going to be a pain in the butt but I'm not going to just lead him straight to the specimen," she thought, as she boarded the plane.

The two and a half hour flight was the perfect antidote for her worries; the scenery was breath-taking. Someone had left a guidebook on the plane and Lettie read all about the place she was going to.

"Patagonia is one of the least populated regions in the world with a population density of 1.9 people per square kilometre."

'I seem to specialise in places like that,' she thought.

"Patagonia is more than four times the size of the United Kingdom and is about two thirds in Argentina and one third in Chile. Patagonia is neither a geographic term nor a political or administrative one, the name comes from the word 'Patagon', used by Magellan in 1520 to describe the native people who were giants, nearly a foot taller than the Spanish. He had spent the winter there before continuing his epic journey and rounding Cape Horn. The name has stuck ever since. The border dividing Argentina and Chile was established by the British Crown in the 19th century but has been disputed ever since. There is even a 50 km stretch where there is no accepted border. Border issues are a continuing source of tension to this day. In Patagonia there is a highly varied topography of steppes, plateaux, glaciers, deserts, volcanoes and, of course, the Andean mountains. The region contains some of the most inhospitable conditions on earth but also some of the most beautiful scenery to be seen anywhere."

"Well," thought Lettie, "I hope I'm not going to an inhospitable bit."

Just then the captain announced that landing at Esquel was imminent. "Wrap up warm," he said, "it will be cold and thank you for flying with us today..."

Esquel appeared a charming town but Lettie was anxious to get to Trevelin as soon as possible and try to find a way to throw Wiseman off. She found a taxi for the 14-mile trip, knowing that Wiseman was behind her and would have instructed his taxi to follow hers. She had asked Silvio della Santa Cruz, General Manager of the Alvear Palace in Buenos Aries, to book her a hotel in Trevelin "The best they've got Silvio please" and he had booked her into the Challhuaquen Lodge, after telling her that Trevelin was apparently very busy for some reason and there were very few rooms left, only expensive ones. "Not a problem," she had replied.

On arrival at the Lodge, followed by Wiseman of course, she had sought out the General Manager, as usual, and found out that the Lodge was now fully booked for the next week because of the local Eisteddfod.

"Now just hold on a moment," Lettie had said. "Firstly, did you say fully booked? So if someone shows up now asking for a room, you have absolutely nothing?"

"That's right. Nothing at all, and I doubt there are any empty rooms in the town anywhere at all. You were very, very lucky, there was a last minute cancellation of your room that I could have refilled a dozen times at any price but just at the right moment Silvio called and, as a favour to him as an old friend, I gave it to you. Anyone else coming in now will have great problems."

'Well, that should get rid of Wiseman for a while,' thought Lettie, as she saw him walk away from reception clearly unhappy and scowling in her direction. "And why is it so busy? Did you say something about an Eisteddfod? I remember roughly what those are but we are about as far away from Wales here as it's possible to be."

"You must know about the Welsh community in Patagonia, surely that's why you are here? It's why everyone else is here. I'm a Welsh descendant myself. Here is a leaflet about all the events and a history of the Eisteddfod. It starts tomorrow." He handed her three pages of information. Just then she noticed the general manager's name badge, 'Pedro Morgan'.

"Are you related to Xavier Morgan?" she asked.

"Yes," came the reply, "there are a lot of Morgans here and I'm a sort of second cousin but I knew him well. He died earlier this year. How did you know him?"

"It's a long story," replied Lettie and she proceeded to tell him a little about Havergal's correspondence with Xavier. "So you knew Havergal did you?" asked Pedro. And then a little more of the story had to come out. "Xavier's son, Roberto, lives in Trevelin and would be just as interested as I am in your research, shall I call him and invite him to meet you?" asked Pedro.

"That would be good," smiled Lettie. "Let's see... it's 6 'o' clock and I haven't unpacked yet. How about I go to my room now and then meet the both of you for dinner at seven o'clock?"

"I'm sure that will be OK," Pedro replied, "See you then."

Lettie's room was everything she could have wanted and unpacking took little time. Then she sat down to read the information on the Eisteddfod. An Eisteddfod, she learnt, is a competitive festival of literature, music and performance all in the Welsh language and Eisteddfodau have been taking place since the 12th century. They take place wherever there are sufficient Welsh speakers and outside of Wales itself also in the USA ("I didn't know that," thought Lettie) Australia, Argentina and England and even the Channel Islands. In Patagonia all the large Welsh towns have an Eisteddfod at different times and each travel to the others as well as quite a lot of visitors from Wales itself, which explained why the hotels were all full up. The programme for Trevelin was set out but, unlike the general description above, it was in Welsh so she couldn't understand it but there did appear to be lots going on. Soon it was time to join the others for dinner; Lettie would ask them to translate the programme for her.

On entering the restaurant she saw them sitting at a table in an alcove, which would be nice and private. Pedro was unchanged from earlier, in his dapper manager's suit with a buttonhole. He was of medium height, with dark hair, clean-shaven, smart and slim, the complete opposite of Roberto, who was large, scruffy but clean, with a luxuriant moustache and a very strong handshake; they were both probably in their mid- fifties.

"Good evening Mrs Brown," Roberto said, in an accent straight from the mid-west of America.

"Good evening to both of you," she replied. "and where did you get that accent from Roberto?"

"I spent quite a lot of my youth in the States." he replied. "Educational opportunities are a bit limited round here and my parents wanted me to have a good education, so they sent me to high school in Chicago and later I graduated from the University of Chicago. I guess I have never lost the accent."

"What subject did you graduate in?"

"Biology and botany," came the answer.

Lettie tucked that piece of information away for later while they talked about the Eisteddfod and the events that would take place and both Roberto and Pedro promised that, between them, they would show her around. "It will all be in Welsh," they told her, "but still enjoyable nonetheless." Then they moved on to ask what she was doing there and by now Lettie felt she trusted them both – Roberto, after all, was the son of Xavier, a friend of Havergal's and Pedro was his relation – so she told them the entire story, including about Wiseman.

"Wow," they both said simultaneously. "Well," said Pedro. "The first thing to say is that you can feel perfectly safe here and with us. I will go and call the police station now."

"Hold on," said Lettie. "I don't know if I want the police involved."

"No, you didn't let me finish," said Pedro. "I will call them just to find out where Wiseman is staying. We are supposed to register passport numbers of all guests with the local police. I didn't bother with yours because any friend of Silvio in Buenos Aries is a friend of mine and the local police chief is also a Morgan, so he won't worry. But Wiseman's hotel, wherever he ends up, will not know him and will certainly register his passport, and my cousin will tell me where he is staying. I'll be back in a moment."

Then Roberto added, "You will be safe and I will help you find the orchid if I can. In fact, I have known about it for quite a long time. I knew my father found an unusual specimen but he sent the only photograph to Havergal, as well as the instructions on how to find it. I asked him many times where he had seen it and he just couldn't remember. First he would say 'here' and then he would say 'there' and I would go to look but I didn't find anything. He was a dedicated botanist all his life. He was always in the mountains looking for things. He found this specimen about two years ago, just as his health was deserting him. He was ill for a long time and his mind was going. He just forgot where it was but now perhaps you have the way to find it? It will be a beautiful tribute for him if we can find it."

"I must just ask," said Lettie. "Did your father die naturally?"

"Oh yes. As I said, he had been ill for some time and into a decline and when the end came, a couple of months ago, it was merciful. Wiseman had nothing to do with it. Dad was 87 when he went; it was just his time."

"And do you know why this orchid is so special?" asked Lettie.

"All I know is what my Dad told me," he said. "He believed it was special for two reasons. Firstly, it is the highest known orchid in the world. Orchids do not normally live in or near glaciers but this one does apparently. Secondly, he said it is the only true blue orchid he has ever seen. Most orchids described as blue are actually shades of purple. All attempts to cross pollinate orchids to produce a true blue have failed but here is apparently a proper and natural blue which will make its molecular structure of particular interest to botanists, but it is also likely to have big commercial potential."

Just then Pedro came back. "My cousin told me that Wiseman is at a bed and breakfast about 12 miles out of town. I know them well, so I called them. They gave him a box room that nobody else had been prepared to take. He is not happy, apparently. I didn't tell them much but they will keep an eye on him."

"Thanks Pedro." Lettie felt increasingly relieved.

"But there is one important thing I must tell you," said Roberto. "If we find this specimen, which I am sure we will, with that photo and those instructions, you will not be allowed to take it out of Argentina."

"Oh really? Why?" exclaimed Lettie.

"There has recently been a new law prohibiting individuals from taking plants out of the country. There have been so many plants removed over the years, especially orchids, that in some areas they've been wiped out and so this law was passed. Customs at the airports check for any plants or living material on the way out."

"He is right," added Pedro. "I had forgotten. To enforce it, all hoteliers are required to explain this to guests. If you look in the folder of hotel information in your room, you will find confirmation of this."

"Commercial exploitation is still allowed if you get a license," added Roberto, "and it is possible, I suppose, that Wiseman, through Kew, has done that, but it is also quite likely that he hasn't because the law is very recent. Apparently, even your friend Ron didn't know about it."

"But now I think about it," said Lettie, "it really doesn't matter. The only important thing is to find this orchid, confirm that it is a new one, publicise it appropriately in the botanical press and then name it

Orchidaceae Morgan-Wyllyams perhaps? Botanists can come here to see it instead of Kew, or perhaps we'll send seeds to Kew?"

"That sounds good to me," said Roberto.

"Tell me Roberto," asked Lettie, "you studied biology and botany, are you still a botanist?"

"Sadly no," replied Roberto. "I'm still interested in it and haven't forgotten what I learnt in Chicago. I used to accompany my father on his trips whenever I could, but botany doesn't really pay the bills around here. There is no Kew Gardens in Patagonia. No, I have a company that offers adventure holidays: skiing, paragliding, trekking, canoeing, anything like that. I still know enough botany to identify our orchid but, even more usefully, I have the 4x4 vehicles to get us to the site, so you don't have to go trekking like you did in Morocco. I can even take along some canoes in case we need those."

Lettie felt truly exhilarated. Everything was falling into place, compared to 24 hours earlier, when things had seemed so bleak. She almost now felt sorry for Wiseman, who was onto a total loser here.

"When can we start?" asked Lettie. "Immediately?"

"I'm afraid I can't," said Roberto. "I'm very much involved in the Eisteddfod."

"I would like to be involved but I can't either," added Pedro. "I've got a completely full hotel until the Eisteddfod is over."

"In which case," Lettie was triumphant, "it works perfectly. I will spend the next few days enjoying the Eisteddfod and when it is over we can all go into the mountains in search of the orchid. In the meantime, Mr Wiseman will probably be following me all over town, tearing his hair out, wondering when something is going to happen."

"As soon as the Eisteddfod is over, we will both be ready to make our trip and in the meantime we won't leave you on your own at any time. Either Pedro or I, or even one of my adventure guides, will be with you all the time," assured Roberto.

"That sounds great," said Lettie. "I am really looking forward to a dose of Welsh culture and I am truly very grateful to you both."

Lettie was indeed accompanied for the entire period of the Eisteddfod and Wiseman was always 50 yards or so away, watching and clearly becoming increasingly exasperated. He had not come all this way for an Eisteddfod!

Chapter 25

The three of them, Lettie, Roberto and Pedro, were sitting in a bar drinking beer. Lettie had developed a fondness for the local Patagonian beer during the Eisteddfod. "This will have to stop when I get home," she thought. Then she realised that when she thought of 'home' she was thinking of 13 Sandown Road; she had not thought of New York for ages. The festival was now over, the bard had been crowned, the speeches all made, the final marching band had played and people were now drifting home. Lettie ordered three more beers. "Well guys, I guess it's time for work now? Should we start tomorrow?"

"Yes ma'am?" they chorused.

"OK, so how do we go about it?"

"We know almost exactly where to go from the poem's instructions" Roberto pulled a folded piece of paper from his pocket and began to read:

> *In the land of loneliness and wind,*
> *no shelter to be had*
> *Near a Welsh mill town called Trevelin,*
> *is a most unexpected friend*
> *Head for Chile, Los Cipresses and then the mountain road,*
> *to Lake Baggilt at the foot of Conico hill where a canyon*
> *leads to the glacier and there, my friend, you will see*
> *a beautiful new friend, which I would like to think*
> *when I am gone, you may name after me.*

"I can use one of my 4x4s to get us there and then there may be a bit of walking at the end but it shouldn't be difficult."

"But there's just one problem," said Lettie gloomily. "Wiseman. He's still around, as we know. He'll follow us and if we're not careful we'll lead him to the site. How do we deal with that?"

"I've been thinking about that," said Roberto, "and I think I have the solution. Pedro and I will go to the site, but not you. You will go on one of my organised trips with half a dozen others to somewhere completely different. You will take your specimen box and equipment as if you are going out collecting and you'll leave about half an hour before

Pedro and I go in the opposite direction to find the orchid. You'll spend the day hiking around the mountains with my group. Wiseman is sure to follow you and by the time he discovers his mistake it will be too late for him to catch us up. Of course, that leaves you out of the action and you'll have to trust Pedro and me, but that is the only way to ensure that our friend finds out nothing."

"I think that is an excellent plan," said Lettie. "Of course I trust you both and since it was your father, Roberto, who found the orchid in the first place, it's quite right you two should be the ones to rediscover it, although I would like to go another time to see the site when every-thing has been sorted out."

The next morning a 4x4 arrived outside the Challhuaquen Lodge, driven by Roberto, with four others in it, one of whom, Paulo, was to be their driver for the day. Lettie got in with her specimen box and equipment prominently on display and introduced herself to Paulo and the three other tourists and off they set, leaving Roberto behind, waving them off and calling out 'good luck'. Wiseman saw all this and had no alternative but to follow. They were on their way on a regular trip for tourists to the Los Alerces National Park and its incredible Alerce trees, some of them 3,000 years old, Lake Futalaufquen and Lake Menendez, then the Cypress groves and the Valdivian rainforest; all in all a wonderful day of hiking, boating and sightseeing. Wiseman fairly soon realised he had been tricked and returned to Trevelin but too late to see Roberto and Pedro depart on their expedition to find the orchid. The plan had worked.

Lettie got back to the Lodge at about 5 o'clock having had a wonder-ful day, she had made friends with the other tourists, who turned out to be an American family from Boston who knew friends of friends and there had been plenty to talk about as well as plenty to see. On the veranda in front of the Lodge she saw Roberto and Pedro, with beers in front of them and huge smiles on their faces. She sat down with them and another beer magically appeared, for her.

"What luck then guys?" she greeted them.

"It has been a very, very good day," beamed Pedro. "You will be pleased to know that the specimen is confirmed and we have lots of pictures, but shall we start from the beginning and take you through it all in order?"

"Yes please, and don't miss anything out," replied Lettie.

"Over to you Roberto, you are the botanist and you speak English better than me," said Pedro.

"Well, we waited until you were out of sight, and of course Wiseman did follow you, and then we set off in my other 4x4, following my father's instructions. It was actually surprisingly easy to find the site, not easy walking but easy to find because the instructions are so clear. We used the 4x4 to get to Los Cipresses and then Lake Baggilt and then we looked for the canyon leading to the glacier. This took a bit of finding but eventually we did and then there is quite a long walk up to the glacier, it was too steep for the 4x4 and then, "fantastico", we saw the orchids, about seven of them. We took lots of pictures, here they are, exactly the same as the picture my father took, and which your friend Ron confirmed was a new species. We took the exact GPS positions, we took some soil samples and noted the air and soil temperatures and then we phoned the Argentinian Botanical society to notify them. I have a friend there and at first he was not very excited. "Just another orchid?" But when I explained about the location and the colour he became much more interested. He will be arriving from Buenos Aries late tonight, so we can go to the site again tomorrow morning. But he said that we should not take any samples, no matter how many specimens there are, until he has inspected the site. Here are the photos. As you can see, it is a very distinctive blue and you can see them growing right by the glacier"

"Yes, it's very beautiful," murmured Lettie in awe.

"We were actually back by lunchtime," continued Roberto, "and there was no sign of Wiseman, so he will have no idea of where the site is."

"I've actually made quite a few telephone calls this afternoon," Roberto continued. "I called the Government environment agency, my friend at the Botanical society suggested I do that, and someone from there is also coming tomorrow. And I called the local press. Another distant Morgan cousin is editor of the local paper, *El Oeste*. I thought this was a good idea, I hope you agree. Firstly, my father was well known in Trevelin and people will be interested in what he found and, secondly, the sooner we get the story out the harder it will be for Wiseman to try to take it over. And finally I called the local Mayor of Trevelin..."

"Another Morgan?" Lettie interrupted.

"No, this is a Davies, Fernando Davies, and I invited him to join us tomorrow as well. Are you happy with all this?" asked Roberto.

"Oh yes! You've done very well. Wiseman will probably follow us tomorrow, but with all those dignitaries he can't possibly hijack anything. This is all very exciting!" Lettie gushed.

"I'll have to get cracking organising some 4x4s for tomorrow," said Roberto. "We'll need a larger one for such a large party and then a smaller one to ferry us up the final ascent. The mayor, for one, will not be able to walk up there on his own."

A very jolly group of eight set out the next morning. There was Roberto, Pedro and Lettie, Fernando Davies the Mayor, a short, very fat and very jolly man who spoke not a word of English but did speak Welsh as well as Spanish, Sergio Ariando the botanist from Buenos Aries, a tall and rather serious man, a man from the environment agency who said very little and never introduced himself, the editor of *El Oeste*, Frederico Davies, another jolly man who knew the Mayor very well and a photographer.

Wiseman observed all of this but made no attempt to follow them when they left for the site.

There was much excitement when they arrived at the site. For most of them it had been a strenuous but enjoyable hike, although for the Mayor and the editor it had been a struggle. Even the small 4x4 had not been able to get very close. Having taken the two of them as far as it could, it then had to reverse all the way back, which is why the others walked.

"I don't know how my father got up here," said Roberto. "He didn't have a 4x4. He must have walked all the way. He couldn't have walked here and back in a day, so he must have been camping."

The botanist from Buenos Aries quickly confirmed that this was a brand new species of orchid, that the location, so close to the glacier, was most unusual and that the colour, so far as he knew, was unique. He then started surveying the entire area, taking soil samples and photographs and readings of this and of that. The man from the environment agency continued to say very little. The editor, Frederico Davies, however wanted a story and the Mayor, Fernando Davies wanted lots of pictures, all of them with him centre stage.

Between them Lettie, Roberto and Pedro gave the editor his story. They talked about Xavier and his passion for plants, his contact with Havergal and who he was, how Lettie fitted in and the letters and photo, their meeting at the Eisteddfod all leading now to this discovery. There was no mention of Wiseman or Kew.

The botanist from Buenos Aries and the man from the environment agency then stepped forward to address the others.

"This is, of course, a most important discovery," said the botanist in perfect English. "But we must point out some problems. Firstly, this is now an important scientific site which must be protected. I've been listening to your press interview and you must not give away the exact position of this site or even its approximate position, and you must not give too many details about why the orchid discovery is so important. If you do then hundreds of amateur botanists will be out in a flash, looking for them and possibly they will destroy the site. I suggest your article..." he said, motioning to the editor, "focusses on Xavier, Havergal and Mrs Brown and not the botany, at least for the time being."

"And the second problem," said the man from the environment agency, speaking for almost the first time, also in perfect English, "is that we are actually in one of the areas that is disputed between Chile and Argentina. For Chile the border is that range of mountains over there," he said, pointing to the East, "and for them we are in Chile, but for Argentina the border is the river over there to the West, and for them we are in Argentina. If we are not very careful, we will start a war, or at least a major diplomatic incident. We must keep this away from the national politicians in Buenos Aries and Santiago and we must get the cooperation of the Chilean Botanical Association. This will have to be handled very, very carefully," he repeated. "The site will need to be properly protected and fenced off, as my colleague has said, but we must do that in cooperation with the Chilean authorities. We will have to talk to them and make sure we talk to the right people, and that could take time, so it is essential that this place is kept secret. You may or may not know that the issue of the border between our two countries is extremely sensitive and if the politicians get involved then this could be a very lengthy matter."

They all glumly agreed that they could see the logic of this; the editor was already redrafting his copy. The botanist then added, "Normal procedure will now be for me take two specimens, one for our records and research in Buenos Aries and the other to send to one of the international botanical centres either in the US or to Kew. I would prefer Kew simply because although I never met him, I knew of Havergal, although I knew him as Huw Williams, and always had the utmost respect for him. But I can't take any specimens yet until I have agreement from Chile, and so we must keep this secret for the time being, otherwise the site will be stripped."

"That sounds as if it might take some time," said Lettie.

"Hopefully only a couple of days," said the botanist. "Chile are very geared up in terms of botany and if we can find the right people then they will see the importance of this and work with us. And I suspect they won't want the expense of fencing this area off and all the signage and they'll be happy to leave it to us. But we do have to talk to them first; anything involving the border is sensitive."

"When you come to sending a specimen to Kew, would you let me know when you do that, I just want to make sure that Havergal and Xavier are properly attributed."

"I heard your earlier conversations," replied the botanist. "I will make sure that the new species is named *Orchidaceae Morgan-Wyllyams* and when the proper scientific announcement comes out, and it will be issued by my organisation, the discovery will be well described and attributed to those two men, and, in fact, when we are ready to send a specimen to Kew, I will request that it is sent to you in London and you can go and present it to Kew yourself, how's that?"

"Perfect!" Lettie said, even though her smile said it all.

The botanist and the man from the environment agency did a good job with the Chilean authorities. "We've found yet another orchid in the disputed area and just in case it's something interesting we'd like to fence it off and put up some signs to keep people out and take one or two specimens," they said, economically.

"I will, of course, have to check with the Minister and get back to you," they were told.

In the end, it took about a week to resolve things. They successfully kept the matter out of national politics and the Chileans had no problem with the fencing, especially as the Argentinians were paying for it. The problem was the signage. Nobody worried about "Keep Out, Site of scientific interest, trespassers will be prosecuted" but the Chileans wanted the sign to be headed "Republica de Chile". They insisted on this because they suspected the Argentinians would put "Republica Argentina" on the signage. In fact the Argentinians hadn't thought about that at all until the Chileans raised it and then, of course, both sides realised that if their national politicians knew this was going on they would be in trouble if they conceded and so both sides dug their heels in and a stalemate temporarily ensued. It needed several calls to Santiago and Buenos Aries before eventually a compromise was agreed. The signage would be headed "The Havergal Wyllyams Conservation Centre". Neither side could object to this and the Welsh were, of course, delighted. Mayor of Trevelin Fernando Davies had a distant cousin in the Chilean government and a number of other contacts in the right places and the Welsh sorted out a problem that the Chileans and Argentinians might well have chosen as a reason for some sabre rattling, and, in their minds, they sorted it out by establishing the ascendancy of Wales, not Chile or Argentina.

The next day the article in *El Oeste* was published. As requested, it was fairly low key.

> *"Much loved local man, Xavier Morgan, who died four months ago, had a friend in England, Havergal Wyllyams who also died recently, but a Mrs Letitia Brown, an American Lady living in London, is researching Havergal Wyllyams (a Welshman) and she has been visiting Trevelin for the Eisteddfod and is pictured here with the Mayor at one of Xavier's camping grounds, where he was doing botanical field research."*

It was not at all what the editor had wanted to publish but he would soon get his chance.

The protective fence was very quickly installed and the agreed signage was put up warning that it was a criminal offence to enter the area; specimens had been taken and so the full story could be told. Now it was the complete story of Xavier, Havergal and Lettie plus the botany and the incredible discovery, and why it was important, although the precise location was still not revealed. Again there was no mention of Wiseman or Kew.

The story pleased Roberto and Pedro enormously and many other local residents came to the Lodge just to shake Lettie's hand. But, astonishingly, it did not stop there. It must have been the silly season in the world's media because the Buenos Aries papers picked up the story and then the Chilean papers and then European and London media and suddenly Lettie was a 48-hour starlet. The story was always the same. "Middle aged battling American woman discovers rare orchid species high up in the Andes from papers left in house she bought." There were telephone calls almost all day for a couple of days and then it all died down. But the story was well and truly out – the orchid was discovered by Lettie, with a lot of help from Roberto and Pedro, as a result of Xavier and Havergal, and was not a Kew or Wiseman discovery.

The previous day they had been unloading the 4x4 and Lettie deliberately left her specimen box outside where the van had been, as if she had forgotten it. An hour later she went out to see if it was there and it was not. The Director of Botanical research at Kew Gardens, Dr Carl Wiseman, had just stolen an empty box. Later that day Wiseman left to return to London. This simply confirmed everything Lettie had ever thought about Wiseman.

Now that all the media interest had died down and the authorities were dealing with the site and the formalities, it was time for Lettie to go home and she was well and truly ready, she was exhausted.

The goodbyes with Roberto, Pedro and many other friends in the town were long and emotional and even the Mayor came along to say goodbye; they all promised to keep in touch and the Mayor threatened Lettie with the freedom of Trevelin, for which she would have to come back. But it was time to go and Lettie was ready for a rest, although she was not sure if she would get one when she did get home.

Chapter 26

Lettie arrived back at 13 Sandown Road both elated and exhausted. A hot bath followed by a stiff drink and then a long sleep in her own bed was her plan for the rest of this day. But first a full debrief to Ron had to be done. She had kept him posted on things from Patagonia (and he had kept Dafydd informed) but this was inevitably only the headlines and not the detail and he clearly wanted to know everything. When she had finished she asked Ron to liaise with Roberto on several important issues; when would a proper announcement be made to the botanical world and could he help with this? When would a specimen be sent to Kew and what had to be done to ensure the proper naming of the discovery *Orchideae Morgan-Wyllyams?* Ron said he would get on with all those things immediately and left Lettie to pursue her plan for the rest of the day. He forgot to mention that there was a letter for her, which he had put on the mantelpiece.

The next day Ron came round after work to see how she was; he had a stack of papers with him.

"I had a good night's sleep," said Lettie, "and now I'm looking forward to doing very little for a while. I'll just catch up with my washing and just enjoy padding round quietly until the things you are working on with Roberto start to happen."

"Oh," said Ron, "you won't be wanting these just yet then," and he gestured to the papers he had brought. "I've sorted out all of Havergal's Madagascan palm papers and there's some very interesting stuff in there, do you want me to go through it with you?"

"Ron, later, please, I'm very grateful to you but I'm just not ready yet, I will be, but just not yet, I still feel very tired."

"I understand," said Ron, a little disappointed, "but did you see the letter that came while you were away?" and he retrieved it from where he had put it. It was from Mary MidLothian-Sutton in Llandysul.

> *Dear Mrs. Brown,*
>
> *Congratulations on your discovery. It was even in the local paper here in Llandysul. They picked up on Havergal having been a local man and your pursuit of the orchid in his memory. Havergal would have hated all the publicity if he had been at the centre of it*

but probably would have secretly enjoyed the fact that you discovered it and not Mr. Wiseman and that you attributed it to him and his friend Xavier Morgan.

I do hope you can visit me sometime here in Llandysul, there is much we could talk about. I don't know when you get back from Argentina but I am sending this for when you do.

Yours sincerely

Mary MidLothian-Sutton

"Wow" exclaimed Lettie "so the story even made the depths of Wales" "it was everywhere for a day or so" replied Ron "are you going to go and see her?" "Yup, but not immediately, like I said, I need a bit of time to myself, I'm not a spring chicken anymore!"

Several days later Ron came around again with some news. The announcement to the botanical world had been made in all the proper scientific journals. This was, of course, just the start. There would have to be much more study to find out how the orchid lived at such high altitude; in the article there was mention of Havergal, Xavier and Lettie but no mention of Kew. Also, the proper authorities had accepted the new name of the species *Orchideae Morgan-Wyllyams*. But the best piece of news came last. The Patagonian authorities would be sending a specimen directly to Kew but would be asking Lettie to formally present it to them on their behalf and would be in touch soon as to the arrangements.

"That will be delicious!" beamed Lettie.

Meanwhile, at Kew, Wiseman had attended a very uncomfortable executive meeting. The Director-General of the Royal Botanic Gardens, the governing body of Kew, had seen the press reports and the proper botanical announcement and the fairly extensive coverage of Havergal Wyllyams and he wanted to know what was going on. "Who is this Lettie Brown?" "You were in Patagonia recently, why didn't you pick this up, and what were you doing there, you didn't bring anything back?" and "if Huw Williams was so good, why did we let him retire?" and on and on. For the first time in his career Wiseman felt very uncomfortable and lied and dissembled as best he could to get through it. But he hadn't brought a new discovery to Kew for quite some time and that was the whole point of his position and just when he seemed to have some possibilities this woman had got in the way of things. He felt threatened and had better do something about it and soon.

The next day Lettie received a hand delivered and handwritten letter from Wiseman. Although she knew that he knew where she lived, it still sent a shiver up her spine to have this confirmed. And as she read the letter it was clear why it was handwritten; Wiseman would never have let a secretary see what he said.

Dear Mrs Brown,

I am writing to apologise for my behaviour. I have made a fool of myself. The only explanation I can offer is that I am a passionate botanist and dedicated to finding new species and you appeared to me to be an amateur who would get in the way of proper science, so I tried to circumvent you and get to Havergal's discoveries as quickly as possible to prevent them being destroyed or found by too many people before they could be properly studied. In fact, although you are not a trained botanist you do seem to have a knack for it, especially in finding help from others.

I wasted 10 days in Patagonia and do not wish to repeat that experience. I therefore propose that in future we cooperate. As I am sure you know the greatest of Havergal's passions were the Madagascan palms and that may be where his most interesting undiscovered species is. I know he researched this at great length and would have loved to make a trip there to see if his theory was true. Perhaps you have details of all this in his papers (which, incidentally, you promised me a copy of).

I would like to suggest we make a joint trip to Madagascar as soon as possible to investigate all this. Please let me know if you are willing.

Yours sincerely
Carl Wiseman

"Well, I never!" exclaimed Lettie. "What do you make of that Ron?"

"I wouldn't trust him any further than I could throw him. It's a trap, don't go with him," came the reply.

"You don't think perhaps he has repented? Odd that he should refer to Havergal by his real name; he's never done that before."

"No, I don't think he's repented. I think he used Havergal's real name just to make you think he has."

"But I could cause him quite a lot of trouble if I ever leaked this letter to Kew, don't you think?" said Lettie.

"Yup, you could. He has certainly raised the stakes, but I still wouldn't trust him," said Ron.

"I guess I'll have to think about it," was all she said to Ron.

Lettie no longer feared Wiseman. He was a fool but a driven fool and she was still understandably very cautious of him, but she thought, instinctively, and despite Ron's advice, that she might allow Wiseman to accompany her; she just had to find a way of rationalizing her decision to herself and then explaining it to Ron.

In the next few days Lettie received any number of calls from the botanical press and even some requests for photographs. She told them all that there would be a formal presentation at Kew and the chance to see the orchid then. A few days later the secretary at Kew, Wiseman's secretary to whom she had spoken before, phoned to make the arrangements. Lettie told her about the press interest and to be prepared for possibly quite large numbers. "I'd better tell Dr. Wiseman about that," she said nervously. "We don't normally have the press at these sort of things unless Dr Wiseman invites them."

"I'm sure there won't be a problem," Lettie reassured her. "Just make sure it is a large room and that press passes are available at the main entrance, I'll be starting to invite people as soon as we finish."

"I'm not sure that Dr Wiseman will be happy with this..." the secretary had never before experienced someone dictating to her boss.

"He had better be," said Lettie and hung up.

The presentation was two days later. There were dignitaries from the botanical world, a representative each from Argentina and Chile, reporters, photographers, senior managers from Kew, including the Director General himself, as well as Lettie, Ron and Wiseman. The room was packed. The Director General opened the meeting by thanking the Argentinian Botanical Association for the valuable specimen they had given to Kew. He thanked their representative who had brought the specimen over and then he informed the meeting that the Argentinian Association, "supported, of course, by their Chilean colleagues" had asked very specifically for the presentation to be made on their behalf by Mrs Letitia Huntingdon-Brown and so he would ask her to come up to the platform and address the meeting.

"Six months ago," she started, "I was in New York and bored out of my skull and I knew nothing whatsoever about botany, so I really can't quite believe what has happened." She then went on to explain about Sandown Road, about Havergal, his papers and her trips to Morocco and then Patagonia, following up his personal research. She said nothing about Wiseman or about Kew, except that Havergal had worked there and was much respected. She tried hard, but not wholly successfully, not to allow the presentation to be an ego trip for her so much as a celebration of Havergal's work, although since Havergal wasn't there, she inevitably collected the reflected glory. She concluded by paying tribute to Xavier Morgan, his son and nephew, the mayor of Trevelin and all the people who had helped her, although inevitably she had to leave out Ron and Rhodri, and then asked if there were any questions.

The first question was whether there were any more potential discoveries in Havergal's papers and whether she had any more trips planned.

"I'm glad you asked me that," she replied. "Yes, there is one more trip, probably the last one. This time it is to Madagascar, looking for a very specific palm that Havergal was interested in. I'm planning on leaving in a few weeks. It'll be a private trip, of course, on behalf of Havergal, but now I think of it," and she turned theatrically to the Director General, "perhaps Kew might like to send someone to assist me, perhaps even Dr Wiseman himself?" The room went completely silent. Wiseman was squirming in his chair, the reporters were scribbling in their notebooks and the Director General was glaring at Wiseman in a less than friendly way.

Two days later Ron practically knocked Lettie over in his excitement as he burst through the door of her house. "Big news from Kew, you won't believe it. Wiseman has gone. He has left Kew. I don't know if he resigned or was sacked but he has gone. There was a staff announcement this morning. It's fantastic, almost everyone has been walking round with a smile on their faces all day, and I think a lot of it is down to you, you made him look such a complete fool at the presentation, no one has ever spoken to him like that before and you did it in front of his bosses." Ron could barely contain himself with glee.

"Well that is good news," said Lettie rather more calmly. "At least I won't have to worry about him following me about in Madagascar like he did in Patagonia."

"Hold on," said Ron, "that's the other piece of news. He's still going to Madagascar. He leaves in three days' time."

"What!" screamed Lettie.

"Yes," said Ron, "the Director General made the announcement about Wiseman going this morning and asked if there were any questions. Wiseman's secretary, or ex-secretary, said that some tickets had come through for Madagascar and asked what should she do with them. The DG said she should send them to Wiseman's home address because he had now paid for them personally and was still going in a private capacity.

"But how will he know where to look or what to look for? We haven't sent him Havergal's papers yet."

"Maybe he's not looking for plants. Maybe he's just intent on getting even with you," said Ron, rather darkly. "But the good news," he continued, "is that I asked the DG privately whether I could take up your offer to go to Madagascar with you. I said I would pay the costs, all I wanted was the time off, but he said, "Not to worry, old chap, Kew will pay, anything to help botanical research," so I'll be coming with you, in case Wiseman does try anything, not that I know much about palms."

"That's a big relief, Ron," sighed Lettie, "and I guess we had better start thinking about Madagascar and what we're looking for. Oh and by the way, you say you don't know much about palms, what is your speciality, you've never told me?"

"Onions," said Ron, "the technical word is Alliums. When you start at Kew you are expected to specialise in something and I didn't know what to do until Havergal told me his favourite flower was *allium schubertii* and so that did it, from then on it was alliums. I've never regretted it."

"I don't know how much use that is going to be in Madagascar," said Lettie. "Now, it is getting late, shall we go through the palm papers tomorrow evening after you finish work and start planning for Madagascar? At least we don't now need to send anything to Wiseman, the fact that you have them means that Kew has them, right?"

"Yes Ma'am" agreed Ron. "I'll see you tomorrow evening."

Then Lettie remembered the letter from Llandysul and dashed off another holding letter to Mary MidLothian-Sutton. She would have to wait until after Madagascar.

Chapter 27

Ron came round to 13 Sandown Road the next evening in a state of high excitement.

"The plot thickens," he announced dramatically.

"Calm down and take a seat and tell me about it," soothed Lettie.

"Wiseman came into the office today. It was just to pick up some of his personal things. I wasn't there at the time but apparently he didn't speak to anyone. On his way out he noticed the Madagascar papers on my desk; they were addressed to him, so he took them. The secretary told me afterwards that she had no reason to say he shouldn't. I had taken the envelope, addressed to him, that we were going to send to him before we heard that he'd left Kew, it was in amongst all my other papers. I was going to post it as we agreed and then, of course, I didn't have to and in all the excitement I just left the envelope on my desk intending to bring it home and now he has it, and, what's more, he knows that I've been helping you, otherwise what was it doing on my desk?"

"I can't see that it matters now that he knows you have been helping me, after all Kew have agreed to finance your trip with me," replied Lettie, "but it's pity he has the papers, I suppose."

"Well, that's the thing," Ron was still very excited, "there actually was nothing new in them. There was a lot of material about Havergal's discoveries over the years, including *Tahina spectabilis*, the Madagascan self- destructive palm, do you remember I told you about it?" Lettie nodded dutifully. "There's a lot on that but that was 10 years ago and there is almost nothing since, so Wiseman will get nothing from those papers."

"Well, what is he looking for then?" asked Lettie.

"Goodness only knows," said Ron, "but I've been chatting to a few people at Kew who knew Havergal and doing a bit of digging around and I think Havergal's main interest in his later career was less in new plant discoveries and more to do with conservation, and Madagascar is absolutely central to that."

"Well, if there's nothing to discover and Wiseman is off on a wild goose chase, then I guess there is no need for us to go rushing after him. We'll just let him make a fool of himself and decide later whether to go."

"But you'd better tell me about Madagascar," said Lettie.

"You're right, there is no rush. As to Madagascar, I've never been there, but it one of the hot spots of the botanical world, in fact, of the entire world of natural history, for all sorts of reasons, some good, some bad. All botanists know about it; they refer to it as "the dream and the nightmare" and although there's no rush I can't wait to go there! Not least because Havergal went there often."

"Well, you'd better tell me everything then," replied Lettie, preparing herself for another lecture.

"OK, I'll give you a potted history. I've been doing a bit of research," started Ron. "Madagascar is an island about three times the size of Britain, about 250 miles off the eastern coast of Africa. Originally Madagascar, Africa, India and Antarctica were all one landmass and Madagascar split from the others about 90 million years ago. Its first inhabitants were tribes from Borneo and its language today, Malagasy, is an Austronesian derivative very similar to the Ma'anyan language of Borneo. It's incredible that it was colonised by people from more than 4,000 miles away in Borneo, how on earth did prehistoric peoples find Madagascar from such a distance without maps or compasses? This migration has been described as "the single most astonishing fact of human geography in the world" and yet hardly anyone outside Madagascar knows it. This all happened in about the 1st century AD and before that it is believed the island was uninhabited, by humans anyway. And another strange thing; the tribes from Borneo settled in Madagascar but, having travelled 4,000 miles to get there, never travelled the extra 250 miles to mainland Africa.

"There are so many extraordinary things about Madagascar. Humans, as we more or less know ourselves today, have been around for about 300,000 years and started in Africa. Then, about 70,000 years ago, humans started to migrate to Eurasia and Oceania and eventually the Americas. The ancient Egyptians were using primitive boats about 5,000 years ago. Yet no one found Madagascar until about 2,000 years ago and so it is one of the most recently inhabited places, by humans, on earth. But there is evidence of prehistoric creatures found nowhere else on earth; elephant birds, lemurs as big as gorillas, pygmy hippos and much else.

"Even the current natural history is unique. About 90% of its estimated 12,000 plant species are found nowhere else on earth. I told you before about all the unique palms; climbing palms, bush palms, alpine palms and especially *Tahina spectabilis*, the self-destructive palm. There are 180 known palm species in Madagascar and 100 of them were discovered by Kew and 70 of them have been discovered in the last 20 years. There are 70 different species of lemur and 240 bird species; there are chameleons ranging from the size of a cat to the size of a thumbnail; there are boa constrictors, indri lemurs, sifaka lemurs, mongooses, the natural history is just incredible. Madagascar has mountains, rainforests and semi-deserts; there is almost every sort of habitat there. It really came onto the botanical map about 50 years ago but for a long time was quite unstable politically and dangerous and difficult to get into, but then it did open up and botanists flocked there. They were finding new plant species continuously and Havergal was one of them."

"The political history is interesting too. Madagascar is one of the poorest countries in the world. English pirates sailed there in 17th and 18th centuries and there are, apparently, pirate graveyards there to this day. There was extensive slave trading until the French invaded and colonised the island at the end of the 19th century. It was briefly German in the 2nd World War, then British for a year or two and then restored to the French after the war and then gained full independence in 1960. And that's when its troubles really started."

"Before the French, local farmers had practiced an ancient form of crop rotation called *tavy*. Farmers would clear a small portion of forest by burning it, then grow rice for one or two seasons and then move on to another area, leaving the first area for up to 20 years to regenerate, which it did. But as a French colony, population pressures were starting, as well as demands by the Mother country for food in France, and farmers were forced to return too soon, so regeneration never occurred, soils became exhausted and the process of forest loss and biodiversity loss began, but this was still in a very small way. The real trouble started soon after independence, when the military took over, and even more so in recent years."

"Sadly, post-independence the Malagasy government has been chronically weak and has been one of the most corrupt administrations on earth. They have made no effective attempt to control the burning, grazing, marble mining, logging and cattle ranching and especially the coffee cash cropping, and deforestation has accelerated. A third of Madagascar's humid forests have been destroyed since the 1970s and it has the highest soil erosion rate in the world, 20 to 40 thousand tonnes per square kilometre per annum. And in recent years, unbelievably, it has actually got worse. Firstly, the population has doubled since 1990. Local traditions say that the ideal family is seven daughters and seven sons, but secondly, foreign governments and corporations have moved in. South Korea has bought a 99-year lease on 3.2 million acres for $12 an acre, to grow corn and palm oil. Chinese steelmakers have acquired exploitation rights for 287 square kilometres for iron ore extraction. Illegal rosewood and ebony foresting is rife; 620 containers of rosewood worth $130m were exported this year alone, even though it is illegal. They do this by getting a license to harvest fallen trees only and then... well you can imagine what they do. The Chinese will take all the hardwoods, especially rosewood that can be cut; they use it for reproduction antique furniture. This logging has increased 25-fold since the current government came into power in 2009. It's an absolute tragedy. Probably less than 10% of Madagascar's original forests remain and 1-2 % continues to be cut down every year."

"And if that's not bad enough, the Malagasy people do not benefit one jot from the destruction of their country. The only ones who benefit are the corrupt politicians, who turn a blind eye and proffer an open hand while all this goes on, and the foreign governments and corporations. Each rosewood or ebony trunk that's logged is worth about $5,000 but the local cutters and hauliers make about £5 per trunk between them. Astronauts orbiting the earth have remarked at the red colour of Madagascar's rivers, suggesting the country was bleeding to death as its denuded mountainsides leach topsoil into its waterways." Ron paused for breath.

"Of course it's symbolic of biodiversity loss and deforestation all over the world, but this is such a unique place to lose and almost no one is doing anything about it, many of the species being lost are unique to Madagascar, once they're gone, they're gone forever, you can't just go somewhere else, like Brazil, and get some transplants, they don't exist."

"I was looking through some press cuttings and even the Duke of Edinburgh, on a Royal visit, said publically, "This island is committing suicide." The heading for the article was "Paradise in Peril.""

"I didn't know all about this," said Lettie, "and you say that nothing is being done to stop the destruction?"

"Well, that's not quite true. There are a lot of people trying to change things. The World Wildlife Fund is trying to save the lemurs and there are lots of others, including Kew, but you apparently get the same answer every time: 'We are a poor country, we have to allow development to create jobs and prosperity for our people,' even though you know that the prosperity will go nowhere near the people. You just have to bite your tongue or you risk getting thrown out. Kew set up its only overseas office in Antananarivo, the capital of Madagascar, the Kew Madagascar Conservation Centre or KMCC as we know it at Kew. Havergal was instrumental in setting it up and visited it regularly. I didn't actually know that until chatting to someone today. He would visit twice a year at least and for him it was about conservation not discoveries. I also found out that since Havergal left full-time employment he had to pay for his trips himself; Wiseman would not allow Kew to pay for it. I find that incredible. He was going to Kew's office to do Kew work and Wiseman would not pay. It must have broken his heart. Whenever I think or read about Madagascar I always remember that Joni Mitchell song, you know the one, "They paved paradise and put up a parking lot."

"Thanks for the lecture, Professor Ron. I can certainly see why you want to go to Madagascar," said Lettie, thoughtfully.

"Yes, I want to see the place before it is totally ruined. I found out a lot of what I've told you by chatting to staff at Kew, including personnel department who, of course, know everything," Ron continued, "but the funny thing is that Havergal never mentioned any of this in our chats at the pub. He never complained about Kew and rarely talked about himself or what he was doing. He was always talking about what I was doing and encouraging me," Ron paused sadly, remembering his mentor.

"I'll give you an example of what KMCC does, and what Havergal was doing. Again, I found out about this in the office today, I didn't know before," Ron continued. "KMCC try to agree sustainability plans with local government and local communities and they work on projects. One that Havergal had worked on was training 50 schoolchildren to conserve one of the world's rarest orchids – *angraecum longicalcar* – which had been brought to near extinction by orchid collectors. The population in the wild was down to 10 plants, so they collected seeds and tended the plants in a greenhouse and the children look after the seedlings. Havergal would visit every so often to keep an eye on things. There are more than 1,000 orchid species on the island, almost all endemic to it and more than half are threatened with extinction, so that's the sort of thing that Havergal was doing in Madagascar."

Ron sat back in his chair, drained by his speech. Lettie asked him if he would like a cup of tea and then said, "It's pretty clear to me that you want to go to Madagascar and so do I. But there really isn't a big rush is there? If we leave it for a while then perhaps Wiseman will have realised he's making a fool of himself and will have left the island and come home. Why don't we plan on a trip in a few weeks' time, I'll be recovered by then."

"OK," said Ron, hiding his disappointment.

About a week later the postman brought Lettie two letters. She recognized the handwriting and postmark on the first; it was from Mary MidLothian-Sutton in Llandysul.

> Dear Mrs Huntingdon-Brown,
>
> I don't like to be a nuisance but do hope you can visit me soon, I have so much to tell you. I understand from your last letter that your next trip will be to Madagascar, I hope you can visit me <u>before</u> you go there.
>
> Yours sincerely
> Mary MidLothian-Sutton

"Yup," thought Lettie, "it is time I visited, I've put her off too many times." Then she picked up the second letter. It was an airmail letter from Madagascar and had been express couriered. She opened it slightly suspiciously.

> Dear Mrs Huntingdon Brown,
>
> I have read about your work in the newspapers here and, of course, your exploits are talked about a lot in this office. As you can see below I work at Kew's Madagascar Conservation Centre and have done for many years. I hope you will visit this office very soon. I want to tell you all about the work that Havergal did here on conservation.
>
> But I also want to tell you about some original unpublished work that Havergal did on the Baobab tree, which is very interesting. At the time of writing, Dr Wiseman is here in the office. He has no right to be here and is making a real nuisance of himself. He has heard about the work on the Baobab tree. I don't know how but he does have some friends (spies) here. I have all the papers and he doesn't know that and I will do my best to keep them away from him. The sooner you can get here the better.
>
> Yours sincerely

Sahondra Rakotomalala
Kew Madagascar Conservation Centre
Antananarivo, Madagascar

P.S. I am Havergal Wyllyams' daughter. I will explain every-thing when we meet.

Lettie picked up the phone and almost screamed at Ron. "Get packed! We're going to Madagascar and we've got to get there as soon as possible!" Then she explained why.

Two days later they were at Heathrow waiting for their flight. Lettie had sent another holding letter to Llandysul. Once again, something more important had come up.

Chapter 28

At the airport the next day there was a bit of a mix up over seating on the plane. Kew had booked Ron's ticket so they had not been able to arrange to sit together. Lettie booked herself an economy ticket, assuming Ron would also be in economy and that they could then try and change seats to sit together. But to her and Ron's surprise they found he was booked into Club class; the Wiseman travel rules appeared to have been extended to Ron, much to his pleasure.

The twelve-hour flight was unremarkable and on arrival they took a taxi to the Carlton hotel in Antananarivo. Lettie's late husband, Arvin, had never had reason to visit Madagascar and consequently she had no contacts there, so she had called her old friend Francesco Molinari, General Manager of the Savoy, and he had recommended the Carlton and said that he would alert the General Manager as to their arrival. The General Manager turned out to be a Welshman, Clive Monmouth Llewellyn, and, suitably warned by London, he escorted the two of them to their suite. It was a beautiful suite overlooking the city, with two en-suite bedrooms, a lounge and an office. As he was leaving, Lettie asked the General Manager, "I notice from your name and accent that you're Welsh. Do you by chance speak Welsh?"

"Yes Maam," he replied. "I was brought up speaking Welsh and although I haven't lived in Wales for 20 years, I can still speak it."

It was late and it had been a hard day's travelling but there was just one thing to do before turning in and that was to phone Sahondra Rakotomalala and arrange a meeting for the next day. It was a short conversation, she sounded pleasant, they would meet at the hotel at 9.30 next morning. Wiseman was still around, so the offices at KMCC were not a good place to meet. And with that, Lettie and Ron turned in, exhausted.

The next morning the General Manager, well briefed by Francesco Molinari, personally greeted Sahondra Rakotomalala and escorted her to the suite, accompanied by a waiter with a silver tray of coffee, tea and biscuits. It must have felt like being ushered into the presence of the Queen of England.

Lettie greeted her guest. Sahondra was medium height, probably in her late 40s, plump and with a ready smile. There was nothing half-caste about her; she looked just like any other middle-aged Malagasey woman. But she was clearly very nervous. Lettie introduced her to Ron and then sat her down and offered refreshments.

For a moment there was silence; no one knew who should speak first or what to say, so Lettie jumped in. "Sahondra, let me tell you my story first and what I've been doing and why."

"That would be a good idea, but please, call me Sandra, or even Sandy if you wish, that's what I am called in the office. Malagasey names are so long and complicated, they always get shortened," she replied.

Lettie then explained everything that had happened to her, the purchase of 13 Sandown Road, the papers, Morocco, Patagonia and now Madagascar, Kew, Wiseman and Ron. "You see, I've sort of become fond of Havergal, I don't know why but I want to make sure his work is recognized and is not stolen and I've sort of become quite interested in botany, for which much thanks to Ron here. Now...." and she hoped she had spoken long enough to settle Sandra down and to convince her that she had no ulterior motive, "that brings us right up to date except for your letter, which I received a couple of days ago and which got Ron and I to come here as quickly as we could."

"I think that probably what caught your attention in my letter was that I am Havergal's daughter," Sandra spoke perfect English without a trace of an accent, "and perhaps I should explain that first. I don't know how much you know of his career. I didn't know much myself until about 10 years ago. He made his first trip here when he was in his early 30s. It was his first trip anywhere. He was just becoming a useful botanist at Kew. Soon afterwards he was part of the team, he may even have led it, that set up KMCC, which I am sure you know about. As well as assignees from Kew, there were several local nationals recruited to work in the office and my mother was one. Everything I've told you so far and what I will be telling you is as told to me by my mother and only a small part of it is from Havergal." She paused and sipped a glass of water. "Was it an office party that got out of hand, or did they drink too much, I don't know, my mother would never tell me, in fact my mother did not tell me that Havergal was my father until about 10 years ago, when she was seriously ill and just before she died. Anyway, I was the result. You might be wondering about my English. Well, I went to a very good English school here and only discovered much later that Havergal had paid all the school fees, for my entire education. I took it all for granted at the time but much later in life I wondered how on earth my mother could have afforded it, she was an unmarried mother working as a secretary in KMCC! It was again only just before she died that she told me. You might also wonder that I am not a half-caste; well, I just can't explain that, I don't seem to have inherited many of my father's physical genes."

"Can I ask something?" said Lettie. "Havergal was coming here regularly over many years but it was only about 10 years ago that you knew he was your father?"

"That's right. I knew him firstly just as 'Mr Wyllyams', a bigwig expert from Kew who I worked with, and then as Havergal, my father, still working with him. It was very strange."

"But Havergal knew about you from birth?" asked Lettie.

"Yes, as I have said he paid for my education and even used to help my mother financially from time to time and although I did not find out until later he got me my job in KMCC."

"What was the relationship between Havergal and your mother? I hope you don't mind me asking?"

"That's a complicated one," replied Sandra and took another sip of water. "They did not love each other. There was no question of marriage or of my mother going to England. It seems, as we botanists say, it was a case of 'random fertilisation', as happens in nature, by the wind or by birds and bees and they just dealt with the consequences of it, in other words, me."

"That actually explains one thing I've often wondered about. For a senior botanist at Kew, who was single and apparently without any expensive tastes, why was he so relatively poor, living in a small house and leaving very little, I believe, in his will. And the reason is that he was supporting you and your mother and, towards the end of his life, because he had to pay for himself to come out here," Lettie glanced at Ron, who nodded.

"When your mother told you about Havergal, did you then discuss it with him during his visits?" asked Lettie.

"Yes, a bit, but not very much. You see no one in the office knew and we wanted to keep it that way. And then I'd known him for so many years as just Mr Wyllyams and not as Dad, it was difficult to change. And by then I had my own family. I am married and have five children and three grandchildren. We did talk a bit when there were private moments, of which there were not many, and I remember one thing he did say, which was, "I don't know much about being a father. You see, I didn't have one myself." He was always kind and considerate, never forgot Christmas or Birthday cards but he was never a father in the traditional sense," Sandra paused again to collect her thoughts.

"Did Havergal go to your mother's funeral and did you go to his?" asked Lettie, knowing full well that the latter had not happened.

"My mother had been ill for a long time but then went very suddenly and unexpectedly. Havergal was away at the time. I think he was in Patagonia looking for orchids. I think he would have come if he could. And no, I didn't know he had died until I had a letter from Mary MidLothian-Sutton telling me, but by then it was too late and I don't think I could have gone anyway."

"Mary MidLothian-Sutton? I didn't tell you but I have been corresponding with her. She wants me to visit her in Wales. Where does she fit in?"

"Well, I've never met her but I know she was a friend of Havergal's. My mother told me he was planning on going back to Wales when he retired from Kew and I assume he told her about my mother and me."

"Can I just ask something?" Lettie never hesitated to butt in. Ron had not yet spoken a word. "You keep calling him Havergal, never Dad or my father?"

"To be honest, for all the reasons I have said, I never really thought of him as my father, just a kind, friendly and generous colleague."

"You do realise," continued Lettie, "that as his daughter there are probate issues. I don't know the legal position but you are entitled to his estate which, so far as I know, is mainly the house which I bought, at 13 Sandown Road?"

"I am not interested in that," she said. "The greatest gift he gave me was my education, which led to me becoming a botanist, just like him and working here at KMCC. That is enough. I have a large family here in Madagascar. I do not want to go to London. My husband and I are both well paid, we don't need another house so far away, so no, there are no probate issues. In her letter Mary MidLothian-Sutton did mention that and I wrote back saying I would not pursue it."

"You know what?" announced Lettie. "I think it's time for a break, perhaps a little lunch? I'll call Clive Llewellyn to send something up; maybe after lunch we'll talk about botany, conservation, the Baobab tree and our friend, Dr Wiseman, what do you guys think?"

No one disagreed.

Chapter 29

Lettie had asked for a typical Malagasey meal for lunch and that is what they got. They started with *Lasopy*, a thick veal and vegetable soup, then *Varenga*, roasted and shredded beef with steaming hot vegetables (*Vary Amin Anana*), a tomato and scallion salad (*Lasary Voatabia*) and rice, all followed by fruit and coffee. It was delicious. Over lunch the main topic of conversation was conservation and the work of KMCC and the botany of Madagascar and this was Ron's chance to join in. Sandra described how Havergal had been a regular visitor who originally had come to find new species, like every other botanist, but his motivation had changed when he saw the progressive habitat destruction and the loss of species and concern over this had been the binding factor between him and his daughter. This was the work that Sandra was continuing to this day and was the memory and the legacy which she treasured. Her mother also had been involved. It was at KMCC that she and Havergal had met and conceived Sandra. Her mother continued to work there for a few years and then left to work at the school where Havergal had trained the schoolchildren to conserve the *angraecum longicalcar* orchid seedlings, and Havergal would visit her there. "So we were all involved you see, we were never really a family but we did all share that," she said, rather sadly.

Lettie was not sure where things would go now and asked, "Will you need to be getting to the office?"

"No," replied Sandra, "I've taken the day off. I told them I would be meeting you and my boss said to take off as much time as I needed. In fact, the whole office knows I am meeting you and they all would like to meet you too. You're a celebrity in the botanical world."

"It should not be me that is a celebrity," said Lettie, "it should be your father. He did the work. All I've done is to make known what he did."

"That's true, of course," said Sandra, " but in their eyes you are a sort of proxy for him. They all loved him. He was so quiet, gentle, patient and encouraging, they couldn't wait for his visits and they would love to meet you."

"And how do *you* feel about him?" Lettie asked quietly.

"Until I knew he was my father, I felt exactly the same as them. But when my mother told me, I didn't know what to think. I didn't really have anyone to talk to. My mother was very ill and soon died and Havergal didn't want to talk about it. There were so many things I didn't understand. He had known I was his daughter for many years when we worked together until my mother told me, but he never did anything fatherly. And then when my mother told me, and he knew I knew, he didn't treat me any differently than before and no differently to any of the other staff. And then it all had to be kept secret from the other staff as if it was a guilty secret. I simply didn't understand and didn't know what to think and realised that I really did not know him and, I think, I became distant from him. That's not what I think a family should be and it's not how I would treat a child of mine, no matter what the circumstances. I have never spoken to anyone about this, not even my husband, and that is why I wrote to you. I wanted to talk to someone about it, someone who either knew him or knew about him. Talking about it has helped me. I hope you don't mind me burdening you with all this? I feel closer to him now and perhaps begin to understand a little bit more." Sandra's eyes were moist as she stopped.

"Of course we don't mind Sandra. I didn't know Havergal either, but you did Ron, can you add anything?"

"He was very private. I wouldn't say I really knew him either. All we talked about was work and botany and that is all that interested him. But he was very kind and generous and thoughtful but above all he was a superb scientist, that was his life."

No one had anything to add to this and they sat quietly for a while.

"You haven't told us about your mother?" said Lettie.

"My mother was lovely, warm and kind; unmarried mothers are not unusual in Madagascar, there are lots of them, and my childhood did not feel empty, especially as I had such a good schooling and University training. As I have said, she told me nothing about Havergal until shortly before she died. She did not marry or have any other children, it was just the two of us and we were very happy." Sandra was becoming moist eyed again and Lettie felt it was time to change the subject.

She asked, "If the whole office know I am here, then Wiseman's spies will know and so will he."

"That doesn't really matter. Wiseman is now banned from the office and his spies, like all cowards, have now turned their backs on him and are being chummy with everyone."

"Well," said Lettie, "thank you for sharing your story with me, we will come to your office to meet everyone, perhaps tomorrow, then we'll do a bit of touring around, perhaps you will show us around, Ron wants to see Madagascar and then I guess we'll head off home in a couple of days."

"Hold on!" Ron spluttered. "What about the Baobab tree... in the letter?"

"Oh yes, I'd forgotten about that," replied Lettie. "What's the story there Sandra?"

"My father," said Sandra, "and do you know what? I think that is the first time in my entire life I have called him that and not Havergal," she paused quietly, "anyway, he was on a conservation trip in the mountains and noticed a Baobab tree that was unlike any other he had seen. He made lots of notes and then gave them to me to keep. I think he was hoping I would complete the identification. He was nearing the end of his trip and didn't have time to do it. Anyway, I've been sitting on his notes for a couple of years and haven't done anything more; I've been really busy with work and family and my real interest is conservation work; new discoveries come second when there is time. I'm a qualified botanist and it would not be difficult but I just haven't got round to it. I put it in the letter because all the publicity about you is to do with discoveries and I thought mentioning it might persuade you to come. I hope you don't think I have deceived you?"

"Not at all!" exclaimed Lettie. "But how does Wiseman know about the tree and why is he so intent on finding it?" "I don't really know how he knows about it. I imagine my father..." Sandra paused, "talked about it in the office and the spies passed it on. I don't really know why he is intent on finding it, but my guess would be that he needs to restore his reputation and he needs a new job and since he always claimed he was so good at new discoveries, he may think finding this one will help him get his career back on track somewhere else. He certainly didn't know that I had the papers but I suspect he does now because he knows I am meeting you."

"Well, what do you say we three trump him again and go find it?" suggested Lettie. This seemed to find universal agreement. "Now... tell me about this Bamboo tree..."

"Baobab," Ron corrected her.

Chapter 30

"OK," said Lettie, "you're both botanists, who's going to tell me about the Baobab tree?"

"We'll do it between us, shall we?" Ron smiled at Sandra. "If either of us misses anything, the other can jump in."

"The first thing to say is that the Baobab tree is not particularly uncommon. It is becoming more rare but that is because of deforestation but there are plenty of species still left," said one of them. "And, of course, Baobab is the common name, the scientific name is *Adansonia*, named after Michel Adanson, a French naturalist of Scottish descent who named it in 1750," said the other. "There are eight species within the *Adansonia* genus, six of them are native to Madagascar, one is native to mainland Africa and the Arabian peninsula and one is native to Australia. The African species, *Adansonia digitata* does also occur in Madagascar but is not native, it was introduced."

"They are known locally as the Tree of Life and I expect Sandra will tell you why in a moment, but in terms of their tree of life, do you remember the botany lesson I gave you what seems like months ago? *Andansonia* is their genus, *Bombacoideae* is the sub family (although there is controversy about this, molecular research is suggesting it is a full family and not a sub family), *Malvaceae* or Mallows, is the family, and *Malvales* is the order and they are *Angiosperms,* or plants whose flowers produce seeds."

"As Ron said, they are known locally as The Tree of Life and this is because they can provide shelter, food and water for animals and humans. The bark is fire resistant, or pyrophytic, and is used for cloth and rope, the leaves can be used for condiments and medicines, the fruit is called 'monkey bread' and is rich in vitamin C and the trunk stores vast quantities of water, which can be tapped."

"And the trunks are frequently hollow and can provide living space for animals and humans. For all these reasons it is one of the national symbols of Madagascar."

"They produce enormous crinkled white flowers that last for only one day and are pollinated by fruit bats. The flowers then turn into woody seed pods that hang down, giving the tree the appearance of another of its nicknames, 'the dead rat tree'."

"But he most incredible thing about the genus is that it occurs in naturally arid areas and stores water in its trunk, anything up to 120,000 litres, to endure the harsh drought conditions. This gives it the most extraordinary shape. Baobab trees can be up to 100 feet high but with up to a 40 foot trunk diameter."

"They are also very long lived, thousands of years."

The facts were coming thick and fast now.

"Most of the year the tree is leafless and with their enormous swollen trunks and small branches they look like an upside down tree with the roots sticking up..."

"A local myth is that the tree so offended God that he uprooted it and cast it back to earth upside down."

Sandra and Ron looked at each other and realised they had unloaded all the botany that they had on Baobab trees.

"Well, thank you for all that," said Lettie. "Now where does Havergal fit into all this?"

"My father," Sandra smiled as she said the word, "was at the other end of the island doing some conservation work when he saw a Baobab tree that looked like none of the others that he knew. He made notes, took photographs and gave them all to me. He was returning to London the next day and, although he didn't ask me to, I suppose he hoped I would do something with the information. I think he was hoping that this was a ninth and new species of *Adansonia* and a seventh for Madagascar. As I told you before, I haven't done anything with the papers but from what I remember of them – and I haven't looked at them for ages – I wouldn't expect any problem finding the site. If it is a new species, can we name it after him?"

"I think we may name it after *you*," said Lettie to herself. "Well, what do you say we go find it?" she announced. No one disagreed. But they did decide first to go to KMCC to meet all the staff, as promised. On the way, Lettie asked Sandra if she wanted to keep the secret of her father to herself or if, perhaps, she might want to share it with her colleagues. "I don't care who knows, I'm not ashamed of it. For the first time I am beginning to quite enjoy being Havergal Wyllyams' daughter."

At the KMCC office Lettie and Ron shook every hand and spoke to everyone. Every face was smiling; everyone was a botanist or devoted to botany. Lettie made a short speech, telling her story and how she felt she had come to know Havergal despite never having met him and what a good friend Sandra had become and what they would be doing next. She did not mention Wiseman. At the end of her speech she said that Sandra had something to add, expecting her to make her announcement, but all she said was, "It has been a great pleasure to meet Lettie and Ron. We have followed their adventures from afar and now they are here with us for yet another adventure. We all love them for continuing the work of Havergal, who was so welcome when he was here with us"

Afterwards Lettie asked Sandra why she had not mentioned her father.

"I've thought about it since we spoke earlier. I think it is best it remains private. I wouldn't want anyone at KMCC thinking I was boasting and I wouldn't want anyone asking why it was kept secret for so long. After all, we are only just beginning to understand my father. How can we expect them to understand as well?"

Lettie said that she quite understood.

"Now then guys, let's get ready for Baobabs! Sandra, where are we going? Are we off tomorrow morning?"

Chapter 31

But Ron had other ideas. They hadn't got very far the previous night with preparations and agreed to meet for breakfast the next day to discuss the next stage of their adventure. Ron had been thinking. For most of his life he had been a quiet, unassuming man, happy for others to take decisions. But after prolonged contact with Lettie he was changing, becoming more confident, more opinionated.

"Lettie, I know you. You will want to dash off and find and identify this specimen and then, once you've done it, you'll rush off home. But this is one of the most interesting places on earth for a botanist and I do not want to rush off home. I may never get a chance like this again and Kew are paying for me to do it. I want to spend a couple of days at KMCC. I want to know everything they are doing there, then I want to travel around a bit and see something of the island. I want to look for *alliums*, my speciality. I want to see the *spectabilis* palm that Havergal discovered. I do not want to rush off home and Kew may well get upset if I stay and you rush off once you've found this specimen. So I've got an idea. Why don't you just take a bit of a holiday while I do my botanical stuff – and I hope Sandra will help me – and then we'll all go and find this Baobab tree and then we can both go home together. After all, it has been waiting a couple of years to be found, so a couple of extra weeks won't matter and Wiseman may well know about it but cannot find it without us because Sandra has the papers, so there is no rush. What do you think?"

Lettie was quite taken aback; she had never heard Ron speak so confidently. "Ron, I have no problem with that, I can see exactly where you're coming from. Although I guess my problem will be that I have never had a vacation in my life and I'm not sure how to do it. Coming to England and buying the house was supposed to be a vacation but that didn't work out. But you are right and let's do that. Perhaps Sandra can tell me some things to do as well as showing you round botanically?" Sandra seemed happy to take on this dual responsibility.

"Another reason that this is sensible," Ron added, "is that Wiseman is still around. If you take some time off, perhaps he will give up and go home."

And so it was agreed. For the next two days Ron would visit KMCC and Lettie would just relax in the hotel; in the meantime Sandra would look for a tour that Lettie could do and would arrange a botanical safari for Ron, both to take about a week or so and only then would they set out to find the Baobab tree.

The next morning Ron set off for KMCC, leaving Lettie with a whole day of nothing to do. This was going to be a trial for her. She had no interest in using the swimming pool or the gymnasium; the hotel gardens were pretty but it was very hot outside; the TV had American channels but she hadn't watched TV even when she lived there, she just about managed to last out the day when Ron and Sandra finally came back from KMCC.

"Fantastic day!" announced Ron. "There are some brilliant botanists at KMCC and some great work is being done. I've never enjoyed myself so much."

Sandra added that all the staff had loved talking to Ron and describing their work. "In the past, Kew never seemed to pay much attention to us," she smiled.

"Tomorrow I should have finished and I've had an idea," continued Ron. "I thought we might invite all the staff to have dinner with us here in the hotel, what do you think Lettie?"

"Swell idea," said Lettie. "I'll talk to Clive Llewellyn to set it up."

"Oh, you don't need to, I've already spoken to him. I don't know how I'm going to get the expenses through at Kew, but I'll think of something!" This was a new Ron emerging.

"And I've arranged a trip for you," Sandra said to Lettie, "starting the day after tomorrow. And I've arranged an agenda for Ron and I, of the same duration, so we are all sorted." Smiles all round.

The next day Lettie was once again on her own as Ron and Sandra went to KMCC. She had the dinner that night to look forward to and the tour the next day but was getting seriously bored now, pacing around her suite. Then the telephone rang. It was Wiseman.

"Good morning Mrs Brown," he said. "I just thought I would give you a call to tell you I am returning to London tomorrow. I came out here to look for the Baobab tree, the same as you. I knew about it because Huw told me about it and I knew someone in KMCC had the details. Now I know it was Sandra and I know that Ron has been helping you all along and so I am not going to find the tree. You have got in my way all along and I want you to know that I take serious exception to what you have been doing. It has cost me my job at Kew and my professional reputation and I will not take that lying down. I don't know how but I will get even with the three of you, but especially you..."

"How dare you threaten me!" Lettie cut him off. "Goodbye Mr. Wiseman!" And she replaced the receiver, shaking.

She paced around the room furiously indignant at Wiseman's threats. "How dare he?" she kept repeating to herself. "I will get even with him for daring to say such things!"

Later Ron and Sandra came back and she told them about the short conversation.

"I wouldn't worry about it," said Ron. "What can he do? Absolutely nothing. It's all bluster, typical Wiseman, all threats but no action. Now, listen, the guys from the department are going to be here for our dinner in an hour or so and Sandra has been making all our arrangements for tomorrow, so we'd better listen to her."

Lettie had told Sandra that she would like a guided tour of as much of the island as possible – the wildlife, the scenery and the people – and not to worry about the cost. Ron had privately told Sandra to make sure it was a tour that kept her very busy and occupied and did not include afternoons on the beach or by the pool.

"I have booked you onto what's called a coast to coast safari," Sandra announced, "starting tomorrow morning. There are five others on the tour, it is quite small, they will pick you up here at 9am. It's 12 days and takes in Majunga, the Ankarafantsika National park, the Andasibe National Park, the Isle Sainte Marie. You will see many different kinds of lemur, you will go whale watching, there are volcanic lakes and thermal baths, you will see many chameleons, frogs, lizards, a pirate cemetery in Isle Sainte Marie, many tortoises and beautiful scenery, from deserts to high mountains to rainforest. You will see a lot of the island, both on the ground and from the air, since there are five flights, in order to get you around as much as possible. Does that sound like what you wanted?"

"It sounds great and thank you," replied Lettie, impressed.

"Now, while you are doing that, Ron and I will be doing some serious botany. He's made a list of all the things he wants to see, including Madagascar's own *alliums* and I have planned out an itinerary to take it all in. KMCC have made available their 4 wheel drive vehicle and we will get back on the same day as your trip ends, so we will all meet up here in 12 days' time. It's a little longer than the week we discussed but there is so much for us all to do."

"One question." said Lettie. "I hope your trip will not be going to where Havergal's baobab tree is. I don't want you solving that without me."

Sandra smiled. "No, we won't be in that area and if by chance we found another one we certainly wouldn't do anything with it until you could be with us."

The departmental dinner was a huge success. Clive Llewellyn and his staff could not have put themselves out more and the staff could not have been happier. After the Wiseman terror campaign, now they were appreciated and acknowledged and there was probably no happier or more motivated group of botanists in the entire world. And Sandra was the departmental heroine because she had brought Lettie and Ron to KMCC. She was glad she had said nothing about her father; this was enough.

After the last course had been eaten, Ron surprised himself. He stood up to make an impromptu speech, something he had never done before. He thanked them all for the hospitality they had shown to him and to Lettie and above all he thanked them for the excellent work they were doing and promised that Kew would be told all about it. And he closed with, "and one thing I will do when I get back to Kew, I will talk to the authorities and ask them to consider giving a new name to the KMCC. I will ask them to rename your organisation, "The Havergal Wyllyams Conservation Centre".

A spontaneous burst of applause followed this. Drinks and happy conversation went on late into the night.

Chapter 32

The next day they went their separate ways; Lettie on her tour and Sandra and Ron on theirs. Twelve days later they all arrived back at the hotel in the early evening and had dinner and a long and animated discussion of their adventures. Lettie had been particularly struck by the leaf-tailed gecko, amongst much else, and Ron had seen more plant species in the wild than ever before in his life, including many alliums. They had both had a wonderful time in their different ways but both were also struck by the desecration of the island. As Lettie said, "I just kept thinking of that Joni Mitchell song. You travel through mile after mile of either derelict scrub land or rice paddies and then get to a nature reserve; you see wonderful and unique things there but you are conscious that it is surrounded by gradually encroaching development. I saw some red ruffed lemurs and they were in a small enclave surrounded by farmland and with a motorway a mile away. Everywhere you go you see something incredible and then you're told that there are only 200 left and they're on the endangered list.

"It's even more stark when you see it from the air," Ron agreed, sadly. "As I told you, the population is exploding and it is still 80% subsistence farming. But the real devastation happened when the big corporations and governments discovered Madagascar and they simply don't care about biodiversity. About the only part of the island that is reasonably untouched, for now anyway, is the north and that's where we'll be going next to look for a certain baobab tree."

Lettie turned to Sandra, "Yep, we've had our fun, now it's down to work, what's next?"

"I've got my father's notes here," gestured Sandra, "and I've reread them. When he gave me the notes originally I just skimmed them, I didn't read them properly. I was very busy on other things at the time and I've never been a big discoverer, as I've told you, and the site is a long way away right at the northern end of the island, as Ron said, and I was not sure how I felt about my father so, in truth, I more or less ignored them and just filed them away. Then Wiseman arrived demanding he be given anything to do with the Baobab tree and I realised they might be important, so I put them somewhere safe. Now

I have read them properly and it is very strange. He gives the exact location and coordinates of the site and there are some grainy photos but they are just general countryside photos, but there is very little botany in his notes, he doesn't say why he thinks the tree is so special or different, all he does say is to inspect the hollow interior of the tree very carefully."

"Where is the site?" Lettie asked Sandra. "It is in the Anjajavy forest at the north west end of the island, a very remote and unspoilt area more than 500 miles from here, which is partly why I did not go rushing off immediately, but the instructions are very clear, it will not be difficult to find."

And so, the next morning, they were up early to catch a flight to Antsiranana, where they would take a local bus to Anjajavy and then hire a driver to take them to the site. They had made no arrangements for accommodation; they didn't know if they would be there and back in a day or not.

All went entirely to plan. The Anjajavy forest was breathtakingly beautiful, with magnificent trees "thousands of years old" Sandra told them "and preserved, for the time being anyway, by being so remote from the centre of the island, that is what my father was doing, I think, trying to set up local protection for the forest."

Eventually the driver arrived as near as he could get to the designated site; the rest of the journey would be on foot. The instructions took them deep into the forest. They were perfectly clear but it was not easy walking. Finally they arrived at the precise spot indicated by the notes and were presented with an enormous and handsome tree. Lettie was excited. "Is this a discovery?" she thought. But Ron and Sandra were silent. Then Ron said quietly, "*Adansonia madagscariensis,* one of the Baobab family of trees, they are common all over the island. What was Havergal up to?" They all stood silently, disappointed and bemused. Then Sandra said, "he did say to inspect the hollow interior of the tree very carefully, maybe there is something interesting there? Would you have a look Ron? I don't like clambering around in musty old trees full of spiders and bats and goodness knows what else."

Ron did as he was asked, muttering, "I'd better take my torch so I can see what I am treading in..."

About ten minutes later he emerged from the hollowed out tree carrying something.

"I looked around and couldn't see anything at first, except lots of evidence of animals. Then I remembered the words "inspect the interior of the tree very carefully". The hollow goes up a long way into the tree and I shone my torch up there and saw something about ten feet off the ground tucked into a hollow, I had to clamber a bit to get to it but this is it and I believe it's yours," he said, offering the discovery to Sandra. It was an old canvas weatherproof satchel and on the front was a label. "This is the property of Sahondra Rakotomalala, Kew Madagascar Conservation Centre, Antananarivo".

Sandra gasped, "That's not mine, I know nothing about it!" She refused to take the satchel, scared of what might be in it and how it had come to be there.

"Would you like us to open it?" asked Lettie calmly.

"Yes please, it's nothing to do with me. How can this have happened? It's like black magic," she shivered.

Ron opened the dusty satchel and took out a letter enclosed in a plastic cover for protection, several instruments and a chronometer.

"The letter is from my father," gasped Sandra, "the handwriting is unmistakable but what are all these other things and why are they all here in the middle of the forest?"

"Maybe the letter will explain things?" opined Lettie.

"Will you read it to me please?" Sandra asked Lettie, "I'm scared to."

"I will, if you like, but it may be a personal letter for your eyes only."

"Lettie, you are now as much a part of Havergal's life as I was, so please read it to me."

Lettie started.

My Dear Sandra

This will seem a strange way for a father to communicate with his daughter. This will be my last trip to Madagascar because Kew won't pay for me any more and I can't afford the fare and, anyway I am getting old. It was always my intention to talk to you this time and to give you the things in this satchel but I never plucked up the courage.

You see I am better with plants than people and I did notice that you have recently become somewhat distant from me. I have been a useless father for you, in fact I have not been a father at all for most of your life. All I can say is that I never knew my father and so never learnt the craft of it. In fact, as you know, it was never my intention to become a father at all, that was a mistake but that does not mean that you are a mistake or excuse my shortcomings. I simply could never, in the circumstances, have been a proper father and so it seemed best to keep it from you but then, on her deathbed, your mother wanted you to know and even if I had been there I would not have stopped her. Your mother was a remarkable woman and I have always enjoyed working with her as indeed I have also enjoyed working with you, whether as colleague or latterly as father.

I am aware and proud of your success both as a botanist, which gives me huge pleasure, and your growing family. Of course your children are my grandchildren, and so on, and it is my great regret that I have never known any of your family; decisions taken years ago are difficult to unravel later, or perhaps I was just a coward.

I wish you the very best in everything you do. The things in the satchel are some things I would like you to have. There are some botanical instruments from my school days that your grandchildren, my great grandchildren, might like to play with (and the thought of that gives me pleasure) and there is my father's chronometer. My father was a Swedish sailor on leave from Pembroke Dock, my mother told me, and he probably only met my mother once but he did, for some reason, leave his nautical chronometer behind and my mother gave it to me and I now give it to you and it just seems oddly appropriate.

Of course, I could have left this letter and these things in the office for you but there was always the risk of somebody else finding them and doing it this way seemed to be a botanist's way of doing things. But there is another reason. If you walk about 500 metres directly due south you will not be able to miss a magnificent Tahina spectabilis, now turn due west for about 300 metres and you will find a rocky outcrop of singy limestone and behind that, on the lee side, you should find some Alliums the like of which I've never seen before. I am not an expert on Alliums but I have a friend, Dr Ron Carter, at Kew who is. I have run out of time, I must get back to Kew for the orchid festival. Would you send specimens and details to Ron, I will not warn him, let it be a surprise.

I hope you will forgive me my inadequacies, at this late stage in my life I wish I had devoted more time to people than to plants. And families are so important, as a botanist you'd think I would have known that.

Your father, Havergal

Lettie could see tears welling up in Sandra's eyes. She handed her the letter and quickly said to Ron, "Lets you and me go for a short walk and leave Sandra in peace to think about her father."

They wandered around for a long time, every so often walking near the tree to see if Sandra appeared ready and then diverting when she didn't look up. It was more than an hour later when Sandra noticed them and called them over.

"I'm sorry," she said, "I got a bit emotional."

"Don't apologise, we are not in the least surprised, in fact I got a bit emotional too," said Lettie.

"And so did I," added Ron.

They all stood silently in front of the Baobab tree, unsure of what to do next, as if it was Havergal's shrine, which in a way it was.

"It's getting late," said Lettie "we need to think about whether we make a run for the airport and go back, or stay locally?"

"Here's what I suggest," announced Ron, in his newly confident style. "I suggest you two stay locally in Anjajavy and I will make a dash to catch the last flight back to Antananarivo, and then come back tomorrow morning and meet you both at about lunchtime. It's just that I didn't bring any kit for Alliums, I came kitted out for giant trees, so I need to go back to get my specimen equipment and reference books so I can do a proper identification."

"Once a botanist always a botanist," thought Lettie. "He gets more like the way I picture Havergal every day."

Lettie and Sandra stayed at a small local hotel with no airs and graces but perfectly comfortable. They had dinner together and then went to bed very early. It had been such an emotional day.

Chapter 33

Sandra hardly slept that night and was still emotional in the morning. Lettie was, unusually for her, very subdued. They ate little for breakfast. Then they went for a walk around the small but charming town of Anjajavy. Sandra cheered up as she described the stores and the vendors and the language, which was a bit different up here, to Lettie. They did not talk about Havergal, neither knew what to say. Still with time to kill before Ron got back they took a local boat trip to explore the mysterious islands of Moramba bay where there were Baobabs in profusion as well as Sakalava tombs tucked high in caves and on ledges in the limestone cliffs. Along the way they Sandra pointed out Lovebirds, Brown Lemur, Chameleons, Coquerel's Sifaka and much else. They had a lovely morning.

Ron arrived just after lunch. Neither Sandra nor Lettie wanted to go back to the site and Ron went off on his own with all his equipment and books. Much later he returned with his specimens and measurements and a confirmation that this was indeed an Allium that was brand new, not in the books and therefore a discovery. "What shall we call it?" he asked. But the two women were not listening, they had lost their enthusiasm for botanical discoveries; they were in the middle of personal discoveries.

"I've been thinking," said Sandra. "I want to share all this with my family and I would like you two to be there when I do. Will you do that for me?"

"Of course!" they both said.

"But why the change of mind?" added Lettie.

"Until your trip here, my father was something I did not understand and I suppose I decided to just put it to the back of my mind and forget it. But all that has changed. Now I am so proud of my father and I want to share him, however belatedly, with what is his family as well as mine. I want to have a family dinner when we get back, at my house, with you both there too, and I want to share it with all the children and grandchildren. I want to give the grandchildren the botanical equipment he left and show them how to use them. I may embroider or edit the story a little, just to make it more understandable, but I don't want to go around for the rest of my life being the only one here who knows all this. I want everyone to know, maybe even, in time, my friends at KMCC. But there is one thing that would really help me and that is a photograph of Havergal. Do either of you know of any photographs?"

Lettie shook her head glumly but Ron said, "Yes, there could quite possibly be some pictures at Kew. He appeared sometimes in the staff newsletter, when the orchid festival was coming up, for instance. he hated being photographed but they insisted. There might also be the original from the picture in his staff pass and, now I think of it, he even did some staff training videos and they might still have those. I will get onto Kew as soon as we are back in Antananarivo. There's no phone reception here but they may be able to send something digitally and quickly if I call in some favours."

Both Lettie and Sandra were wide-eyed with excitement.

"Then let's get back to Antananarivo as quickly as possible," said Lettie. "Oh, and by the way Ron, how did you get on with your onions?"

Back in Antananarivo they were all very busy. Ron was in contact with Kew about photographs and onions, Sandra was busy organising a family dinner and trying to fit in some work at KMCC, they didn't mind, and Lettie was busy interfering with everyone else. They were all very excited and went round with permanent smiles on their faces.

Then Ron received some news from Kew. They gathered eagerly round.

"I'll get the boring stuff out of the way first," he said. "The *Allium* we found in Anjajavy is a new discovery. I sent photos to Kew for confirmation and we are at liberty to name whatever we want and they will arrange a press release in our names, not Kew's, when we get back."

"Great, but what about the real news?" said Lettie.

"Well, there are photos and they will be sending the best one digitally and it should arrive anytime now on the hotel computer. I have a friend in personnel who has been very helpful. In fact, she has gone through all the files and not just found photos but also some very interesting correspondence which could be very damaging to Dr Wiseman. She wouldn't describe it on the phone or send copies here but she has taken private copies, which she should not have done really but she said that if ever Wiseman becomes difficult then she has them. They apparently show how badly Wiseman treated Havergal."

"I'm not sure I ever want to see them and I sure hope we never have to use them," replied Lettie.

Just then there was a ring at the door. It was Clive Llewellyn. "The file from Kew you were expecting Dr Carter, has come through. There was only one photograph but I have copied it several times and the original file is on CD, all in here."

"Thanks," said Ron taking the envelope. He passed copies to the others. Lettie could hardly contain her excitement. The others had known Havergal but all she had seen was the tiny passport photo left in the house, together with Ron's description, and now she would see a proper picture of the man who been such a part of her life for such a long time. Would he be as she expected? Would this be a disappointment? Before she looked at the photo she asked the others, "Is it a good photo? Is this what he really looked like?"

"Yes," they both trilled.

"It's actually quite a recent picture, probably about five years ago, taken, I think, at the opening of that year's orchid festival," added Ron. So Lettie looked at the picture.

Havergal was a distinguished looking man, tall and slim, in his early 70s by the look of it, smartly dressed in the picture. He had penetrating eyes and a prominent nose, he was greying but still had a full head of hair, which was swept back. He had a serious look but there was a clear kindness about him.

"Well how do you do, Mr Havergal Ulric Wyllyams?" whooped Lettie.

The family party was a great success. It was a large gathering: Sandra's husband Josoa, their five children, with three husbands, one wife and one girlfriend, three grandchildren, Lettie and Ron. Language was a bit of a problem, since very few of Sandra's family spoke English, although most spoke French, even though Lettie and Ron did not, but somehow they communicated and they certainly smiled a lot.

Sandra made her announcement to her family in Malagasy. It was quite short. Afterwards she told Lettie and Ron that she had decided not to make a big fuss of it; it had never been an important factor in their lives. All she had said was that she had discovered, quite by accident, who her father was, he was an Englishman ("they wouldn't have heard of Wales") who was a friend of Grannie's and she had found a photograph of him and some possessions. She had passed around the picture and gave the botanical equipment to the grandchildren to play with. The microscope and the magnifying glass kept them happy for hours. She said that she had already told her husband the complete story and would tell her children more over time, filling in the details, "but I didn't want it sound like some earth-shattering announcement that was going to change their lives and get them worried, even though it has changed my life!"

It was late in the evening when Lettie and Ron said their goodbyes; they were flying back to London the next morning but promised to keep in touch. Ron told Sandra that there would be an official announcement about the *Allium* discovery and she would be expected in London for that. Sandra smiled, her life was different now. In fact, it would never be the same again.

Chapter 34

Safely back at 13 Sandown Road, Lettie found the usual pile of junk mail and two real letters. One was from Llandysul and wished her well with her trip to Madagascar and looked forward to meeting in due course at Llandysul.

"Yup, I really must make that trip soon, I've messed her about too much already," Lettie said to herself.

The other letter was from Wiseman. It read as follows:

> *Dear Mrs Brown,*
> *I am writing to notify you that I am in the process of commencing legal proceedings for damages against both you, personally, and against Kew for unfair dismissal. Between the two of you my career has been wrecked and my reputation sullied and it is my belief that this was not accidental but a concerted campaign in a misguided attempt to rewrite and reinvent the limited botanical contributions of Huw Williams. I don't know why you have such an infatuation for someone you have never met but I have certainly suffered from it. I shall be seeking a full public apology from you and an apology and damages from Kew. You may expect to receive papers from my solicitors soon.*
> *Yours sincerely*
> *Dr Carl Wiseman*

"What a bastard!" exclaimed Lettie. "What an absolute bastard!" she repeated several times. "OK, he wants a fight, he can have a fight, I can look after myself, I've done it before!" She immediately called her lawyers in New York, or rather Arvin's old lawyers. She asked for Hiram J Kneival III, who she trusted.

"Hey Leddie, how're yer doin ?" he greeted her. Lettie had almost become anglicised by her months in England but now the real Noo Yoick accent reminded her of home. She described the circumstances at length to Hiram. He thought for about three seconds and then gave his opinion.

"Leddie, whatever you do, don't say "see you in court". As a lawyer I shouldn't say this, but if you do go all the way to court then you will end up, after two years of anxiety and a bill for $100,000 bucks plus, and you'll be sitting in a courtroom hoping that your slippery, twisting lawyer is smarter than his slippery, twisting lawyer and hoping that the judge stays awake through the whole thing and praying that the judge did not go to the same school as the father of Wiseman's lawyer. It's always a lottery. Head it off if you can. Chances are that Wiseman has no intention of going all the way to court and this is just bullying in the hope that you and Kew will cave in, but my strong advice is to head it off."

"How do I do that?" asked Lettie.

"Oh I dunno, think about it, there's always a way; launch a press campaign, hire a hitman, go talk to Kew, that's it, they're at the centre of this, go talk to them and go see those files you mentioned, there could well be some useful dirt there."

"That's what I will do," said Lettie, "I will talk to Kew. Thanks Hiram, you've been a great help."

"You bet Leddie," replied Hiram, "and Leddie... this call has taken more than an hour of my time. I'm not going to charge you for it, for old time's sake, Arvin put plenty of business our way and never quibbled about fees, but if you can't head it off and I have to come over to defend you, then the clock will start ticking and it could get mighty expensive." They rang off.

Once again, Llandysul would have to wait. There was the *Allium* announcement to be made soon but, above all, Lettie hated having legal things like this hanging over her and was determined to deal with it. She called Ron at Kew and described what had happened. She must see those files and the Director General as soon as possible.

"That really won't be a problem," Ron assured her. "I'll arrange it for tomorrow. I've briefed the DG on our trip and he is very happy with what we achieved and you are totally flavour of the month. I'll set up both meetings straight away."

"Great, oh, and by the way, make sure I see the files before I meet the DG please," added Lettie.

The next morning Lettie was sitting with Melody Markham, the new personnel director. The previous one, Eileen Tinker, had left shortly after Wiseman, "which surprised nobody", Ron had said. Melody opened with, " It's a bit unusual showing someone's personnel files to a member of the public but the DG has approved it so here they are," she gestured to a small pile of files. "It's probably best if I leave you to read them on your own. Would you like a drink while you do?"

"A cup of coffee would be nice, thank you."

And Lettie began reading.

What she found shocked her profoundly. After removing all the bureaucratic stuff, the rest of the papers could be arranged into two piles, one about five times larger than the other. The larger pile was all letters of appreciation from botanists and botanical organisations all over the world thanking Havergal (usually Huw) for his contributions and expressing their admiration for his abilities. There were also letters and appraisals from Sir Lancelot Swann, Wiseman's predecessor, similarly glowing and appreciative.

Then there was the smaller pile and this was all correspondence from Wiseman to Havergal, annual appraisals, notes to file and so on and they were all negative. "You are much too secretive." "You must share what you are doing with me and the rest of the department." "You do not seem to have realised the new commercial imperative for the department and are not doing enough in this regard." "I will handle the naming and announcement of the species you brought back from South Africa." (This many times from different places)

Lettie knew, from Ron, that the distance from Havergal's desk to Wiseman's office was about 15 yards in the Kew department. Why did he write these things and not just talk to Havergal? "I shall expect a weekly briefing on what you are doing" and "I shall not be extending your employment beyond your retirement date, even though you requested this. The composition of the department has now changed, it is now younger and more commercial and your profile no longer fits" and "post retirement I shall allow you access to departmental facilities but only on a supervised basis whereby I know exactly what you are doing and there will be no provision for travel expenses" and "in departmental meetings I do not take kindly to being contradicted, if you have a disagreement speak to me privately" and on and on but the crowning glory was a letter from Wiseman to Havergal on the date of his official retirement.

"Dear Mr. Williams, I wish you a long and happy retirement and thank you for your work at Kew."

Havergal's surname was spelt wrongly and the signature was pp'd by a secretary.

Lettie was very shocked by all this and now wanted to see the Director General. Melody agreed, when asked, that she could take the files with her.

Lettie was shown into the office of Sir Gervaise White-Hampshire, Director General of the Royal Botanical Society. As she was being ushered in, he bounded up.

"Mrs Brown, so pleased to meet you again, do come in."

"Thank you Sir Gervaise," said Lettie, unsure whether to curtsy or not.

"Bill!" he boomed, "everyone calls me Bill. My second name is William and I prefer Bill. At Harrow they used to call me Gerry, which I hated, may I call you Lettie?"

"Of course," she replied, slightly overwhelmed for once.

"Let's go and sit somewhere comfortable." He ushered her to a coffee table with two comfortable chairs. "We met briefly, of course, for your Patagonian orchid discovery but you were a bit surrounded by the press and we didn't really talk, so now it's a pleasure to meet you properly. Carter has briefed me on your trip to Madagascar, which was a great success by the sound of it, and great fun too. Congratulations, we'll be having a press day to announce it. Carter is organising everything and, just like last time, you will be the centre of attention."

"I'm looking forward to it," said Lettie, "but what I want to talk to you about right now is Dr Carl Wiseman."

"Had a feeling you might... OK, off you go."

Lettie showed him Wiseman's letter, then described the nuisance he had been in Morocco, Patagonia and Madagascar and then showed him the personnel files.

"Well," sighed the DG, "where do I start? We've had a letter from Wiseman as well. Something similar. He hasn't got a leg to stand on. I've been through it all with Legal and Personnel. He was guilty of gross misconduct and, in the circumstances, he was treated very well, better than he deserved. In fact, we paid him to go away. We could have just sacked him outright. It was cowardly really but we wanted to preserve the good name of Kew. He signed a full and final agreement, which the lawyers call a 'compromise agreement' and he has breached it by these letters. He must know he has no chance of success against Kew and my Legal Director in effect told me to forget about it. If he continues against us we can take action against him to recover his settlement for breaching his confidentiality agreement. So he is doing this, I guess, just to get at you, he knows he cannot succeed against Kew."

"I've been through legal actions before with my late husband's contested probate and I don't want to do it again," said Lettie quietly.

"I think there is something we can do which will stop it stone dead," replied the DG. "I could talk to Wiseman personally and tell him to stop. Because of Kew's position, I have it in my power through contacts to make sure Wiseman never works again in the field of botany anywhere in the world, although he probably won't anyway. But I think the best proposition is, in fact, the *Allium* press launch. If the right question comes up, then I could humiliate Wiseman publically and that will stop him. And the reason I can do that is because he breached the undertakings."

"But what if the right question does not come up?" asked Lettie innocently.

"I know the press; I can make sure it comes up. Lettie, please don't worry. This will be history very soon. Wiseman was not one of our best decisions, a most unfortunate appointment, we got things badly wrong. Havergal should have had the job, not Wiseman, and if anyone had a case for unfair dismissal it was him, not Wiseman. All we can do now is try to put things as right as we can."

"And now to happier things!" Bill boomed. "Carter has told me about his idea to rename the KMCC to become the Havergal Wyllyams Conservation Centre and I have agreed and I think we should announce that on the press day. That will also give us the chance to talk about Havergal and give him, belatedly, the attention he deserves."

Lettie left the DG's office feeling much happier.

Chapter 35

It was the day of the Allium announcement at Kew. Lettie had invited Sandra and her husband from Madagascar and Dafydd Myrddin Rhodri from Newcastle.

"While you're here you can tell me about the poems," she had told him when she called, but he had arrived late the night before and there had been no chance to do this, so it would wait until after the announcement.

They set off for Kew not quite knowing what to expect and were greeted by the DG.

"Call me Bill," he told everyone. He turned to Lettie. "The format is that I will open the proceedings, then Carter will give a brief account of Alliums and the discovery, or at least I hope it will be brief," and he winked at Ron, "then I will ask you to speak and then we will take questions. I am told to expect a large press interest, as many from the general press as from the botanical press. You see, you've become a bit of a star!"

Lettie blushed.

DG "Bill" then opened the meeting.

"Good morning everyone and welcome to Kew. As a humble botanist I am always excited when a new species is discovered and today we are delighted to facilitate the second species discovery made by Mrs Huntingdon-Brown and I am also delighted to see so much interest in Alliums, although I rather think it may be our guest speaker, Mrs Huntingdon-Brown, that you have come to listen to. Anyway, I will ask our Kew expert on Alliums, Dr Carter, to kick things off by describing the species and what is unique about this find and then I will invite Mrs Huntingdon-Brown to describe to you the circumstances of the discovery; so, may I introduce Dr Carter?"

Ron, with his newly found self-confidence, strode purposefully to the front.

"I don't think I have ever in my entire life spoken to so many people at the same time about Alliums," he started. "Normally when people ask me at parties what I do and I tell them I study onions, they move off somewhere else as soon as possible." The hall tittered. "But they are a fascinating genus and I will tell you why..."

"The word *Allium* is Greek for onion and most, but not all, species have an onion odour or taste. The layman's description is that Alliums are herbaceous perennials with flowers produced by *scapes* or runners. But of course botanists need to be more precise than this and for years we have struggled with Alliums; they are taxonomically difficult to define and species boundaries are unclear, and this discovery, I think, will either add to the confusion or may just help it. The present definition of *Alliums* is that they are *Angiosperms*, that just means flowering plants. They are *monocots*, that is, their flowers are *trimerous*, they have petals in multiples of three (i.e. 3, 6, 9 and so on) and not *dicots*, which have petals in multiples of four or five. Their order is *asparagales*, that is *phytomelon* is present in all of them, giving a black pigment in the seed coat creating a dark crust. Their family is *Amarylidaceae*, that is they are herbaceous, perennial and bulbous, and then we have a sub family called *Alliodeae* and then the genus which is *Allium*. The controversy has centred on the subfamily, *Alliodeae*. Until recently this was a separate family, broadly, Lilies, and then the APG III, that's the Angiosperm Phylogeny Group redefined it to be a sort of step-parent of the *Alliums* and botanists have been debating ever since if that is so. Lettie's discovery could help considerably to resolve this. *Alliums* do not like cold, exposed or waterlogged conditions and that is where these were. Oh, and I should have mentioned, there were numerous specimens and so we felt it was safe to bring some back and there is one in front of the Director General." (Most of the audience had assumed this was just a table decoration.) "And you will see it is definitely an *Allium* but with some very Lily-like characteristics."

"So, in summary, this species is an *Allium* in a habitat where *Alliums* shouldn't be and it hopefully will assist greatly in the taxonomy of the species, but there is much work now to be done. Thank you for listening."

Ron returned to his seat with the DG beaming at him, some of the audience scribbling like mad in their notebooks but most with a rather glazed look on their faces.

"Thank you Dr Carter," announced the DG, "and now may I introduce Mrs Letitia Huntingdon-Brown." The entire audience was now interested.

"I'd like to start by thanking the Director General (she couldn't bring herself to call him either Bill or Sir Gervaise) and Kew for hosting this event. And I want to make one thing very clear, this discovery was not mine, it was originally made by Havergal Wyllyams and, from his notes, it was found by Ron Carter, who you've just heard from, and Mrs Sandra Rakotomalala of the Kew Madagascar Conservation Centre, who is here today. Stand up Sandra..." Sandra stood up bashfully. "I just happened to be there at the same time. We found the species from notes that Havergal had left with Sandra on his last trip to Madagascar. I can't tell you enough about the good botanical and conservation work being done at the KMCC by Sandra and her colleagues, supported over many years by Havergal. I guess that's about all I have to say but if there are any questions, I'll be happy to try and answer them," said Lettie, rather pre-empting the DG who, as chair of the meeting, was supposed to be the one to invite questions.

The first two questions were from representatives of the botanical world and Bill passed them to Ron.

The next question was from a broadsheet journalist.

"Director General, may I ask why Dr Wiseman has left Kew; was it under a cloud? He always used to be big on new discoveries; was he involved in this one or the last one at all?" he asked, apparently innocently.

"Thank you for that question, Peter. I thought it might come up so I have prepared a statement. You will appreciate I am choosing my words carefully, since this is a public forum and this is all I am going to say and I will not take any further questions on this subject after this. Mr Wiseman was sacked from Kew for misconduct and under performance. We became dissatisfied with his performance of his duties some time ago but then he absented himself for months, making a nuisance of himself all over the world, running up unnecessary costs and harassing certain individuals, so we agreed a very generous severance with him, which was in full and final settlement of his employment contract and which stipulated total confidentiality by both parties. Since then he has continued to make a nuisance of himself and is actually threatening legal action against Kew and against Mrs Brown. Since this is in breach of the agreement that was signed, I am able to say these things, which otherwise I would not have said. Needless to say, what he alleges is utterly ridiculous and is just another example of the bullying personality he exhibited while he was here at Kew. It is my hope that after these words he will see sense and stop his bad behaviour and get on with something else. As I have said,

I will say no more on this but I hope this was a helpful clarification. Next question?"

Kew's legal director, Tony Turner, was sitting in the front row and looked rather uncomfortable. He was new to the job, the previous legal director having been a Wiseman acolyte and having now left, and Tony had been warned that the DG had a tendency to stray off-message. The DG hadn't strayed off-message, in fact he hadn't uttered a single word of the agreed statement Tony Turner had prepared for him. As he had prepared to answer the question the DG had remembered the files he had seen and his fury came back in his answer; he had said exactly what he felt, as he always did. For a few moments the room fell silent, absorbing what had been said and stunned to be hearing this, at Kew of all places. There were a few questions trying, unsuccessfully, to squeeze more out of the DG. Then the subject changed.

"A question for Mrs Brown; last time we were here you told us you were off to Madagascar looking for a palm but you've come back with an onion, what's going on Leddie?" asked the London correspondent of the New York Times.

"We thought we were looking for a palm but Havergal played a little game with us; his instructions took us to a place in the north-western part of the island but the palm there was an ordinary one, but, there were further instructions there on how then to find this *Allium*, which Dr Carter did."

"How's that again?" persisted the New York Times. "He played a trick? Why? And where were the further instructions? Were they hidden in the tree?"

Lettie was not sure how she was going to answer this when Sandra stood up at the back of the room. "Perhaps I can help with this..." And she came to the front to address the audience.

"I am Havergal Wyllyams' daughter," she said. "The details don't matter. My father set up the KMCC in Madagascar, where I have worked for nearly 20 years, and he visited regularly to encourage us. He never really accepted me as his daughter; he did not dispute it but could never come to terms with fatherhood. Needless to say I was an unplanned arrival. He was kind but could not be a father emotionally. On what he knew would be his last trip to Madagascar he had intended to talk to me but in the end he couldn't and instead left me a long letter. He didn't want to give it me directly and didn't want it discovered accidentally in the office, so he set up a reason for me to go to a place where he would leave the letter as well as some mementos for my grandchildren, who are his great grandchildren. It was only when Lettie and Ron came to KMCC recently that they encouraged me to go to this place and find the letter. It was a long and emotional letter which, almost in parentheses, referred to the *Alliums*. So, that was the trick as you call it. This is all very personal for me and I hope you will excuse me if I say no more."

There was stunned silence. Then a journalist asked, "Could someone please tell us a bit more about Havergal Wyllyams?"

The DG could see Sandra's eyes moistening and he took the question. "Havergal, or Huw as we knew him, worked here at Kew for more than 40 years. He was one of the finest botanists I have ever known. He should have been made head of research and not Wiseman, that was a big mistake that we made. Wiseman for years furthered his career by stealing the work done by Huw and keeping Huw away from the limelight for fear he would be exposed." The DG saw his legal director squirming. "Don't worry Tony, I have proof of that. Havergal was treated very badly and I regret that. I did not know until now that he had a daughter but am delighted that she is already a member of the Kew family." He turned and smiled at Sandra. "I will do everything I can to acknowledge, however belatedly, Huw's contribution and we will make a start by renaming the KMCC the Havergal Wyllyams Conservation Centre."

Since it was a time for statements, several more followed.

"And I," said Ron, "worked with Havergal here at Kew for 15 years and he was the kindest and most gentle and encouraging man you could ever wish to meet."

"And I bought Havergal's house after he died," now it was Lettie's turn. "I didn't know it was his house, I just wanted a house in London, but in it I found all his papers, botanical, personal and so on that eventually led us here."

"And I," it was Rhodri's turn, "am a bit peripheral to all this but just for completeness I am a policeman and I was on duty when a death was discovered and I attended the house with a colleague, only to find a man originally from my village in Wales. My parents had known the Wyllyams family. Some of the papers Lettie talked about were in Welsh and, as a Welsh speaker, I have translated them, although Lettie hasn't seen them all yet."

And so it all came out, except that Sandra would not add to what she had said.

The final question was to Lettie.

"Do you have any more trips planned, any more discoveries?"

"Nope, as far as I know I think that's about it for now," she replied, "although I'll tell you something more. Havergal has been the inspiration for us all in this but there has been another inspiration for me and that is Marianne North. I have been involved in just two discoveries over the past few months and that is about all now. Marianne was a Victorian Lady who spent most of her life touring the world collecting in pictures hundreds of specimens, they are all displayed here at Kew in the Marianne North gallery and I recommend you go see them to understand how inspiring botany can be."

As they left the meeting one seasoned old hack turned to another. "I didn't realise the world of botany could be quite so interesting."

"Yeah, I thought I'd drawn the short straw being sent here by the office, but I've got enough material for a week."

"What you going to do with the onion story?"

"Probably nothing at all; I didn't really understand it."

After all the Press had gone the DG took Sandra to one side.

"I never realised Havergal had family but , as I said just now, I am genuinely delighted that he did and that you are part of the Kew family."

"I hadn't intended to say anything," said Sandra. "It just came out and I certainly didn't say it because I wanted to be treated differently. I love what I am doing and want to continue."

"I understand, my dear," said Bill comfortingly," and it is high time I made a trip to the KMCC, or as we now know it the HWCC. I've never been. I'll ask Carter to organise something."

"You will be very welcome," smiled Sandra.

Back at Sandown Road, Lettie announced to Ron, Rhodri and Sandra and her husband, "OK guys, we're off to the local pub for dinner, it'll be my treat." They were a very happy group, who almost took over the Crow's Nest with their excited chatter. There was much to talk about. But Lettie had one question in particular she wanted to ask Sandra. "Why did you decide at the last minute to announce that Havergal was your father?"

"The discussion until then about my father had been so impersonal and I suppose I felt that way once, but not now. He was a real person and I wanted them to know that. I hadn't planned on saying anything, it just blurted out, but now I have said it I am pleased."

"Will you now tell them at KMCC, or HWCC I should say..." continued Lettie.

"There'll be no need," interjected Ron. "It will be all over the press in the next few days, I guarantee you that, certainly the botanical press, and, if it's not, then the Kew grapevine will probably get there first anyway."

Ron was right. When they got back to Sandown Road the answering machine was completely full of messages asking to speak to Ron, Sandra or Lettie. There was even one message from the Llandysul Enquirer asking for Rhodri.

"Let's leave all that till the morning," said Lettie. "I'm tired, but what a great day!"

Chapter 36

The extent of the media interest exceeded all their expectations. Rhodri, who had come down to London to talk about the poems, became their telephonist/receptionist, handling all the incoming telephone calls and passing them to whoever was asked for and handling callers to the house asking for interviews and photos; the poems would have to wait. Initially most of the calls had been to Kew but they would only respond to botanical questions and not the personal ones and definitely nothing further about Wiseman and, when asked, they gave out Lettie's number. She didn't mind, she was loving it.

The bombardment lasted several days. The day after the announcement, the botanical press carried botanical stories and Wiseman stories and the general press ran Lettie stories and Havergal stories. Then the other media picked up on the stories and then the provincial and foreign press picked up on it and then the weeklies and the weekend papers ran in-depth articles and interviews and so it went on.

Kew's press office had a cuttings service which monitored the coverage worldwide and they sent copies each day to the house. Unsurprisingly it was highly varied, frequently inaccurate and often lurid. Apart from the botanical press there was scarcely a mention of Alliums.

One tabloid headed it's piece "**Lettie Brown goes to town**" – Lettie Brown, the inveterate botanical battler took on a bruising bully called Wiseman, on behalf of her hero, Havergal Wyllyams, and won against all the odds....

Another piece focused on Wiseman. "**Wiseman not so wise?**" – head of botany at Kew, Carl Wiseman stole botanical secrets from his staff and was only found out by a member of the public and is now disgraced...

There was widespread coverage of Wiseman's downfall in most papers and surprise that this had all happened at the Royal Botanic Gardens, of all places.

One of the Welsh papers did a piece on Havergal. "**The quiet Welsh botanist**" – he just got on with his work despite the fact that it was being stolen... was dedicated to his work and wanted no fame or fortune.

One of the American papers headed it's coverage, **"It took an American to sort out Kew"** – Lettie Brown from NYC got to the bottom of a scam at Kew involving a nasty creep called Carl Wiseman...

Oddly, there was a similar story in one of the British papers, **"Why did it take an American to sort out Kew?"** – Kew's DG admits Wiseman was a mistake so why did they allow it to continue for so long? Why didn't they do something much sooner and so prevent someone's life being destroyed?

There was even a call from a management magazine enquiring why it had taken so long to discover the ineptitude of a senior manager.

"You'd better ask Kew that," Lettie had replied.

"We have already called them and they won't comment."

"Well, I think the same had better apply to me."

The Llandysul paper carried a piece about Havergal being a son of the village who never came back but reached the heights of the botanical world without ever bragging about it. Rhodri shared with them a little of his family history.

Rhodri's old station sergeant also called. "I hope you are not revealing confidential information? Just joking, well done, son, I always knew you had something in you."

The Trevelin paper *El Oeste* called following their coverage of Lettie's Patagonian adventure and, once again, featured the Welsh connection.

Several of the journalists tried to get them to say things about Wiseman but they had agreed beforehand not to. One asked, "can you at least tell us where we can contact him, his phone doesn't answer, there's no one at his house, where is he?"

"I have no idea, try Kew," Lettie had answered, but they had already tried Kew with a similar result.

There was one thing almost none of the journalists could understand; why had Havergal allowed Wiseman to steal from him and done nothing about it and no one could really give a satisfactory answer.

The BBC programme "Woman's Hour" interviewed Sandra; their interest was in how she had come to terms with a father who apparently rejected her but then at the very end accepted her.

The "Today" radio programme interviewed Lettie, asking if she had a personal grudge against Wiseman.

Even Sandra's husband received a call from a Madagascan paper. "What's it like discovering that you have an English (sic) father-in-law who is so famous?"

In amongst all this, Lettie's New York lawyer, Hiram J. Kneival III, called.

"Hey Leddie, I've seen all the press coverage, you're quite a star, lemmie tell you, you won't hear from Wiseman again, you've totally skewered him, well done and it was pure genius getting the Director General of Kew to do your dirty work for you. Arvin would have been proud of you!"

"It wasn't quite like that," replied Lettie. "The DG didn't need any persuasion at all, he just said what he thought was right, and that kind of restores your faith in honest people. But, you really think that is the end of Wiseman do you?"

"No question," replied Hiram. "Wiseman cannot now do anything against you and I doubt he could do anything against Kew. They must have got the contract right. All he could do is try and sue the Director General for defamation – but do you know who he is?" asked Hiram.

"Not really," replied Lettie.

"I checked him online this morning. Sir Gervaise is a member of the House of Lords, a 3rd cousin of the Queen, Lord Lieutenant of Dorset and he has a string of directorships. Only a madman would try and take him on and even Wiseman can't be that stupid. OK Lettie time for me to go, have a good life, a good botanical life, will we see you sometime in the Big Apple?"

"You know, I'm kinda happy here," she said, as they rang off.

Sandra received a call from KMCC; it was Julian ("Jules" to everyone) Waddilove, the director of KMCC and her boss. "Congratulations Sandy, you're a star, what great coverage for our work here as well as Kew and conservation in general. I'm really proud of you."

Jules had joined Kew about 10 years after Havergal and had been taken under his wing and they had been good friends ever since. When Havergal had set up KMCC he had not wanted to run it from then on and had suggested Jules do it for a 5 year assignment. "Good training for a young botanist," he had said. Jules had never gone back to Kew. He had married locally and was perfectly happy working and living in Madagascar with his family.

"Of course," he continued, "it must have been a surprise to many that you are Havergal's daughter, and you were very brave to announce it, but I must tell you now that I have known for a long time. I've got quite a lot to tell you. I could have waited until you were back here and talked to you personally but now seems the best time to tell you, not in a week's time. When you first joined KMCC your father asked me to look after you and be a sort of godfather to you, he never explained why and you never actually needed any help anyway. Then, when your father found out that your mother had told you about him, he shared that with me because he did not want any hint of favouritism or preferment and I told him that you had never actually needed any help but that I would keep things confidential. On his last trip he asked me to give you the letter and the presents but I told him I thought that would complicate things for you; you would wonder why I knew and you didn't. So we devised a trip for you to make, but you never went, until very recently of course, and it would have been strange if I had ordered you there, so Mrs Brown eventually was the unsuspecting catalyst. Your father, as I am sure you know, was a very kindly and generous man but also unique. I knew him as a friend for as long as you did but could never say I understood him. When Wiseman came barging in to KMCC I knew what he was looking for and why, and did everything I could to stop him. Unfortunately I had not been told officially by Kew that he had been sacked so I couldn't ban him from the office and I just crossed my fingers every day that you would give nothing away, which you didn't. The sad thing is that everyone knew what Wiseman was doing except the authorities in Kew until the very end, he was a very nasty man." Jules stopped to let all this sink in.

"Thanks Jules," said Sandra, "almost every day I learn something new about my father. It's so sad that never happened while he was alive but, as you say, he was a unique man."

"Just one more thing I want to say," added Jules, "as you know I'm retiring at the end of the year, I'll be staying here in Madagascar and perhaps doing a bit of part time work, just as your father did, but retiring from full-time work. Kew have asked me to recommend a successor and I have recommended that you take over from me. Would you take it on?"

"I would love to carry on working at the Havergal Wyllyams Conservation Centre in whatever capacity you think I am capable of," replied Sandra.

After all the broadsheets and tabloids had taken the story as far as they could, mainly involving Lettie and Sandra, the botanical journals began to occupy Ron and the Kew in-house magazine wanted to do a feature on Sandra and the renaming of KMCC but things now were definitely calming down now.

All the activity had not gone unnoticed in the street; who could miss a BBC outside broadcast van parked in the road and a constant stream of visitors, and the next time Lettie was walking down the road, on her way to buy some coffee, she ran into Delbert and Nelbert.

"Allo Missus!" they chorused. "Been following you in the papers and on the radio. You're famous now."

"It shouldn't be me, it should be Havergal Wyllyams who is famous but the papers always get it wrong, they don't like a complicated story."

"But, I tell you what," said Delbert, "you should get a blue plaque put on the house saying *Havergal Wyllyams lived here.*"

"You're going to have to tell me all about that sometime," replied Lettie. "Sorry guys, can't stop, we're still kinda busy."

The next day Ron came in with some news.

"Do you remember that Wiseman lives just a few houses from me?" he asked

"Yes"

"Well, there's a "For Sale" board outside now. He's finished; he's going away."

"That's good," said Lettie, remembering what Hiram had said, "and we've done pretty much all we can to acknowledge Havergal; although Delbert next door had an idea, he suggested we put up a blue plaque to him, what do you think? And what is this blue plaque business any-way?"

"Blue plaques," explained Ron, "were a Victorian idea, started in the 1860s, I think. They simply proclaim that such and such a famous person lived in that house between this date and that. There are about 850 plaques in London dedicated to Mozart, Nelson or more modern people such as Jimi Hendrix. But you have to have been famous to get a plaque, so I doubt if Havergal would qualify."

"Well, who runs the sceme?" asked Lettie.

"It's run by an organisation called English Heritage."

"I wonder if Sir Gervaise might have any contacts?" mused Lettie, remembering the potted history Hiram had given her.

It just so happened that Sir Gervaise had been a classmate at Har-row of 'Binky' (now Lord) Fortesque, chairman of English Heritage...

Chapter 37

As peace slowly returned to 13 Sandown Road it was time for PC Rhodri to talk about the poems he had been translating. This was the main reason he had come down from Newcastle and he would have to return to work soon and was running out of time. The three of them put the telephones on hold, bolted the front door and sat down to listen to him.

"While you lot have been gallivanting all over the world, collecting glory," Dafydd started, good-naturedly, "all I've been doing is either working or going through the poems, nothing else, look at them..." and he gestured at a pile of papers nearly seven inches high.

"I haven't translated everything, there's far too much and it would take too long but I have read everything and it's been fascinating. I am not a proper poet and just translating word for word from Welsh to English doesn't work, you go from beautiful rhymes and cadences in Welsh to clumsy jarring words in English that don't rhyme, but some of the poems have translated , only a handful, and I will read those to you; otherwise you'll have to rely on my interpretation of them. You see, Havergal's life is played out in his poems, they chronicle his life, the ups and the downs, the dreams and the joys and the sadness, I didn't know him but his personality comes through."

"He obviously just loved poetry, possibly as much as botany, both reading it and writing it. He certainly seems to have written it all his life, there is even some early schoolboy stuff in here which I won't embarrass his memory by reading. He also appears to have almost only ever written in Welsh, although there are a couple of poems in English written by him and he collected and wrote out a number of English poems by others that he obviously liked. One that he liked was by Dylan Thomas, remember he heard him reciting in 1952, I'll read it to you and it will be pretty obvious why he liked it."

The force that through the green fuse drives the flower
Drives my green age; that blasts the roots of trees
Is my destroyer.
And I am dumb to tell the crooked rose
My youth is bent by the same wintry fever.

The force that drives the water through the rocks
Drives my red blood; that dries the mouthing streams
Turns mine to wax.
And I am dumb to mouth unto my veins
How at the mountain spring the same mouth sucks.

The hand that whirls the water in the pool
Stirs the quicksand; that ropes the blowing wind
Hauls my shroud sail.
And I am dumb to tell the hanging man
How of my clay is made the hangman's lime.

The lips of time leech to the fountain head;
Love drips and gathers, but the fallen blood
Shall calm her sores.
And I am dumb to tell a weather's wind
How time has ticked a heaven round the stars.

And I am dumb to tell the lover's tomb
How at my sheet goes the same crooked worm.

"It says, of course, that we are all part of nature and brings botany and poetry together quite beautifully. I heard it before at school but never really appreciated it until now."

"Most of the poems he wrote are dated and so I've been able to put them in order and they are probably written for his own pleasure since they are final versions. Then, about 20 years ago, or perhaps a bit less, it changes, some poems are still dated but many are undated and draft with scribbled changes, implying that a final version was then produced and sent to someone; he seems to have found a soul mate, perhaps a fellow poet."

"There are lots of poems in his early life with pastoral and botanical themes; poems about nature and wildlife, the birds and the bees and so on. One of his very early poems, perhaps written when he joined Kew, starts as follows;

One day a young student went along to Kew
Little did he realize how little he knew
So much to learn and so much to know
The young student started, his face all aglow

"There's lots more but those words translated fairly easily into English and I think they are charming and so true. One of the English poems I mentioned is also lovely; I didn't realize it was in English until Ron saw it, you'll understand why when I read it, I'll just read the first two verses, there are quite a lot more"

Abelia, Dahlia, Wisteria and Mahonia
Verbena, Santolina and our old friend Paulownia
Trillium, Allium, Orontium and Lamium
Skimmia, Uncinia, Robinia and Taxodium

Caducous lenticels flabellate Calyptra
Indehiscent deltoids come into the vista
Cladophyll verticils from faraway Bicester
Cross with epiphyllous rhizomes to make a half sister

"The first verse is plant species and the second is botanical terms," explained Ron "maybe he used it as a crib help before some exams or, more likely, just enjoyed playing with the words and the rhymes."

"Another one Ron enjoyed which translated very well from the Welsh is about his old boss, Lancelot Swann, the one before Wiseman, who was a lepidopterist.

A handsome blue butterfly
Chanced just then to flutter by
Like a shot, net in hand, Lance went and got
That fluttering blue buttery fry

"I enjoyed translating that; it works as well in English as in Welsh, it's only short but it took me several days to translate it properly as a rhyming verse rather than just doggerel."

"It works perfectly," added Ron, "all Lance cared about was butterflies and Havergal often helped him and there's an affection in the poem; they were great friends."

Then there is a poem by another poet which he obviously liked because he copied it out and may have sent it to someone, it's called "Solutions" and is by Edmund Blunden.

The swallow flew like lightening o'er the green
And through the gate-bars (a hand's breadth between)
He hurled his blackness at that chink and won;
The problem scarcely rose and it was done.

The spider, chance-confronted with starvation,
Took up another airy situation;
His working legs, as it appeared to me,
Had mastered practical geometry

The old dog dreaming in his frowsy cask
Enjoyed his rest and did not drop his task;
He knew the person of "no fixed abode",
And challenged as he shuffled down the road.

These creatures which (Buffon and I agree)
Lag far behind the human faculty
Worked out the question set with satisfaction
And promptly took the necessary action.

By this successful sang-froid I, employed
On "Who wrote Shakespeare?" justly felt annoyed
And seeing an evening primrose by the fence
Beheaded it for blooming insolence.

"I really like that one," said Dafydd and I've done a bit of research. Blunden is mainly known as a poet from the First World War, with Siegfried Sassoon and others, and that is one of only a few poems that Blunden wrote about something else. But in a way it is about war because it is saying that answers, or solutions, lie in nature and, with all our brains, we humans are still not actually that bright, we think too much and are not instinctive or natural enough. You can see why a botanist would like it"

"Another one he copied out is a fragment from Keats' Hyperion"

As when, upon a trancèd summer-night,
Those green-robed senators of mighty woods,
Tall oaks, branch-charmèd by the earnest stars,
Dream, and so dream all night without a stir

"There are lots and lots of poems just like that; light, joyful and humorous, mostly written by him, he just enjoyed words and the sound of words and almost everything he wrote was about nature. But things began to change about twenty years ago in quite a lot of different ways"

"There's a fairly bleak period when I think he must have lost his mother and some rather dark poetry that sounds quite guilt ridden, although I suppose everyone feels like that when you lose a parent, then he seems to perk up a bit and then he starts to write to someone, almost all his poems are draft with the originals presumably having been sent to whoever it was. The poems gradually become more and more affectionate as well as increasingly metaphorical and difficult to understand. There is one long poem about a fish, in fact a trout, riding a bicycle underwater and upstream against the current. The fish reaches someone's house but is then told to go away and jumps back in the river, leaving his bicycle behind. Now, I've got no idea what that means and it would probably take me a month to translate it. But here's one I did translate, I had to play with the words quite a lot to get rhymes and sentences but I'm quite pleased with it."

> *A Waterfall of golden tresses cascades about her face,*
> *Red rivulets and streams collide in a glorious river race,*
> *What joy to swim and splash in that heavenly watery place,*
> *Flaxen haired, Saxon haired she is spun in filigree lace.*

> *Flame crested, wode chested the shrill warrior cry*
> *of the Celtic virgin she-Queen splits the lowering sky,*
> *Willing men follow her, ready to do or die,*
> *Victory swift and bloody she's gone, back to her eyrie on high.*

> *Which, Muse, are you, she Warrior or girl Queen?*
> *Or are you neither but just a figment, never to be seen?*
> *Just imagined and remembered, like a heady summer's dream,*
> *A beautiful Muse woman, an illusory Warrior Queen.*

"Wow, that's pretty powerful stuff," exclaimed Lettie. "Who on earth was that written for?"

"I don't know," said Dafydd, "but whoever it was he must have been pretty close to, maybe it was the woman in Llandysul who keeps writing to you?"

"I'd forgotten about her," replied Lettie. "I must go and see her soon."

"You said almost all the poems were drafts but he still wrote some for his own enjoyment?" asked Lettie.

"Yes, in a way," said Rhodri, "although I wouldn't necessarily call it enjoyment. He wrote several poems about birds, almost like the

Hitchcock film, and especially a big black crow that stole things and had an evil personality and Ron has told me that the timings of these are soon after Wiseman joined Kew and Havergal was overlooked, and Wiseman must have started stealing from Havergal almost from the beginning and this was another dark period. But this only lasted a few months and from then on almost all his poems are draft and so for someone else and he appears to have reconciled himself to Wiseman or just ignored him, he doesn't write about the black crow again."

"Then the poems start to get dark again towards the end of his life, but this is not Wiseman it seems to be intimations of mortality and a degree of self-questioning and evaporating confidence. To be honest with one exception they are almost untranslatable, the Welsh is very dense and the language is highly metaphorical, they presumably mean something to the person they were written for but not to me. But there is one sort of poem towards the end which is in English. And it's a strange one. The national song of Wales is "Land of my fathers" or "*Hen Wlad Fy Nhadau*" in Welsh. It was originally written in Welsh in 1856 and it is sung at all national events, sporting contests, eisteddfods and so on. The original Welsh version is written in very Victorian Welsh – thee, thou and so on – and so were the first English translations. But over the years there have been many updated versions since it is more often sung in English than in Welsh these days. What Havergal has done is to take a fairly modern English version and then adapt it. I'll read it to you in its recognized form and then in his adapted form. I don't think he sent this to anyone; it's a final version. There are three verses and a chorus sung in between each verse. The first verse goes like this, and remember this is normally sung not spoken;

> *The land of my fathers, the land of my choice*
> *The land in which poets and minstrels rejoice*
> *The land where stern warriors were true to the core*
> *While bleeding for freedom of yore.*

"Havergal has written

> *The land of my mother, father had I none*
> *A bastard boy and a bastard son*
> *Was I a stern warrior, true to the core?*
> *Or did I abandon my birthright and more?*

"The chorus then goes

~ 179 ~

Wales, Wales, favourite land of Wales
While sea her wall, may naught befall
To mar the old language of Wales

"And Havergal's version of the chorus was

Wales, Wales, when will I see you again?
Will er' I cross the sea, back home to be,
to speak again the old language of Wales?

"He didn't change the second verse which goes

Old mountainous Cambria, the Eden of Bards
Each hill and each valley excite my regards
To the ears of her patriots how charming still seems
the music that flows in her streams.

"But he completely rewrote the third verse; normally it goes;

My country tho' crushed by a hostile array
The language of Cambria lives to this day
The Muse has eluded the traitor's foul knives
The harp of my country survives

"And what he wrote was;

My country was abandoned by a selfish son
The loser was me tho' the language lived on
The Muse still awaits me and what shall I do?
Will I ever go home, can I er' again be true?

"I'm not a poet and certainly not a psychiatrist but I would interpret that that he is missing his home country, perhaps feeling guilty he neglected his mother, he seems to have decided he cannot now go back home and is worried he may be letting someone down, presumably the Muse, who may be this person in Llandysul, and all in all he's feeling pretty low; it's a very powerful poem even if it is a personalized version of an old favourite, and even the old favourite, Land of my fathers, it's one of those things you belt out watching a rugby match without thinking about the words but when you read them they are really quite beautiful. He was obviously a Welshman until the day he died but, like so many of us, once he'd left he couldn't go back."

"And so there you have it," continued Dafydd wistfully, "a man's life through his poetry. I've only translated a tiny portion of the total but his life is reflected throughout and I hope I have done it justice in what I have told you."

"Dafydd," said Lettie, "thank you so much for all your time and effort, it must have been very difficult fitting all this in with your own work and I think you've become a bit of a poet yourself, certainly with the translations I've heard. It's pretty clear that the key missing link now is to find out who the drafts were written for and that road would seem to lead to Llandysul, or at least that's the only remaining piece in the jigsaw puzzle, and so I guess that's my next trip."

"But tell me," she continued, "do you think we should publish these poems, perhaps publish in Welsh as they are or even get a professional translator to produce English versions?"

Ron interrupted. "I think you would have to get permission from the owners of those poems and in the case of the drafts we don't know who that person is and in the case of the others the owner is presumably Sandra."

"You're right, I hadn't considered that."

"I'll be quite happy to leave all those poems with you now, it's been exhilarating but also quite depressing reading through them all; exhilarating when you find beautiful soaring poems about nature but depressing when you read the big black crow poems and you can't help thinking – I wish I could do something to help.

Since finishing all of Havergal's works I've actually begun writing myself a bit, just for fun. I really enjoy it, but mine are in English not Welsh. I've probably lived in this country too long, it's not just knowing the words it's also the getting the atmosphere, and anyway, 70 years ago when Havergal was growing up, Wales was very Welsh, far more than it is today or when I was growing up."

"Will you read us some of your poetry?" asked Lettie.

"I thought you might ask that," replied Dafydd. "Not tonight, it's getting late now, but perhaps another time, they're not very good but I'm not ashamed of them."

Chapter 38

Lettie was sitting quietly in the kitchen at 13 Sandown Road enjoying a morning cup of tea. Yesterday's poetry reading had been quite emotional and she didn't know what to think. She felt as if she was invading someone's private life even though he was dead. What had started as a botanical adventure, taking on Wiseman and righting wrongs, was now getting intensely personal and she wasn't sure if she wanted to take things any further by going to Llandysul. But she knew she had to, after all she had been asked to come several times and so, reluctantly, she wrote to Mary MidLothian-Sutton suggesting some dates in the near future when she would come down to West Wales.

Almost by return an answer arrived accepting one of the dates, which would be in a few days' time, and so Lettie now prepared for her next and hopefully final, trip. She checked the maps and the satnav and found that Llandysul was about a five hour drive from London so she would leave the next day, stay in a hotel and meet Mary the day after. She did not know what to expect from the trip; she expected Mary to be just be a friend with whom Havergal exchanged local news and gossip and who had a liking for poetry, in fact she hoped that that was all Mary was whilst suspecting that there would be more to it than this, but this was the last piece of the jigsaw and Mary had seemed so anxious to see her and so Lettie set off wondering what would be the final twist in this story of a remarkable man who had occupied her life for so many months now.

With such a long drive to make, Lettie would need places to stop and, rather than leaving it to chance, as she had on her drive to Newcastle, she consulted Ron.

"Havergal didn't visit Llandysul very often but he did tell me once that when he did go down there he would sometimes stop at Avebury and sometimes at Abergavenny to have a walk in the Brecon Beacons. And sometimes he would call in at the National Botanic Gardens of Wales, they're the Welsh equivalent of Kew so he was bound to be interested, but that won't help you much because the gardens are only about 15 miles from Llandysul, so stopping there won't break your journey very much."

"Thanks," said Lettie, "so it sounds like the two "A"'s - Avebury and Abergavenny, don't tell me about them, let it be a surprise for me." Later, having Googled the two sites, Lettie could contain her curiosity no longer and she asked Ron, "why do you suppose he chose those two places? A pile of stones and a small market town?"

"He never said why but I think I can guess," replied Ron. "The pile of stones, as you put it, and just wait till you see them, were put there nearly 5,000 years ago by the Celts, in other words, the Welsh. Maybe he thought of it as a Welsh outpost in England and he was paying homage to his forefathers. Maybe he thought, "If the Welsh can achieve this, what can't we do?" And as to Abergavenny, again he didn't say but when you cross the bridge into Wales the first county you come to is Monmouthshire, which has been part of England, then Wales, backwards and forwards over centuries, and it is only when you get well into the county and to Abergavenny that you get into the real Welsh speaking Wales and I would think that is what he looked forward to."

"He was a real patriot wasn't he?" asked Lettie.

"Yes, I think so, again he didn't talk about it and he certainly didn't hate the English, but I think he was like many expatriates, idolising the country you have left."

Dafydd Rhodri had been listening to this and added, "funny you should mention Monmouthshire, there's a poem that Havergal copied out by a Welsh poet from Monmouthshire, and maybe he was talking about the Brecon Beacons, I'll go and get it, it's rather charming." A few moments later he returned. "Here it is, it's called Leisure and it's by William Henry Davies and it's one of those poems that everyone knows the first two lines of but not the rest."

What is this life if, full of care
We have no time to stand and stare

No time to stand beneath the boughs
And stare as long as sheep or cows

No time to see, when woods we pass,
Where squirrels hide their nuts in grass

No time to see, in broad daylight,
Streams full of stars, like skies at night

No time to turn at beauty's glance
And watch her feet, how they dance

No time to wait till her mouth can
Enrich that smile her eyes began

A poor life this if, full of care
We have no time to stand and stare

"Well, that is rather lovely," said Lettie.

"And it does sum up the life of a botanist," added Ron. "Lots of time spent standing and staring and thinking and wondering. Havergal must have been bursting to get out into the real countryside when he came home and headed straight for the Brecon Beacons."

Dafydd was listening to this and added, "It sums up the life of a poet as well. We spend lots of time standing and staring."

Lettie noted the "we" in what Dafydd had said and wondered what the Newcastle police force thought about their Bardic Bobby.

And so the next morning, bright and early, Lettie set off for Llandysul. She had looked up her two stops and had them plotted in her satnav and even knew a bit about them from the internet. Her journey was long but quite simple; the M4 motorway took her almost directly to where she was going with just small diversions for her two stopping places. About two hours after leaving home Lettie drew into Avebury and was amazed by what she saw. First stop was the toilets and then a coffee but Lettie could not wait to look around.

Having joined the National Trust, who own the site, she joined a guided tour of the incredible monuments. "Neolithic, nearly 5,000 years old, the original purpose not really known, probably used for ritual or ceremonial purposes, still used by pagans and druids to this day ("was Havergal a Druid?" Lettie thought, but then quickly abandoned the notion) much was destroyed over the centuries and has been carefully reconstructed" and more and more, she could imagine Havergal just standing and staring at the wonder of it, but it was time to go or she would never get to Llandysul.

Back on the M4 Lettie set her sights on the next stop, Abergavenny, about two hours away.

Abergavenny was a beautifully picturesque town surrounded by hills and mountains, it described itself as "the gateway to Wales" and perhaps it was this self-anointed title that had appealed to Havergal. But the real attraction was the hills, mountains and rivers around the town but Lettie would have no time for those today; she would have to make time on the way back and just contented herself with a wash break and another coffee before setting off on the last stage of the journey, a further two hours to Llandysul.

It was about 6pm when Lettie finally arrived at her destination. Llandysul was a beautiful large village lying in the valley of the river Teifi and built around the 13th century church of St Tysul and surrounded by heavily wooded hillsides. Unusually, Lettie had not made any advance arrangements for accommodation, she was getting more confident now. She stopped at the first place she saw, the Kings Arms Hotel in the High Street. Yes, they had rooms, they were smaller than she was used to but perfectly clean and comfortable and within half an hour she was installed and sitting in the bar ordering some food. The barman was inevitably intrigued. What had brought a middle aged American Lady to the depths of Welsh Wales? Was she there for the garden festival? Lettie was tired from her journey and didn't really want to chat and certainly she didn't want to give the real reason for her trip, so she steered the conversation into generalities. "How do you pronounce the name of the town?" The closest she could get was Clandysul but the barman seemed happy with this. She retired early for an important day to come.

The next morning after a full Welsh breakfast she made her way to the address Mary Midlothian-Sutton had given her, which was very close to the hotel.

Mary lived in a small cottage on the outskirts of Llandysul, with a front garden brimming with flowers and plants and a bright red front door. Lettie knocked at the door and it was opened by a strikingly attractive woman with long flowing golden hair. "Can that be natural?" Lettie thought, and then she remembered the poem read by Dafydd Rhodri.

A Waterfall of golden tresses cascades about her face
Red rivulets and streams collide in a glorious river race...
Flaxen haired, Saxon haired, she is spun in filigree lace

Suddenly Lettie was very excited. This was, without doubt, the woman Havergal had been writing to. She had piercingly intelligent grey/green eyes, she must have been a contemporary of Havergal's but had an ageless serenity that made her seem twenty years younger.

"Hello, you must be Mrs Brown, I recognise you from the photo in the local paper, do please come in," she said, in a well-spoken and only slightly Welsh accent.

"Thank you and if I may call you Mary then I hope you will call me Lettie?"

Mary suggested tea and cakes and they sat down in a warm and welcoming lounge and then indulged in small talk about Lettie's trip but eventually the formalities were done with and Lettie opened the proceedings by asking, rather abruptly, "So you knew Havergal then, did you?"

"I've known him practically all my life. I've got so much to tell you. I've been desperate to talk to someone for a long time," said Mary quietly.

Suddenly Lettie felt again like an intruder. "I am sure we've both got a lot to tell each other, maybe it would be best if I start first, I want you to know you can trust me and that I have Havergal's best interests at heart."

And so Lettie started her story.

She described Arvin and her life in New York, why she had then come to London, the papers, Ron, Dafydd Rhodri, her trips, Wiseman, Kew and her intention to carry on Havergal's work and become a botanist herself and maybe even eventually work at Kew (in fact she surprised herself, she had never before thought such things but, somehow, subliminally, it had blurted out, she wanted to become a proper botanist!) By the time she had finished her story it was lunchtime and Mary said that she had prepared a few little things that she hoped Lettie would like and that she would start her story after they had eaten.

Over lunch they did not talk about Havergal or botany. Lunch over, it was Mary's turn.

"It is all so complicated and there is so much to say, I will take it slowly and start from the very beginning..."

"As I said, I have known Havergal, off and on, for practically my entire life. We lived just a few houses apart in a terrace of houses near here. Havergal was best friends with another local boy, Dai Llewellyn. He lived in the same terrace and for a while they would have nothing to do with me, a mere girl, but then they grew up a bit and we became a gang of mates, always together, we all went to the same local school, and we were in the same class, we would go rock climbing, tree climbing, camping, scrumping, looking for snails, looking for plants, playing in the river down there, always outdoors. I was a real tomboy and we were very close friends and had a wonderfully innocent childhood. Havergal was always the leader of our gang. Then, as always, hormones kicked in, we started to notice that we were different and a threesome became awkward. I would either have to leave the gang or pick one of them and break it up. If we went to the local youth club and there was music playing, who did I dance with? We were still very innocent but beginning to realise that the next stage of life was beginning. I spoke to my Mum about it. She totally shocked me. "I don't want you getting involved with Havergal, he's illegitimate, he hasn't got a father!" she had said. "Dai's a nice boy, go to the dance with him" It had never occurred to me that Havergal not having a father was important and my mother had never mentioned it before. I was really amazed but that's how things were in those days in small villages. I didn't know what to do. Havergal had always been the one I preferred, in fact he even carved our names on a tree in the soppy way that youngsters do. I remember Havergal saying he would carve it on a Quercus because it would still be there in 60 years' time and it still is."

"Will you show me sometime?" asked Lettie.

"Of course. And we even talked of running away, Havergal's mother would have helped, but in the end I couldn't face upsetting my parents and then, anyway, events took over. Havergal went away to university and eventually to London, the gang was broken up and I married Dai."

"Havergal kept in touch in the early days, mainly with Dai, we would swap letters and birthday cards and Christmas cards and on the very occasional times he was in Llandysul he would always call in but the gang was finished."

"Then Dai had a terrible accident and died about twenty years ago," Mary paused. "He was a farmer, he inherited the farm from his parents and I still run it now; one day he was cutting back a huge tree that was too close to someone else's house, it was a very windy day and he shouldn't have been up there; he just fell out of the tree and broke his back. I was devastated. Not just losing him of course but I also had four children to bring up one of which was born just three weeks before his father died. Havergal came to the funeral of course and was pretty broken up. He said to me that he would look after me now, he said that several times in a very meaningful way. But how he was going to do that when he lived in London he never explained."

"But you are Mary MidLothian-Sutton, not Llewellyn?" asked Lettie.
"I am really Mary Llewellyn but I just choose to use my maiden name,

I've done that ever since Dai died, I don't really know why, my two sons are both Llewellyns and so were my two daughters until they married. And I've got three grandchildren now, although one of them is in Australia because one of my sons emigrated to Manly in New South Wales, I miss them terribly."

"What Havergal did do was to start writing regularly to me and he did visit Llandysul a bit more often, just to see me, but still not very much. Anyway, I coped somehow. Then gradually Havergal's letters became more affectionate and he started writing poems for me. He would write one every week in Welsh, regular as clockwork. We were becoming quite committed to each other but only in correspondence. He did ask me several times if I would come to London to live with him, but that was never really a possibility; I have my children and grandchildren here, I have a farm to manage and I'm a governor of a local school and I did an arts degree as a mature student and my studio is all set up here, I am a farming, teaching artist and that would never fit in to south London."

"I've seen drafts of the poems he sent you and a couple have been translated and they are very good; would you ever think of having them published?" asked Lettie.

"No" said Mary, "they are personal. They are the very best of Havergal and I am going to be completely selfish and keep them for myself. There are a huge number of them and what my kids will do with them all when I'm gone I don't know and I don't really care but while I am alive I don't want to share them. I read one or two of them every day."

"I completely understand," replied Lettie.

"Havergal loved poetry," Mary continued, "both writing it, in Welsh and English, and reading it. One of his favourite poems was "Solutions" by Edmund Blunden, do you know it?"

"As a matter of fact I do," replied Lettie, "there was a copy of it in his papers."

"It sort of became our poem," continued Mary. "Havergal would call himself *Hen gi* which is Welsh for *old dog*, do you remember the verse? He thought of himself as that old dog."

> *The old dog dreaming in his frowsy cask*
> *Enjoyed his rest and did not drop his task;*
> *He knew the person of "no fixed abode",*
> *And challenged as he shuffled down the road.*

And he called me *Fy Gwen bach* which is Welsh for my small smile but it's a bit of a play on words as well because the Welsh for swallows is *gwenoliaid* and the real reference in the name was to the first verse of Solutions when *the swallow flew like lightning o'er the green,* he meant I was his little swallow, he was always amazed at how busy I was."

The swallow flew like lightening o'er the green
And through the gate-bars (a hand's breadth between)
He hurled his blackness at that chink and won;
The problem scarcely rose and it was done.

"But then, quite recently, he wrote that he would be finishing with Kew soon, his work was done, and he would like to come back to Llandysul and could he live with me? He more or less proposed without using those words. I wrote back that it was not out of the question but that I thought we should talk about it first when he was next down. If he was going to propose to me I wanted him down on one knee not doing it by post. You see I wasn't really sure if he meant it, he had said several times before that he would come back and we could get together but then something always came up, he was always onto something new."

Lettie smiled at this as she remembered Arvin's proposal to her. She and Arvin had been at the Waldorf Astoria entertaining his business friends. As they moved from group to group, working the room, Arvin had said, "Hey, we work well together, we should get married."

"Is that a proposal?" she had replied.

"I guess so, well, what's the answer?"

"Yes, I would like that," replied Lettie.

"Swell, now let's go meet some very old friends of mine over here."

Ten days later they were married.

"And that brings us up nearly to the present day," continued Mary. "He sent me the photograph of the orchid and I immediately thought something was wrong. He had never done anything like that before, so I tried to phone him from the call box here, several times, but I couldn't get a reply and so I decided to go to London to see him. I had keys for his house. He had given them to me long ago when he hoped I would come up to London, perhaps for a weekend just to try it and in case he was out when I arrived. He worked such long hours at Kew. I went to the house and found him. I didn't know what to do. I knew immediately he had gone, he was cold. I took his red file, there it is on the sideboard," she gestured. "You see he wrote a weekly poem for me and this week's poem was there in his file, he told me that once a week he would stay up all night composing the poem and so I wanted to have it but I probably shouldn't have taken the whole file. Then I just ran straight out of the house, went to the station and straight home. I was crying all the way. I should have called the police, I know, and I suppose someone else has had to do that, but I just couldn't bear the thought of the indignity for my poor Havergal and so I just ran. Afterwards I was scared to death for weeks because my fingerprints would have been there and someone may have realised the file was missing and so I might be a suspect but once the funeral was over I knew that would not happen."

Mary heaved a sigh, glad to have finally shared all this with someone, and someone she knew would care and that she could trust. "I'm really pleased to have shared this with you, excuse me please for being a bit emotional," she said.

"What sort of a man was Havergal?" asked Lettie quietly.

"He was a passionate and emotional man, although if you met him you would never know it; it was all inside and only came out in his poetry and his work. He was utterly committed to his work; his passion was his plants. But he was also a complete gentleman although he was a little bit otherworldly; he struggled with reality and real life and people."

"What do you think he died of?" asked Lettie. "There have been suggestions that Wiseman may have tried too hard to get hold of Havergal's papers or perhaps the photograph of the orchid."

"I think he died entirely naturally," replied Mary. "He just felt his time had come and it was time to go. His last poem more or less says that; it was very dark and sombre, I will show you if you wish but it is in Welsh. He just felt that his work was done, he had finished with Kew, thanks to Wiseman, he was worried about coming to Llandysul and was worried about coming to live with me and so it was time to go."

"So in a sense Wiseman did kill him by taking away his will to live?" asked Lettie.

"Yes, that is perhaps true, but I think he was also worried about me. I think all along he had felt he ought to marry me without necessarily knowing why or wanting to in reality and now the time was coming closer he worried. You see he often called me his Muse, his dream, his inspiration, but real life isn't always the same as dreams, real life is about babysitting, screaming grandchildren and dirty washing and I think he felt worried about all that. Muses are often most appealing from a distance and are not quite the same close up and I think he knew that; he had allowed himself to romanticize a vision and then perhaps realised that I was not a dream, just an ordinary person."

"But he did have a child, in Madagascar, did you know about that?" asked Lettie.

"Yes, I know about Sandra," replied Mary, "he told me all about it once when he was nearly thinking about coming here and felt he should declare everything. But, and I think you should keep this secret, Sandra was not his child. When Havergal was setting up the Kew office in Madagascar, one of his team got very friendly with Sandra's mother, whose name I've never known. She was very young, only 17 at the time, and the inevitable happened and the next time Havergal was there the mother came to see him, distraught. She was now very pregnant and she would lose her job and could not afford to bring up a baby and what about the hospital fees? Floods of tears and so on. Havergal, being the gentleman he was, said he would help financially and she would not lose her job. But the mother wanted to know how she would explain a half-caste baby and Havergal said she should tell anyone who wanted to know that it was his. He never wanted to adopt Sandra and he didn't want her to know about the help he had been giving but then it all came out when Sandra's mother was dying and told her that Havergal was her father, even though he wasn't, I don't think anyone knows who the real father is."

"The reason Havergal told me all about this was to explain why he was so poor. He never had any money. He was well paid I assume at Kew but for many years he was supporting his mother who had no source of income and then he was supporting Sandra's mother and paying for Sandra's education and when Wiseman came on the scene at Kew he was even having to pay for some of his botanical trips. But there was, I think, an emotional cost as well, for the best part of 25 years Havergal was supporting someone; either his mother, or Sandra's mother or Sandra and I think all of that wore him down and, I think, it also preyed on his mind that if he came down he would have to rely on being supported by me."

"Sandra does not know what you've just told me, in fact she is very proud of who her father is and so, as you say, this must remain a secret between the two of us."

"I agree." replied Mary. "I was not going to tell anyone but I trust you implicitly and am happier now that I have shared it."

"Let me just get some timings right," said Lettie. "Havergal's mother died just over 20 years ago and your husband died a year or so later?"

"That's right," said Mary

"So by then Havergal must have finished paying for Sandra's education and then about six or seven years after that Wiseman was appointed at Kew?"

"That sounds about right."

"That's when he should have come down here, isn't it?" asked Lettie.

Mary did not reply.

"Would you have married him if he had asked properly?" said Lettie.

"Yes, of course I would, even if only out of loyalty for our youth and the long correspondence. But I did worry about it and so, I think, did he. You see I'd almost given up waiting for him. I had my own life with my family, the farm, the school and my artwork. I never really expected him to come. And in a way we were in awe of each other. We'd become such different people since our childhoods. He was single with really only one passionate interest, I have a family and lots of interests, none of which interested him, he was only ever dutifully interested in my children and grandchildren, I think he may have even felt slightly threatened by all my interests. So, yes, I would have married him but really I'm glad in a way that it didn't happen, we were both a bit long in the tooth to change for each other; he'd just been away too long." Mary dabbed her eyes.

"There's something else I think I must tell you," continued Mary. "I wasn't going to tell you but now I will. I suffer from chronic lymphatic leukaemia; it is incurable and eventually terminal. I was diagnosed about 10 years ago. I had been feeling very tired for ages, I was fed up with it, I am usually a very active person and eventually I went to see the doctor. She couldn't find anything obviously wrong and suggested having some blood tests and they showed that I had this disease. They told me that I could take steroids and other medications but that they don't get rid of it they just manage it for a while until eventually the leukaemia becomes resistant to them; they told me I had a maximum of five years to live until that happened, but, as you can see, I'm still here. When I was diagnosed I put up that motto on the wall, she gestured to a framed motto

"What is difficult can be done with ease,
what is impossible can be done with difficulty"

I was determined to try my best to fight it and not just lie down, there's nothing really you can do except be positive, get on with life, put it out of your mind and do healthy things. One thing I did do was to move out of the farmhouse, it was just too big, and into this small cottage, the farmhouse is now used for holiday lets. I wasn't going to tell you all this and I haven't told my family and I didn't tell Havergal. Perhaps I should've told him, after all he was talking about moving in, but telling people is like giving up and I wasn't going to do that, but, as you can see, this wasn't very conducive to making long term plans and commitments. I didn't want Havergal to come down and then immediately find he had another burden to deal with. At the moment I'm fine, I just get tired sometimes that's all. I'm sorry, I think I am burdening you with too much."

They both sat quietly for a while.

Then Lettie decided to change the subject.

"What was in the red book?"

"It's over there if you want it," replied Mary. "He kept all his precious things in it, all my letters to him, some botanical things that I don't understand, names, addresses, photos and so on, and, of course it had his final poem to me in it when I found it. Do you want to see it?"

Lettie did not answer but got up and wandered over to look at the red file on the sideboard. It was a battered old file stuffed with papers.

"You know, at one time just about everyone at Kew was looking for this, especially Wiseman, all I heard was "have you seen his little red book?" and now it seems curiously unimportant. Not to you of course, but botanically, I mean," she added quickly. Realising she had unintentionally said something that could be hurtful she changed the subject. "It's not actually so little, you must have had a job getting this back on the train?"

"It's not large but it is heavy, it's got a lifetime's memories for him in it, and it is very important to me. What should I do with it?"

"You must keep it," replied Lettie, "unless, perhaps, you might want to give the botanical stuff to Kew, to Ron?"

"That would be best, before you go I will sort through it and give you all the scientific stuff to take back, I don't understand any of it anyway."

"I hope you don't mind me asking all these personal questions?"

"Not at all, I want to talk about it," said Mary.

"Well... did you love him?" asked Lettie.

"That's a very difficult question to answer," said Mary. "How can you really love someone if you hardly ever see them? I think the best way I can put is to say that because of our shared childhood I loved him as a brother. It was always, of course, platonic. In fact, he died a virgin, in every sense of that word. I was his Muse, as I have said, we almost never met just corresponded, I might have liked it to develop further at one time, but it never did, it just remained a dream," she said quietly, dabbing her eyes again. "I never really expected him to come back, so many Welshmen, when they leave Wales, never do come back."

"How did he actually die?" asked Lettie. "People can't just switch themselves off."

"He died because his heart was broken. His passion was his plants and his dream was me, and when he couldn't have the first and realised the second would not work he was scared of the future. His work was done, he was finished at Kew, he realised he did not really know Llandysul any more or even me, he had lived his dream and there was nothing left and he just felt ready to go. I don't know how you explain that medically but that is I believe what happened. In some of his last letters he was even asking me if I felt it was a good idea for him to come to Llandysul and then his last poem was very dark."

"Can you translate his last poem?" asked Lettie.

"I could but I really prefer not to," Mary replied.

"I understand completely. You will miss him won't you?" asked Lettie.

"Yes, but in a way I feel I have had the best of him, I have had his poetry and his warmth and I will never forget those."

Lettie was thinking about what Mary had said and was not convinced.

"People surely don't just switch themselves off?" she thought "what happened to survival of the species and all that?"

Mary must have sensed her doubts. "Do you think something happened then?" she asked.

"I don't have any evidence of anything else," Lettie replied, "but I do have one small question, something that's been troubling me; when you got to the house was the front door double locked?"

"No," Mary replied. "I remember that very clearly. It was just closed but not locked; I thought perhaps that meant he was in the house and everything would be alright, then of course I found he was in the house but it was not alright."

"And how was he when you found him in his study."

"He was sitting back into the chair, his eyes closed and a faint smile on his lips and he was holding his pen, which I found strange, he must have passed away just as he finished writing."

"Which hand was holding the pen?" asked Lettie

"He was holding it in his right hand, which I thought was odd because he was left handed."

Lettie decided to leave things there but these two pieces of information worried her considerably. She would talk to Dafydd about them.

"After he died," continued Mary, "I went to see him in the hospital mortuary to say goodbye, it was the saddest day of my life, I cried for days afterwards. Then I saw the probate notice asking for anyone who knew him to make contact. But I didn't want to profit in any way from his passing and I didn't want to have to tell a complete stranger, especially someone called Roger Whalley, about our relationship, which was private. I've shared it with you because you have become almost part of the family; you devoted yourself to Havergal, just as I in a different way was also devoted to him. Now I think I've told you everything. Would you like me to walk you round Llandysul and show you the school we went to, the houses where we lived, my farm and perhaps the school I now run and perhaps my studio as well?"

"I would love that," said Lettie enthusiastically, "and I'd like to see the carving please."

From Mary's cottage they walked back to the main street and then turned into Albion Road and a terrace of houses. Mary pointed out her parent's house, Havergal's and Dai's, all within yards of each other. Mary's old house was number 17, Havergal's was number 13 ("just like Sandown Road" thought Lettie) and Dai's was number 12 on the other side of the road. As they passed number 13 a very old Lady came out of number 11.

"Prynhawn da Mary" she called to them, in Welsh.

"Good afternoon Glenys" replied Mary. "Glenys is 97 years of age and has lived here all her life, we all knew her well when we lived here," said Mary.

"And a right bunch of scallywags you all were!" replied Glenys.

"So you'll have known Havergal and his mother? asked Lettie.

"Yes, I knew them both," replied the old Lady, "do you want to come in and have a cup of tea?"

Settled into Glenys' front room with cups of tea, the conversation started. "Of course I knew Havergal and his mother very well, this is a small town and we were next door neighbours for many years.... Havergal's mother was a lovely person, so kind and thoughtful, she doted on Havergal, she was so proud of him but he hardly ever visited her, he was so busy ... he wrote letters and she would tell me his news, some new discovery... but she was so sad not to see more of him after he left ... I remember the kids playing, Mary, Havergal and Dai as if it was yesterday ... Havergal was such a handsome boy ... you should have married him, Mary..."

Eventually the reminiscences were tiring Glenys and it was time to go. Next stop was the school they all attended, a Victorian brick building that had not changed to this day. Then to Mary's farm. "Of course I am just a tenant farmer, I don't own the land ... I just keep a few cows and sell the milk and make some cheese...it doesn't really make any money... I have to employ people to do the work, can't do it myself now although Dai and I used to ... eventually I'll have to give it up ... but not until I have to ... none of the kids are interested, it's too much like hard work."

Lettie noticed that the farm was called Sweden Farm and asked about it.

"I've no idea where the name came from," answered Mary, "it's always been called that, seems strange doesn't it, and there is a bit of a story there too; Havergal's father was reputed to have been a Swedish sailor on leave from Pembroke Dock, the local folklore at the time apparently was that he ended up in Llandysul because he had heard about Sweden Farm and wanted to jump ship and thought there might be a job for him there, but there wasn't and then he somehow met Havergal's mother, but it's probably all nonsense."

And now it was time to go and see the carving. They walked to the outskirts of the town to where a huge oak tree overlooked a small green and as they approached there it was, clear as anything after all these years.

HUW
L
HMS

"I'm sure if he'd known he would become a botanist he wouldn't have done it," said Mary "but the tree doesn't seem to have suffered."

"But it's HMS not MMS?" asked Lettie.

"Yes, there's a bit of a story about that. I'll tell you when we get back to the cottage," said Mary mysteriously.

Back at the cottage and with more cups of tea for refreshment, Mary explained.

"Havergal always called me Helena, or Helen, when we were young. It's because of the house we lived in. It was only a terraced house, as you've seen, it's number 17 now but back then the neighbours started giving their houses names rather than numbers, it was a sign of gentrification I suppose, and next door to us, number 15, named their house Victor Villa, I've no idea why they chose that name; anyway, my father was a farmer but he loved reading and studying in his spare time, he was always going to the library, and he must have been reading about ancient Greece at the time and he decided to call our house Troy Villa, just for a laugh I think, but from then on I was always Helen of Troy; so Havergal carved HMS not MMS. But that was a childhood thing; after Havergal left I was always Mary and never Helen again. Except once, quite recently, just a few years ago, he wrote me a poem which made me out as a Celtic warrior Queen, I could probably find it, but it is in Welsh"

"I think I may know it," replied Lettie "I think it is one that Dafydd translated, and I have it here, is it this one?" and she read;

A Waterfall of golden tresses cascades about her face,
Red rivulets and streams collide in a glorious river race,
What joy to swim and splash in that heavenly watery place,
Flaxen haired, Saxon haired she is spun in filigree lace.

Flame crested, wode chested the shrill warrior cry
of the Celtic virgin she-Queen splits the lowering sky,
Willing men follow her ready to do or die,
Victory swift and bloody she's gone, back to her eyrie on high.

Which, Muse, are you, she Warrior or girl Queen?
Or are you neither but just a figment, never to be seen?
Just imagined and remembered, like a heady summer's dream,
A beautiful Muse woman, an illusory Warrior Queen.

"Yes, that's it" said Mary quietly and a bit sadly. There was silence for several minutes. Lettie was conscious of having intruded again into a very personal matter. Then Mary brightened up. "Dafydd has done a very good job on the translation, it's as good in English as it is in Welsh. I look forward to meeting him. But I'll tell you a funny story about it. I had to get him to change a couple of words in the poem. At the start of the second verse he had written something like, "Bare breasted, wode chested," in Welsh of course. It was most unlike him to write anything saucy like that, I told him to change it, I didn't want my children, or anyone else, reading that, what would people think of me? And at my age, so he changed it to the Welsh equivalent of "red haired wode chested" and Dafydd has done a lovely job making it "flame crested wode chested". He told me afterwards that he got the original idea from Marianne, Delacroix's painting of Liberty leading the people. And he got that idea because of a Kew Christmas outing to see Les Miserables, goodness knows how they persuaded him to go, that wasn't normally his sort of thing. So the poem is a bit of a mixture of a Celtic warrior Queen and Marianne leading the French revolution. But it is, I think, my favourite of all his poems."

They sat quietly for a while as Mary dabbed her moistened eyes.

"And there's another story I can tell you," continued Mary. "I don't know why Havergal saw me as a Celtic warrior Queen but he used to say that he would stop at Avebury on his way down here and imagine me assembling all my Welsh warriors there, in readiness to attack Abergavenny to retake Wales. He was a real romantic with such strange ideas"

It was time for Lettie to go and as they parted Mary said, "I am so sorry to have brought you all this way and caused you so much trouble on behalf of Havergal."

"It has been no trouble at all, I can assure you," replied Lettie, "but I'd like you to promise me one thing. Please come and visit me in London. I will take you to Kew and show you where Havergal worked, where he had his lunch and I will show you his orchid which I brought back from Patagonia. I'll also show you a very unusual palm the he discovered in Madagascar, *Tahina spectabilis*, it's a massive and spectacular palm which dies immediately after it has flowered, it's work then being carried on by its seedlings, it just seems so appropriate for Havergal."

"I promise I will come to see you," replied Mary.

"In fact," continued Lettie, "what I will do is organise a party for everyone who knew Havergal, you're invited of course, and that will be the opportunity to take you to Kew and you'll meet Dafydd and Ron and all the others!"

As Lettie started the long drive home she could not help mulling over all the things she had learnt. Havergal was such a strange and complicated man, a mass of contradictions. He didn't really have any friends, even with Ron he just discussed botany and Kew yet he would help complete strangers. He lived all his emotions and feelings through his botany and his poetry. He had a "daughter" he took little interest in until he knew he wouldn't see her again. He helped his mother but rarely visited her even though she longed to see him. He helped Sandra's mother for years but otherwise took little interest in her. He had a Muse in Llandysul but couldn't bring himself to move down, "if only he had gone to Llandysul 15 years ago when Wiseman appeared it might have all been different, Mary would have sorted him out" she thought to herself. But above all she could not stop thinking about the front door not being locked and that he had been holding his pen in his wrong hand when he died.

"Maybe this mystery is not over yet..." she thought.

Lettie had promised herself a stop in Abergavenny and perhaps a walk in the Brecon Beacons on her way home but now there was too much on her mind; that could wait for another time and she raced back to London as quickly as she could.

Chapter 39

All the way home Lettie had been trying to make sense of things and especially the front door and the pen; she was convinced there was more to this than a man simply switching off because "his time had come". She must speak to Dafydd. "He's a policeman; he'll know what to do," she thought.

Dafydd was politely unimpressed. "People often forget to lock their front doors, it's one of our biggest problems in the police. If only they would take more care there would be much less crime. And as to the pen, well, I'm right handed but I still hold things in my left hand sometimes, if I want to scratch myself for instance, I really don't think this adds up to very much and I can guarantee you one thing; the police will not reopen the case just for this, you'll need to find something else to get them to look again and there probably isn't anything; remember we found no traces of forced entry and no evidence of violence and the doctor said that death was from natural causes."

Dafydd was being defensive. After all, he had been on the case that day and Lettie was feeling a bit foolish, he was probably right, but she wasn't going to give up quite that easily. "When you made house to house enquiries that day," she asked, "did you speak to every house in the road?"

"No, about a third of them, all the others were out, but that was a good enough sample and no one had anything suspicious to report."

"Did you speak to the house directly opposite, on the other side of the road, over there," she gestured through the lounge window.

"No, I think they were out as well."

"I'm just going to try them now, just for fun," said Lettie and walked over the road to number 12 Sandown Road.

Number 12 was occupied by a Polish family. They were very friendly and accommodating and had seen pictures of Lettie in the papers and been aware of all the fuss in the road when the press had been besieging number 13. They felt honoured she had called on them. Lettie told them that she was trying to piece together Havergal's life now that she had done all the botanical work; she carefully avoided giving any hint of her suspicions; she just wanted to know as much as possible about the man himself. "I might write a book about him," she had said.

Marek Zylinski spoke first. "We probably can't help you very much, I'm afraid. We didn't really know him at all. I don't think we ever spoke." His wife Teresa nodded at this. "He seemed to be a very private man; he would nod in recognition if we passed in the road but did not want to talk. I often saw him writing and working in his study late at night or early in the morning, you see I work nights as a security guard and I am often coming home at dawn and there he would be writing away."

"He was writing more or less on the day he died," said Lettie.

"I know," said Marek, "I saw him, as I was coming home from my shift. It was only a day or two later that the police arrived and his body was eventually taken away."

"Did you tell the police you had seen him?" asked Lettie.

"No, I didn't think anything of it, there's nothing unusual about a man writing is there?"

"Did Havergal have many visitors?" Lettie changed the subject.

"Very few that we ever saw, although there was a visitor that day that I came home and saw him writing. After my night shift I was getting ready to go to bed. I wasn't just staring out of the window, but as I was getting my pyjamas on I noticed a man ring the doorbell. Then, when I had brushed my teeth and passed the window again, I saw them both in the study upstairs talking, they seemed to be having a bit of an argument, there was a bit of arm waving, and then a bit later, just as I was going to bed I glanced again and saw the visitor helping Havergal into his chair. And then I went to sleep."

"Did you know that the police asked at each house if they had information?"

"Yes, I know they knocked at each door, a neighbour told me, but I was asleep when they came here and my wife was out because she works daytimes; we don't see much of each other!"

"Could you describe the visitor?"

"Not really, it was only just dawn and I wasn't staring, just glancing and it was several months ago now."

"Thank you both for your help," Lettie returned to number 13, her head spinning.

"OK, Dafydd, is there something that wants looking at now?"

"Well, perhaps there is, perhaps you're right, but I'm afraid the police would still not reopen the case just for that, we'll have to find out who the visitor was. It might be something entirely innocent."

"Yeah, and pigs might fly! It was Wiseman, I'll bet, and what's more I'll find out too."

Despite the Press having had such difficulty in finding Wiseman, Lettie found it remarkably easy. She wandered round to Wiseman's old house, noted the estate agent's particulars from the "For Sale" board, and called them.

"Can you please help. I am a neighbour of Carl Wiseman, such a lovely man, he loaned me some garden equipment which I haven't given back, I've only just come back from a month away and see that he has left, can you give me a contact number so I can return the things to him, he'll be such a loss to the neighbourhood." They were delighted to help.

Now Lettie had to call Wiseman. She was very nervous, even with Dafydd sitting next to her. But she found Wiseman surprisingly unintimidating.

"Mrs Brown, you continue to plague my life even when I thought I had seen the last of you, what do you want now?"

"Mr Wiseman, I'm trying to get to the bottom of how Havergal, or Huw, died and I'm told, by neighbours, that you visited 13 Sandown Road on the day that he died. Is that correct?"

"Yes, it is correct," replied Wiseman. "I called in on my way to Kew. It was very early. I always liked to be the first in the office and the last to leave, it encourages the staff, you see. As I was passing Huw's house I saw him working in his study and thought I would call in."

"So you just barged into Havergal's house then, uninvited and early in the morning?"

"No, not at all. Huw had phoned me the previous evening, saying he wanted to talk to me. I said I was busy just then but would call in on him as soon as I could. I hadn't planned to call in that morning but since I saw him there, and I had time, I thought I would. He hadn't said why he wanted to talk to me but I did want to talk to him to tell him how disappointed I was in how unhelpful he'd been and I wanted to give him one last chance to tell me about the orchid since I was on my way to a meeting of the executive committee and it would have been good to have been able to tell them something about it. When he opened the door he was obviously angry at being disturbed but asked me to join him in his study upstairs. Then he started to become quite insulting and aggressive towards me in a way I'd never seen before. It was clear that all he wanted to do was to berate me and get rid of all his frustrations and I told him that I would not put up with that and I prepared to leave."

"Did you see his little red book, because it was there wasn't it?" asked Lettie calmly.

"Yes, it was there, and I told him, as I was going, that I wanted to look at it to be sure that there were none of Kew's papers in it that he shouldn't have. He refused to let me inspect his file, saying it was personal and then he went very red in the face and shouted and eventually collapsed on the floor, he must have had a fit or something. Anyway, I helped him back into his chair, he said he would be alright and would carry on with his writing so I handed him his pen and left."

"Did you call a doctor or check on how he was later?" asked Lettie.

"No, he said he was OK and asked me to go. I was off to a very important meeting and then the next day I was off on a trip, that's why I called that morning, otherwise it might have been weeks, and it was only when I got back that I discovered what had happened."

"Did you think of contacting the police?"

"No. He was fine when I left him, there was nothing to report."

"Why didn't you just take the file when he collapsed?" asked Lettie.

She knew he didn't have it, Mary did, and she knew exactly why he didn't take it, and she knew she had skewered him.

"Er... I was in a hurry, I was late for my meeting, I just forgot to look in it," he lied.

"I know why you didn't take it. You knew Havergal was in a bad way, perhaps even dying, and you couldn't risk taking the file because if it was later found in your possession you would have had some questions to answer. That's what happened, isn't it?" Before Wiseman could answer, Lettie exploded.

"You bastard!" exclaimed Lettie, surprising even herself with her vehemence. "You killed Havergal. He had had a stroke or a seizure or something, caused by you threatening him, and if you had called for help then he might be here today. You were just totally thoughtless. How many hours, maybe days, was it before he died? You just left a man in need of help and walked away, that's criminal!"

"Mrs Brown, how dare you accuse me of murder. If you repeat that I will talk to my lawyers and if you really believe that then go to the police. When I left Huw he said he was alright and he asked me firmly to go and so I did. I have nothing to be ashamed of and I would be grateful if you never contact me again." And with that, he put the phone down.

"Well, what do you make of that Dafydd?" asked Lettie.

"I think he's telling the truth," replied Dafydd. "He didn't try to hide or deny anything. He confirmed about the pen without being asked to but, fundamentally, no matter how nasty a man he is, I cannot imagine a director of Kew murdering anyone just for an orchid or even a red file. I don't think it is murder or even manslaughter but it was clearly the final straw for Havergal that broke him."

"He must have had a heart attack or something, if only there had been someone who could help but his bad luck was that the only person there was a thoughtless, selfish bastard called Wiseman, and that's why he died, it was murder by neglect."

"And I'm afraid there is no law against that," added Dafydd.

"But there is one other thing," added Lettie. "Mary said that when she found him he had a smile on his face, that doesn't fit with a struggle does it?" They both thought about this and then Lettie said, "well maybe it does, maybe Havergal was pleased because he had finally told Wiseman exactly what he thought of him and maybe Mary was right and he had decided his time had now come, he had written his last poem, blasted Wiseman, which he should have done years ago and now the was the time?"

"Maybe," replied Dafydd, "we'll never know."

"Dafydd," said Lettie. "I think we'll keep all this to ourselves, shall we? I don't think we need to spoil Mary's memories."

But Lettie was still not totally convinced and later, when Dafydd was elsewhere, she decided to call Hiram J Kneival III, her New York lawyer and she relayed the whole story to him.

"Leddie," he said, "you know what? I have just been involved in a case here that is quite similar to yours. It was a probate case and no one could believe that the deceased could be perfectly fit one day and gone the next. Everyone thought there had been foul play. We called in some expert medical witnesses and they said that it is not uncommon. The human psyche is a bit of a mystery and we are all capable of talking ourselves out of things and into things. It's called psychosomatics or something like that. How a person is feeling in their mind can be just as important as how they feel in their body. Of course I don't know anything about Havergal, except what you've told me, all I will say is that it is certainly not impossible that he just decided it was to time to go and to switch himself off. But, as a lawyer I will also say that even if the truth is something else, and I don't think it is, you haven't a snowball's chance of proving it when there were only two parties involved and one of those is dead."

"Oh and by the way Leddie, this call has taken an hour of my time but there will be no charge, on one condition."

"What's that?" said Lettie suspiciously. "That you invite me to your party. I'd like to come over for it. I've sort of got to know all these folks, from you, and I'd like to meet them. And there may also be some useful connections I can make, Sir Gervase for one."

"Consider yourself invited," replied Lettie.

Chapter 40

Lettie had promised a party to just about everyone and now was the time to do it. The invitations had gone out and fortunately everyone could attend. In her inclusive enthusiasm it was only late in the day that Lettie had realised she could not possibly accommodate everyone at 13 Sandown Road and Kew seemed a natural alternative choice. She had approached them through Ron and was amazed that Ron had asked for, and the authorities had agreed, that they could have the Orangery, which would be closed to the public for the afternoon for the first time in its modern incarnation, such was Havergal's reputation now – or was it Lettie's? Delbert and Nelbert had said, "leave the catering to us missus, we know someone who'll do it perfectly," and they were right.

Lettie invited all the staff at Kew to attend and was delighted to see the three guides she had met; Isobel Gardiner, Clemacy Hill-Hughes and Candida Moore-Templeton. Not all of the staff would have known Havergal before, although many did, but all would know him afterwards and would spread the word in their tours, and this made the Orangery the perfect venue since it would allow a staggered attendance; they could not, after all, close Kew down for the afternoon just for her. She invited Roberto and Pedro Morgan and Fernando Davies from Trevelin, Sandra and her husband and Jules from Madagascar, she put notices in all the houses in Sandown Road for anyone who had known Havergal; Delbert and Nelbert obviously were there, the Kew DG, Sir Gervaise White-Hampshire (Bill) was there, and Hiram J Kneival III was working the room and especially the DG, and Sir Lancelot Swann, now frail and aged, was there; it was friends past and present. Of course Mary (who had brought Glenys with her), Ron, Rhodri and Ottoline the typist were all there and the Kew in-house magazine had staff there interviewing and taking pictures for a future edition. In the middle of the room, on a table, with pride of place, sat the (not so) little red book with the initials H.U.W and many of the Kew staff wandered over to gaze at it.

It was a very merry affair. Lettie had decided that it would be just a social gathering in honour of Havergal and it would not be a succession of speeches but she knew there would have to be at least one speech and she knew who would have to give it. At an appropriate moment, when the party was in full swing but before it started getting too noisy she clinked a glass and walked to the front.

"I'm so pleased to welcome all of you here to Kew, which seems such an appropriate place to commemorate the life of Havergal Wyllyams. Please don't worry, this is not a long speech, we are here to meet each other and enjoy ourselves and have fun and remember a man, not listen to speeches. We all leave a footprint in the sand, some larger than others, Havergal would never have thought of himself in those terms but he left a footprint larger than most; for a quiet man he touched so many lives, all of us here for a start, but with the exception of his own, because he was almost entirely selfless. Of course, I never knew him but somehow I feel I have come to know him and it seems to me that sometimes very creative people struggle with real life; the creative process can be all consuming, driving everything else out, and that's the way I think he was. But no life is in vain and his certainly wasn't, everyone here is happier because of him and there can be no finer tribute to him. I think it is fair to say that very few, if any, of us really knew Havergal, but many of us, me included, have been profoundly affected by him and, in many ways, owe parts of our lives to him. Enjoy yourselves, the bar is open all afternoon and I'm looking forward to meeting everyone."

When the applause had died down and some tissues had been put away, the DG, Sir Gervaise White-Hampshire (Bill) asked Lettie if he could say something.

"Don't worry, it will be short! There have, of course," he addressed everyone, "been two stars here today, Havergal of course, but also you, Lettie," he paused for another round of applause for a deeply embarrassed Lettie. "But for your determination, none of Havergal's story would have come out, both his personal story as well as his botanical story and we are all deeply grateful to you for that." More applause. "Thankfully this marks the end of a very unhappy period in the department for botanical research here at Kew, and you all know what I am talking about, and so I am delighted to announce that a new and happier era is starting today because the new director of the department will be Dr Aaronovitch Carter, who will carry forward the ethos and the work of Havergal Wyllyams, who was his mentor and friend." Loud applause. "Lettie's achievements and determination made possible this appointment and if you couple this with her plant discoveries on behalf of Havergal and the trip she made to Madagascar and the renaming of our centre there, she has had a considerable impact on Kew which is not dissimilar to that made by someone I know to be a hero of hers, namely Marianne North. And so, on behalf of the Royal Botanical Gardens, dear Lettie, I say a simple thank you."

More thunderous applause and embarrassment, until Lettie called out.

"That, I promise you, is all the speeches, now let's have some fun!"

The first thing Lettie did was to corner Ron.

"Where the hell did Aaronovitch come from?"

"That's my real name," replied Ron. "Like Havergal, I'm from a one-parent family, my father was from Russia and was apparently called Aaronovitch and so my mother called me that too. My mother didn't tell me anything more than that and I didn't ask. I haven't been called that for years, since my school days in fact, I've no idea why the DG used it, bit embarrassing really, he must have gone to the personnel files and decided to spell everything out in full."

"What an exotic bunch you botanists are!" murmured Lettie.

There was some background music at the party and Lettie whispered a request to Ron and a few moments later Lettie asked everyone to "just listen to a song I heard that just seems to sum everything up, this is for all botanists and for Madagascar in particular." and Joni Mitchell started singing:

They paved paradise and put up a parking lot...

This was now Lettie's song and if she wasn't determined already to be a botanist (and she was) that song clinched it.

Later, Lettie showed Mary all the things she had promised at Kew; the seat where Havergal had lunch, the tree, his desk and she made a big fuss of both Mary and Glenys. Mary and Dafyyd had some long conversations about poetry, and the Joni Mitchell song got played rather a lot.

As she looked up, in the Orangery, Lettie noticed a carved quotation "The infinity of nature" Van Gogh.

"That kinda sums it up too," she whispered to herself.

Ron heard what she said and added, "I know what you mean, but in a way, it should be the finiteness of nature; once a species is gone, whether it's a plant, an animal or a bird, it's gone forever. You see the rain outside?" they both glanced out at the drizzle "Havergal used to call the rain 'dinosaur tears'"

"How's that?" asked Lettie.

"You see, the earth is a closed system. The rain falling outside now is the same rain that might have fallen on Henry the 8th, a Roman soldier or even a dinosaur; it's just recycling all the time. But if we blow a hole in the ozone layer and start losing our water, then we are in real trouble," said Ron glumly.

"In which case lets go talk to some people who, like us, are going to try and do something about it, shall we?" and Lettie took Ron's arm and steered the Director of Botanical Research at Kew back into the party. She was so proud of him, in a motherly way, so smart in his suit and tie.

Later, Lettie's thoughts turned back to Havergal and the seeming infinity of impressions and perceptions there were of him. To the cleaner he had been just a source of income and then a source of shock, to Whalley he was just another case to be processed, to Ron and many others he was a hero, to Dafydd Rhodri he was a part of his history, to Wiseman he was a threat, to Sandra he was a father, Mary thought he died of a broken heart, Lettie knew it was more complicated. In fact, Lettie felt as if she was the only one who really understood him and she was the only one who had never met him, perhaps that was why.

Epilogue

Ron became a highly successful director of botanical research at Kew. He never married, so wedded was he to his work; in fact so similar was he to his mentor Havergal that his departmental nickname was 'HaverRon'. He regularly visited Sandra in Madagascar, now the Havergal Wyllyams Conservation Centre, where she succeeded Jules as director and worked for the rest of her career.

Dafydd remained a beat Police Constable all his life, he never wanted more than that, he never went back to Llandysul but he did continue to write poetry and some was published; he was known as "PC Poet" in whichever force he was working in, and his works were critically acclaimed, at least amongst his friends.

Mary stayed in Llandysul but, now freshly inspired, her art took off and she had numerous exhibitions mainly in Wales and occasionally in London. Her medical condition never troubled her, she lived many more years and died naturally, Lettie went to the funeral.

Lettie never went back to the USA; she found that living in a small house with no servants and no responsibilities suited her just fine. She had surprised herself when she blurted out to Mary that she wanted to become a botanist and continue Havergal's work. She had spoken to Ron about this and he suggested she sign up for Kew's diploma in Horticulture, he would get her in. This was a one year course, three days a week of study and two days a week working at Kew. She would be comfortably the oldest student but that would not be a problem. She passed it with flying colours and now works as a volunteer, unpaid gardener at Kew. They had wanted her to join the staff fulltime but she wanted no responsibilities. In fact Kew had even asked Lettie to become honorary Life President as a tribute to Havergal, but she refused. "We Americans don't do that sort of thing, being a gardener is enough!"

She still lives at 13 Sandown Road. She sold her property in New York and made a bequest to Kew for the construction of a Havergal Wyllyams building devoted to teaching botany to schoolchildren; Ron curated it. She had been much inspired by the Marianne North bequest of her paintings and wanted to emulate her. Lettie never travelled overseas again, except once to the Isle of Wight. Her annual holiday is two weeks hiking in the Brecon Beacons, she has become a hiker as well as a botanist. Her old NYC friends would never recognise her.

Lettie, Ron, Dafydd and Mary all keep in touch with each other and visit each other regularly. Sandra and Mary's families have become Lettie's family and she is now the matriarch of a large and growing family who all visit her. She has become a sort of unofficial grand-mother to them all and thus finally has her own family, albeit adopted and rejected by Havergal, which inspired her all the more to make up for that.

By his actions and the publicity that followed Carl Wiseman had made himself unemployable, certainly in the world of botany. He set up his own business buying and selling second hand cars in Brighton and readers are advised to have nothing to do with him.

Postscript

It is often said that only a newly born baby can write pure fiction, for everyone else our imaginations are coloured by a lifetime of experiences, books read, people met, things seen, all melding together in ways we do not realise.

When I started this story I had three cameos in mind. The first was the opening scene at 13 Sandown Road, which I had had in my mind, almost word for word, for years. The second was the desert scene when the beetle is crushed, not quite so clear in my mind, and the third was the ending in Wales, very dimly imagined. The reason I wrote the story was to do something with these cameos which I had been carrying round for so long; until starting I had no shape for the overall story and no characters.

The name Havergal Wyllyams is a Christmas name. In the usual desperate scramble for Christmas presents one year I saw a CD by Havergal Brian, an underrated Welsh composer, and decided to see if it might be a brand new discovery which my wife would appreciate. She didn't but the name stuck and, of course, from then on he had to be Welsh. The next Christmas a Tesco wine leaflet arrived and the head of wine for that firm was Steve Wyllyams and so Havergal found a surname. The character of Havergal, as it unfolds during the story, was never deliberately based on anyone but, having written it, it is now clear to me that it is a fusion of two family friends, one dead the other alive. The address of 13 Sandown Road, was chosen deliberately to sound bland and ordinary, just like Havergal apparently was, but both concealing some exciting inner stories. So I had three cameos and a main character with a name who was Welsh and who I had fairly clearly in mind, and an address. But, where next?

The desert scene, with the beetle and the cactus, led to botany, which in turn led to Kew. The story then developed a life of its own; I tried to make each chapter a mini story ending with a conundrum (my wife described it as "just like the Archers" but I don't think this was meant to be unkind) There had to be a baddie, Carl Wiseman, and there had to be someone to unfold the story, Lettie. Being a Welshman